The Song of THE SEA

Jenn Alexander

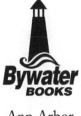

Ann Arbor
2019

Bywater Books

Copyright © 2019 Jenn Alexander

Print ISBN: 978-1-61294-151-6

Bywater Books First Edition: June 2019

Printed in the United States of America on acid-free paper.

Cover designer: Ann McMan, TreeHouse Studio

Bywater Books
PO Box 3671
Ann Arbor MI 48106-3671
www.bywaterbooks.com

This novel is a work of fiction.

To my grandpa, Gerald Alexander,
who shared with me a love of words.

You are missed.

Foreword

On November 7th, 2015, I lost my wife, Sandra Moran, and the world lost a talented writer and learned scholar. Sandra was a professor as well as an author, and she shared her talents as an instructor and a mentor with the Golden Crown Literary Society Writing Academy. In 2016, the Golden Crown Literary Society established a scholarship in Sandra's name in order to honor her memory. The scholarship is given to a Writing Academy student who has displayed the potential to make a significant impact on lesbian fiction.

It was meaningful to me to present the second Sandra Moran Writing Academy scholarship to Jenn Alexander in July 2017. Today, it is my great honor to introduce you to Jenn's debut novel, *The Song of the Sea*. Sandra would be so proud of Jenn and her first published book.

I know you will enjoy *The Song of the Sea*. And we can all look forward to the next book from this talented author.

Cheryl Pletcher
Asheville, NC
June 2019

Chapter One

The first time Lisa Whelan had ever listened to the singing of the ocean she was seven years old, sitting with her grandfather on the rocks along the shoreline, trying to make sense of her grandmother's death.

"Do you hear that?" her grandfather had asked as they stared out at the rolling waves. "Do you hear the water?"

She had nodded, listening to the soft rush of the surf as it rolled toward shore, then back out to sea.

"It reminds me of music."

She remembered seeing her grandfather, his face tilted up toward the sun, eyes closed, head swaying as though he heard an entire symphony.

Lisa had mimicked him, trying hard to hear the song. At first, she heard nothing more than the steady back and forth of the water, but eventually she began to pick out the melody laced above the rocking rhythm of the waves. She heard the gulls and the boats and the distant voices—sounds blending with one another to create harmonies and accents.

"It's the song of freedom," her grandfather had said. "Don't you think?"

She hadn't known what to say, so again she nodded.

"Your grandmother's not in there." Her grandfather had motioned back toward the grief-filled house. "She's out here. You can *hear* it."

As a child, she had been too young to attach much significance to her grandfather's words, but twenty-six years later, that moment occupied her every thought, as she found herself desperate to hear the song.

Lisa drew the paintbrush across the page, a curving shoreline stretching out toward the horizon. She gave herself over to the smooth brush strokes of the blue, curling waves. Along the shore, she outlined the water with a line of white, creating the foam of the breakers, which she also speckled above the crests of the waves. Lines of gray formed the jagged boulders that stacked upon each other, until they reached the grassy field above the cliff.

She set her brush down and closed her eyes, visualizing that moment. She wanted to capture the soothing rolling of the waves, the gentle swirling of the clouds, the calming sun that shone in fat, distinct rays down onto the water like lights from Heaven.

A bird circled over the water in search of fish, and she opened her eyes, dipping her brush in dark brown paint and painting the small line of its wingspan in the distant sky.

She closed her eyes and remembered the briny scent of salt water and seaweed, the comfort of her grandfather's solid figure settled in beside her, the feel of the cliff rising up to support her.

She didn't hear the music.

She *did* hear the ring of her phone, jarring her from her thoughts. It was the third call that morning, and she frowned at the cell phone that lit up and vibrated along with the tinny ring tone from her kitchen counter. She should have turned it off. Her agent had been calling all week, inquiring about the frames she was supposed to have sketched for the new book. The deadline was fast approaching and she had yet to start.

She exhaled slowly and then got up and crossed the room to silence the phone. She could answer and ask for an extension, but she didn't have the energy. Her brother's name lit up across her phone instead, so she hit "talk" and placed the phone to her ear.

"Hey, little brother." She leaned against the counter with the phone to her ear.

"Hey, Lise," Andrew Whelan answered. "How's everything?"

Lisa straightened the stack of unopened mail piled next to her coffeemaker and moved the dishes on her counter onto the pile of dishes building in her kitchen sink. "Good. You?"

"I'm good," he said, but the intonation to the words suggested otherwise.

"You need help hiding the body?" Lisa asked.

He didn't laugh.

"What's the matter?" she pressed.

"Nothing's the matter. I'm good. Really good, actually. I just, well, I have some news. I wanted to call you first so you don't hear this from anyone else."

"Okay?" She waited, unsure if she should brace herself for whatever Andrew was about to say.

"Sarah's pregnant."

At those two words, everything stopped, Lisa's breathing included. The air was knocked from her chest as though she'd been punched. She could feel the walls of her apartment tighten around her.

"I needed you to know first before we tell anyone else," he continued. The words only barely registered. They were distant, hollow background noise.

"Thank you."

"Are you okay?"

She shook her head, and reminded herself to breathe. Somehow she managed to form words. She could hear herself answer, as though she was an outside observer. Her own voice was as distant and muffled as her brother's. "Of course. Congratulations. Kara and Susie will be such great big sisters."

"They will be." Andrew's voice lifted, his excitement breaking through. "Susie, she carries around her little baby dolls, feeding them bottles, and wrapping them in blankets, and I can see her with the baby, you know? She'll be so gentle. And Kara, she's such a goofball and an entertainer. I'll bet you ten bucks now that she gets baby's first giggles."

"I'm happy for you," she said. "I mean it."

"Thanks, Lise."

"Listen, I've got to go, though. I would love to talk more, but I'm waiting on a call from my agent about the new book. Say hi to Sarah and the girls for me."

"Bye, Lisa. Love you."

"Love you, too," she said, already pulling the phone away from her ear to end the call. Her chest was tight, her breathing shallow, and she didn't trust that she could get another word out without her voice breaking. There was only so much she could fake.

She turned off her phone and set it on the counter. She stood in her kitchen, not sure what to do with herself. Her hands itched to hurl something or hit something, but there was nothing. The anxious energy pulsed through her with nowhere to go. She bit back the tears that stung at her eyes. It was so easy for Andrew. He and Sarah had the twins, and now a baby on the way. Four years ago, when Sarah was first pregnant, he had come over to see Lisa in a panic and had gotten drunk off his ass at the thought of being a dad.

God, he's your brother. She hated the jealousy that burned in her chest. She wished she could be happy for him, but the pain swelled up within her until a sob choked out.

She had wanted to be a mom for as long as she could remember. She'd wanted to be a mom so desperately she'd been willing to do it all single. She'd decorated the nursery, bought the onesies, and even chosen schools for Mitchell. She'd conceived him in her heart years before she'd ever gotten pregnant.

But she never got to lay him in his carefully curated nursery. She never got to dress him in the onesie she'd selected as his "going home" outfit. She had had only a few short hours with him, just long enough to hold him against her chest and feel his little heartbeat.

She took in the painting through the blurry threat of tears. That solace she'd felt as a child she needed to feel again. There had to be some comfort somewhere. She couldn't bear to stay in the pain.

She went to the bedroom, careful not to look at the closed door to Mitchell's nursery on her way past. The door was a painful enough reminder on a good day. Seeing it now would crush her.

She didn't know what she was going to do until she had already pulled her suitcase out of her closet and begun filling it with clothes.

This place was suffocating her. She needed to breathe. She couldn't ever move forward staying in this apartment with its closed doors and closed dreams.

Lisa packed her necessary belongings, then pulled open her laptop to check for flights.

The speed limit dropped, the first indication that they were nearing the small town of Craghurst, on Nova Scotia's Cape Breton Island. The Cabot Trail circled the northern half of the island, cutting through all of the coastal towns along the way, and the speed limit was an accordion as traffic slowed in towns and sped up for the open stretches of highway in between. Lisa stared out the window in silence while her great-aunt, Eloise, drove the two of them from the airport in Sydney to the small Whelan family cottage by the sea.

"The place is just like I remember it," Lisa said. The ocean lined the right side of the highway, while homes and buildings made up the town to the left.

"Yeah," Eloise answered. "Nothing much ever changes around here."

It didn't matter how old Lisa got, or how long since her last trip to the island, the town remained the same, and she needed that stability at the moment. Even her aunt looked the same, despite it having been a handful of years since they'd seen one another. Eloise's hair was slightly whiter, and her skin perhaps a tad more aged, but otherwise Lisa could have been convinced she'd last visited Craghurst just yesterday.

The road pulled away from the ocean, the highway curving inland, while a narrow, one-lane road continued to hug the coast. Eloise pulled onto that narrow road, and drove to the cottage which was nestled up atop a cliff. They pulled into the small driveway, and Lisa stepped out of the car.

Breathing in the salt air, she felt as though she had arrived home, despite never having lived by the coast. It was as if the ocean was in her blood, a genetic link passed down from her grandparents. Her grandfather had passed away three years earlier, but she could feel him next to her on that thick sea breeze. It steadied her, as it had when she was a child. Her first experience navigating grief had been with her grandfather at her side, and now she hoped to find some of that same comfort.

"I made up the loft bedroom for you," Eloise said, her blue eyes shining with warmth. "I hope it's not too small."

"It will be perfect." She rolled her suitcase up the little cobblestone path. "I really appreciate you offering to let me stay with you. If I start to overstay my welcome, though, you make sure to tell me. I don't want to impose."

"Nonsense, dear." Eloise waved away her concern as she unlocked the house. Her golden retriever, Roxie, rushed to greet them both. "I'm thrilled that you're going to be staying with me. It's been rather lonely the past few years now that I'm the only Whelan left on the island. It will be good to have some company around here."

Lisa reached down to pat the dog's head and then tugged her suitcase over the ledge of the door.

Everything about the small house was so much homier than her apartment in Toronto. Handcrafted decorations lined the walls, and candles gave off the soft scent of cinnamon. The last time she had been in Auntie Eloise's house had been on her trip back to the coast for her grandfather's funeral. Still, despite the heavy memories, the house gave off a feeling of comfort that enveloped Lisa like a blanket. She stepped in and breathed a sigh of relief.

"I'll let you get settled," Eloise said. "Take your time. I'll be puttering around down here."

Lisa pulled her aunt into a hug, burying her chin against Eloise's shoulder. "Thank you."

"It's good to see you again, kid," Eloise said, squeezing her. "I've missed you. You know that I'm always here for you, and you can talk to me anytime, right?"

"Thank you," Lisa said, wanting to do no such thing. More than anything she wanted to be alone. She lifted her suitcase up the stairs to the loft bedroom. It was a tight space, with hardly enough room for the double bed and small wooden desk, but the large bay window overlooking the harbour gave it an open, spacious feel.

She smoothed her hand over the floral bedspread. She hadn't asked to stay with her aunt, and she wouldn't have wanted to impose, but when she had mentioned to Eloise that she was thinking of spending the next year on Cape Breton Island, Eloise had insisted that she live with her. Lisa had made the obligatory protest, but really she was glad for the invitation. As much as she would never admit it, and as much as she wanted privacy, she was afraid that if she was left alone, she'd never reemerge. And besides, this place was home, and she was glad to be home.

She didn't bother unpacking her suitcase. Instead, she cracked the window and inhaled, filling her lungs with the thick ocean air.

Then, as when she was seven, she tilted her chin up, closed her eyes, and listened, waiting for the song of the ocean to wash over her. Her grandfather had heard his wife in the whispered melody. She wondered if she'd ever hear Mitchell.

It's the song of freedom.

God, she hoped so.

Chapter Two

Declan wasn't in his classroom when Rachel went to pick him up from school. Her son's classmates loitered in the coatroom, stuffing thin paperback books and brightly colored folders into their knapsacks. They struggled with shoelaces and coat zippers, and laughed with their friends. Declan, however, was nowhere in sight.

She didn't need to wait for his teacher to come over and explain. It was the fourth time since school had started only three weeks earlier that she had arrived at the school to pick up her son and found that he had been sent to the principal's office.

"Ms. Murray," Joanna Steward, the school principal, said, standing to greet Rachel when she arrived at the office. "Please, have a seat."

Declan was seated on a chair across from Mrs. Steward, his legs not quite reaching the floor and swinging beneath the seat. He had his elbows on his knees and his head in his hands. He kept his gaze down when Rachel entered the room, his face fixed in a scowl directed at the far corner of the floor.

"What happened?" Rachel made herself ask, taking a seat next to Declan whose lips were pursed, as though he could keep the story sealed. Whatever he had done this time, it wasn't good.

"Why don't you tell your mom what happened," Mrs. Steward urged.

Declan's eyes flashed to Rachel before returning to the floor.

"I kicked Mrs. Harvey." He spat out the sentence as though it was all one word.

"You *what?*" she asked. "Why would you do that?"

He shrugged. "I was mad."

She would have given anything to be anywhere other than the small, claustrophobia-inducing office. "I'm so sorry," she said.

"Declan, why don't you go wait outside with Miss McLean," Mrs. Steward suggested. "I'd like to talk to your mom in private for a minute."

He slunk from his chair and headed out of the office to go wait with the secretary, and Rachel attempted to brace herself against whatever was coming.

"His teacher tells me he's having a hard time making friends in class." Rachel felt as though she had been the one sent to the principal's office. Mrs. Steward's gaze rested on her, and she knew she was supposed to say something, but she didn't have any answers.

"I'll talk to him," Rachel assured her, unsure what else she was supposed to do.

Mrs. Steward gave a small nod that Rachel could have sworn held a hint of disappointment in that answer.

"I know grade one can be a big adjustment," Mrs. Steward offered.

She gladly took the olive branch. "I don't know what's gotten into him."

"Talk to him," Mrs. Steward suggested. "I know his teacher's been trying to connect and facilitate friendships within the class, but she's got twenty other students, and unfortunately there's only so much we can do on our end."

"I understand," she said. "Thank you."

The conversation finally over, she stood and met Declan outside of the office. She motioned for him to follow, and he leaped out of the chair, as eager as she was to leave the school.

Neither spoke as they made their way out to their truck, which was parked on the side of the road. Declan climbed into the backseat, sliding the seat belt over the lap bar of his booster seat, and Rachel turned the key in the ignition, driving away from the school in silence. She didn't know what to say. Her kid had *kicked* his teacher. The week before, he'd given a boy a nosebleed in an argument over who got to go down the slide first.

"Why were you mad at Mrs. Harvey?" she asked, once she was sure she could keep the anger out of her voice. She wanted her son to feel like he could talk to her.

He stared out the window and didn't acknowledge that he'd heard her question.

"Declan, honey, I can't help you if you won't tell me what happened."

"She made me go inside," he stated. "I was still playing."

"At recess?"

"Yeah. I wasn't done with my game."

She took a moment to think about how to respond. "Do you know why Mrs. Harvey sent you to the office?"

"Because it's wrong to kick people," he said in a mocking tone.

"It *hurts* people when you kick them."

"I didn't mean to," he said, exasperation in his small voice. "I just got so angry."

"You've been getting angry a lot lately. What's going on?"

"Nothing."

"Sorry, that's not good enough this time. You hurt your teacher. This is not the first time you've been sent to the office, Declan."

"I said I didn't mean to!" His voice rose in both pitch and volume.

"Fine, don't talk to me." She stared at the road, her jaw set, the silence heavy as it hung between the two of them.

"Do you have to work very late tonight?" he asked, eventually ending the cold war between them.

"Not too late, but there's going to be no television at the restaurant tonight. While I'm working you can make Mrs. Harvey an apology card."

"But Mom!" he protested.

"No 'buts.' Behavior has consequences. You can write your

card, work on your reading for a bit, and then it will be time to go home."

"That's no fair," Declan grumbled.

She didn't bother arguing. She pulled her truck into the small parking lot behind Catherine's Restaurant, then got out and opened the door for Declan, who jumped down and sulked past her, slinging his knapsack with a grinning Mickey Mouse on it over his shoulder as he pushed his way through the back door and into the kitchen.

"Hey, buddy." Rachel's dad gave Declan a big bear hug that lifted him off the ground. "How was school?"

"Not so good," Declan admitted. "I got in trouble again."

Frank met Rachel's eyes before focusing his attention back on Declan. "Well then, it's a good thing the day is over, isn't it?"

Declan nodded.

"I thought I heard voices in here." Eloise pushed her way into the kitchen with a smile.

Eloise, a retired librarian, had taken the job as head chef when Catherine's opened ten years earlier. She didn't ask for much money, saying that the job kept her young and gave her something to do. Rachel knew, however, that the restaurant would never have managed without her.

"Has it been busy?" Rachel asked.

"A handful here and there," Frank answered.

"We've only got two here right now," Eloise added. "Enjoying the quiet I'm sure."

That was what Rachel had expected. Business was beginning to slow for the year as the colder weather transitioned the tourist destination into the sleepy winter off-season.

"Why don't we go get you settled?" Rachel asked Declan, leading him out into the restaurant.

He climbed up onto the seat of the booth nearest the kitchen, throwing his knapsack down beside him and pulling out his yellow folder and pencil case.

She sat across from him. "Do you have an extra piece of paper?"

He opened his folder and took out two plain white sheets of paper.

Rachel took one of the sheets and selected a blue pencil from his pencil case. "What do you want to write to Mrs. Harvey?"

"I'm sorry for kicking you."

"Will you do it again?"

"No," he promised.

Dear Mrs. Harvey, she wrote on the piece of paper. *I'm sorry for kicking you. I will not do it again. From Declan.*

She slid the piece of paper across the table for her son to copy the letters.

"That's a lot to write." He frowned at the paper.

"It is."

He took his own sheet of paper and folded it in half like a card—a lopsided attempt with the edges not quite matching up.

"Are you hungry?" she asked.

He shook his head and riffled through his pencil case until he selected the colored pencil he wanted. His auburn hair, the same shade as his dad's, fell across his forehead, hiding his furrowed brow.

"Let me know when you are, and we'll make you some dinner."

He nodded.

"All right, I'll be back and forth between here and the kitchen if you need me."

"'Kay," he said.

She slid from the booth and went to the kitchen where she took her maroon apron from the rack and tied it around her waist.

"Are you all right?" Frank asked as he scaled and filleted a large salmon.

Rachel leaned against the counter and closed her eyes as though she could shut off the world for a moment. "This is the *fourth* time he's been sent to the office. What am I supposed to do with him?"

"I'm sure he'll settle in soon," her dad offered.

12

"His principal said that grade one can be an adjustment, but how many other kids are consistently misbehaving like this? He's always in trouble, and apparently he's having a hard time making friends."

"Declan? But he's such a friendly little guy."

"Dad, he keeps hitting people!"

He exhaled audibly and frowned. "That could be a problem."

He was only trying to help, but there was no point sugarcoating things. Declan wasn't doing well, and ignoring that fact wouldn't help anyone.

The soft jingle of bells drifted into the kitchen. "I should get that," Rachel said, pushing away from the counter, glad for the distraction.

Since the start of the school year, she felt as if she did nothing but worry about Declan. It didn't seem to matter how much she tried to get him to talk to her, he wouldn't open up, and it didn't seem like anything she said got through to him. If she knew what she was doing wrong, she would fix it. She knew she was failing as a parent, but that was all she knew. She had no idea how to turn things around.

Lisa sat by the bay window sketching mindlessly, doodling really, when her phone vibrated on her nightstand. She'd been expecting the call. She had sent off the frames for the new book that morning, knowing full well she hadn't sent off her best work, but having no energy left to be concerned with the publisher's response. Sure enough, when she checked her phone, her agent's name lit up the screen. She was tempted to let the call go to voicemail, but at the last minute she decided to answer and get the call over with.

"Hello?"

"So your phone does, in fact, work," Natalie Culver said. There was only a hint of reprimand in the simple statement, which was mostly spoken in her usual warm and friendly tone.

"I'm sorry I've been so elusive. I had to get away for a bit."

"You finished the frames," Natalie said.

"I did."

"I was starting to have my doubts."

So was I, Lisa thought, but she said nothing.

"The publisher liked them and wants to know if you're interested in sketching for another book of theirs. It's in a similar vein. Young adult graphic novel. They said think *Hunger Games* meets *Star Wars*."

"I'm not interested."

"You haven't let me get to the best part yet," Natalie continued, enthusiasm clear in her voice. "They've already signed a contract with the writer for a four-book saga. *Four* books, Lisa. They think these are going to be big."

"I'm not interested," she said again.

There was a long beat of silence, and she ran her hand through her hair, exhaling slowly before allowing herself to explain. "I need to take some time. I tried to bury myself in my work, and all I did was bury myself in procrastination and deadlines I couldn't meet. Have you seen the frames I turned in? They're shit."

"They're not that bad," Natalie said, in a way that confirmed Lisa's assessment. "The publisher was happy."

"That's not the kind of work I want to be known for."

"So take a month, get your head back in it, and then sketch these next books," Natalie suggested. "It'll be good for you. You need to be doing *something*."

She could hear the concern in Natalie's voice and knew that it had more to do with concern for her than for sales. The two of them had always connected easily, which was partly why they worked so well together. But she didn't need anyone's concern. She just needed to get away from it all.

"I need to do some art for myself right now," Lisa said. "I'm stuck. I can't move forward. I can't take on new projects. I just *hurt* all of the time."

"I know and I'm worried about you," Natalie said. "I push you because it's my job, but I really am in your corner. You're not just my client. You're my friend."

"I appreciate that," she said. Natalie could be a hard-ass when she needed to be, but she was a hard-ass who'd made Lisa a good deal of money and allowed her to draw for a living. She couldn't shirk her financial responsibilities for good, but she also knew that until she found some way to process her grief, she would continue to be more-or-less useless in all aspects of her life. She needed to find some way to stitch up the giant hole that had been ripped open in her heart.

"I won't disappear for good," she promised. "But I need some time to take care of myself."

"Give me a call in a month or so to let me know how it's going?" Natalie asked.

"I will," she promised. She had no idea if it was a promise she would keep.

Natalie hung up, and Lisa set her phone on the end table. She went back to the doodles she had been working on. She couldn't get her head cleared again, so she picked up her Nova Scotia guidebook and began flipping through the pages, reading about all of the things she would have to see and do.

She stopped on the page that mentioned a restaurant called Catherine's. Auntie Eloise worked for Catherine's, but she had neglected to tell Lisa the place was so renowned within Craghurst. The small write-up called her great-aunt's clam chowder one of the "must-tries" of Cape Breton cuisine.

Lisa didn't hesitate; she grabbed her coat and headed out into the crisp fall air. It was only a few short blocks between her aunt's home and the restaurant, and she took the time to enjoy the fall air with its biting chill. The late afternoon was overcast and gray as she walked down the main road that cut through town. She carried her sketchbook under her arm. A change of scenery and a quiet afternoon sketching and sipping clam chowder seemed the perfect way to get her mind off the call with her agent and get some work done for herself.

She wasn't dwelling.

Catherine's Restaurant was a quaint yellow building with blue lettering, situated between a hardwood shop and a bakery, on the side of the road overlooking the ocean. She pushed open the door and was greeted with a wave of warmth and the soft aroma of seafood and spices. Her stomach rumbled as she stepped eagerly inside, only then realizing just how hungry she was.

"God, it smells amazing in here."

"I'm glad you think so," a woman answered, pushing out of the kitchen.

It was clear from the hurried way the waitress moved that she was busy, probably juggling multiple responsibilities. But the warmth of her smile caught Lisa off guard.

She felt a lightness bloom in her chest, and she couldn't help but mirror the smile.

The waitress was pretty, with dark brown curls pulled back in a ponytail, a few loose strands falling free to frame her face. Lisa took in her soft curves as she strode to the front to greet her, but it was that smile that she was really drawn to. Warm, and genuine, and contagious.

"Table for one?" the woman asked, and Lisa was pulled out of her head and back into reality, feeling her face redden as though she'd been caught staring.

She nodded, surprised at the direction her thoughts had taken. It had been too long since she'd noticed another woman, and even then, she didn't usually feel the same magnetic pull.

"How about a booth by the window?" the waitress asked.

"That would be great," Lisa said.

The restaurant was small, no more than ten tables. It was simply decorated with wood paneling and gray and navy trim, following a nautical theme. Photos of fishing boats and fishermen adorned the walls, as well as photos of a young family out by the ocean. It wasn't hard to recognize the waitress in the childhood photos with her dark curly hair and bright smile. On one side of the restaurant sat an elderly couple talking and laughing over bowls of soup, and at the table nearest the door to the kitchen sat a little boy, coloring a piece of paper. Lisa's gaze landed on the boy, and she felt the familiar pang of grief as she looked at him, so impossibly small in the large booth. He frowned down at his paper with slumped shoulders, and it was that whole-body defeat that held Lisa's attention beyond what should have been a cursory glance. But she hadn't moved to the coast to be reminded of the kids' menus and coloring pages she was missing out on, so she forced herself to look away and follow the waitress.

Lisa was led to a booth in the far corner with windows on two sides, offering an expansive view of the harbor. She sat on the side of the booth that faced away from the boy.

"I'll give you a minute and then I'll be back to take your order," the waitress said before disappearing back into the kitchen.

She already knew what she had to order, but she read through the menu anyway, more to ground herself than to explore her dining options. She had to admit, though, there were a number of tempting seafood dishes. Everything sounded fantastic, and she had to close the menu to keep from wavering in her decision.

The waitress returned a moment later, placing a glass of water in front of Lisa. "If you have any questions, feel free to ask me."

"I already know I have to try the clam chowder," she said. "Apparently my aunt makes a brilliant chowder she's never shared with me."

"Wait," the waitress interjected. "Eloise is your aunt?"

"Great-aunt technically, but yes."

"You must be Lisa! Eloise is so excited to have you here. She's been telling us so much about you, and I was hoping we'd get the chance to meet. I'm Rachel."

Lisa's cheeks reddened. She had no idea she would get such a warm reception from being related to Eloise. "It's good to meet you also."

"I'll be right back. Just wait one minute." Rachel dashed off, returning a moment later with Eloise at her side.

"Well, this is a surprise," Eloise said. "I thought you'd be hard at work today."

"Sent in my final frames this morning."

"What is it you do?" Rachel asked.

Lisa opened her mouth, but Eloise beat her to answering.

17

"She's an artist. You should see her work. She's really good."
Pride was evident in Eloise's voice.

"I illustrate graphic novels," she clarified.

"Really?" Rachel asked with obvious interest. "What kind of graphic novels?"

"Science fiction mostly." She took a sip of her water, looking at the glass instead of Eloise and Rachel who were both acting like she was some sort of celebrity. Anyway, she *wasn't* working on a science fiction project, and she didn't want to talk about what she *was* working on, so she changed the subject.

"Auntie Eloise, how come I had to find out from my guide-book what a great cook you are?"

"It's nothing." Eloise waved away the compliment. "I picked up a few recipes over the years, and the Murrays here were crazy enough to hire this old broad."

Rachel rolled her eyes. "You're the only crazy one around here. We'd have never gotten off the ground if it hadn't been for you."

"Well, I'll go get cooking." Eloise patted Lisa on the shoulder. "Then you can decide for yourself."

"I can't wait," she said, as her aunt pushed through the doors to the kitchen.

"She's been a godsend," Rachel said.

She met Rachel's warm gaze—drawn in by the unique sea-green shade of her eyes.

Rachel broke the eye contact, tucking a soft brown curl that had come loose from her ponytail behind her ear. "I'll be back and forth between here and the kitchen while Eloise makes your chowder. Just wave me down if you need anything."

"Will do. Thanks."

Rachel returned to the kitchen, and Lisa flipped open her sketchbook to a blank page. She sat back in the booth and gazed out the window to take in the view. It was a windy day, and waves pummeled the shore. Down at the point a lighthouse stood sentinel on a rocky outcropping.

She picked up her pencil and began to sketch the lighthouse. Gentle lines, barely pressing the graphite into the paper, formed the ghost of an outline. Eventually she got lost in the gentle scraping of her pencil on the paper. She drew the wooden door, the dusty windows, and a beam of light emanating from the powerful lamp that would guide ships through the storms. Then, she began sketching the creatures hidden in the darkness beyond that light: wiry little bodies that covered the rocks like coral, with reaching hands and bared teeth. The image drew her in until nothing else existed in that moment.

"Cool."

The tiny voice pulled her from her work to find the little boy who had been sitting next to the kitchen standing beside her table holding a blank piece of paper and a red pencil. The boy's eyes were the same shade of green as Rachel's, and they were wide open, fixed on Lisa's page.

She felt the urge to close the sketchbook and hope the boy went on his way, but the memory of him sitting sad and small in that booth stopped her.

"Thank you," she said instead.

The boy stood there, studying the picture, scrunching up his face as he took in all of the details.

"How did you learn to draw so good?"

Her heart twisted. In her head she shouted for him to leave. But outwardly all she said was, "Lots of practice."

She watched as he chewed over those words before he extended his own piece of paper toward her.

"I need help with some words," he said.

She took the offered paper, not at all sure what she could do to help. "Okay."

"I'm trying to write a letter to my mom, but I don't know how to spell all the words. Can you write them so I can copy them?"

Her chest further tightened in what was quickly becoming a vise. "What should I write?"

The boy chewed his lower lip for a moment before he answered. "Mommy, I'm sorry I got in trouble." He paused to think some more. "Next time I'll be good."

Lisa looked at the boy, really *looked* at him for the first time. He couldn't have been older than five or six, but the expression on his face was *so* serious and sad. For an instant, she was hit with an overwhelming desire to scoop him up and hug him. That feeling was followed by an overwhelming need for him to leave. He wasn't Mitchell. Not her son.

Go away, she pleaded internally.

Steadying herself, she took the offered pencil and wrote out each word, careful to print clearly enough that he would be able to read each letter, and then she handed the paper back.

"Declan," Rachel called, emerging from the kitchen with a tray of food. "What are you doing?"

"Nothing." He hid the piece of paper behind his back. "I just needed help with some words."

"What kind of words?" Rachel asked as she stepped toward the two of them. She set a bowl of chowder on the table in front of Lisa and tucked the tray under her arm, turning her attention back to her son.

"You'll see later," he said.

Lisa watched Rachel press two fingers against the bridge of her nose. "Okay, but don't bother other people. Come get me the next time you need help."

"'Kay," Declan said and scampered back to his seat.

"I'm really sorry about that," Rachel said, her gaze holding Lisa's.

"Don't be," she said, but her voice was not as warm as she wanted it to be. Her lungs felt small. She wanted air.

"He's a good kid," Rachel rushed on, "he's just . . . it's just the two of us, and so he has to come to work with me after school, and today, well, it's been a day."

Rachel was visibly frayed and flustered, and Lisa softened. "It's fine," she said, far more gently than her earlier comment. "He's cute."

Rachel offered a tentative smile. "I really am sorry."

She took Rachel's hand to stop her. "He's a kid. There's nothing to apologize for."

Rachel gave her hand a gentle squeeze. Her skin was warm

and soft, and when she pulled away, Lisa noticed the absence more than she would have liked.

"I should let you eat your dinner before it gets cold," Rachel said.

Right. The chowder. She'd all but forgotten about it.

Rachel slid into the booth across from her son, who quickly covered up the letter he was writing.

Lisa was no longer as hungry as she'd been an hour ago. She forced herself to turn away from the mother and son, forced herself to stop wondering about the what-ifs and the should-have-beens. She turned to a blank page in her sketchbook and began to draw, putting her feelings into images.

The chowder was cold by the time she took her first sip.

Declan didn't give Rachel the card until later that evening, just before his bedtime.

"Wait," he said when she told him to get into bed so she could tuck him in for the night. "I have to get something."

"Declan. It's bedtime."

"I know. Just wait," he said, rushing off.

Rachel sat on the edge of his bed, waiting for him to return so she could put him to sleep and have some time to herself.

"I made this for you, Mommy." He handed Rachel a folded piece of paper. He usually called her "Mom." "Mommy" was an endearment saved for rare moments.

Rachel looked down at the card he had given her. On the front was a picture of the two of them: smiling stick figures labeled "Mommy" and "Declan" with a lighthouse standing next to them, a tall gray tower with a yellow beam of light shining out of the top.

She opened the card, reading the two carefully printed sentences a number of times, swallowing the lump that grew in the back of her throat as she did so.

"The lady helped me write the sentences," he said. "I couldn't ask you because it was a surprise."

She turned to her son, taking his chin in her hand and meeting his eyes, which shone with pride. She didn't understand how this could be the same boy who'd been sent to the principal's office *four* times.

"I love you." She brushed his messy brown hair back to kiss his forehead. "You know that, right?"

"Love you too, Mommy."

She pulled him into a tight hug, trying not to let herself cry in front of him. Then she pulled back his covers and motioned for him to crawl underneath them.

"It's time for bed, kiddo." She pulled the covers up to his chin and squeezed him one more time. "Have a good sleep."

"Night," he said.

She flipped off the overhead light and closed the door most of the way, leaving it open enough that the light from the hallway would still seep into his room.

Then she went to the living room and sat down on the couch, reading the card again, this time not stopping the tears as they welled in her eyes.

Mommy, I'm sorry I got into trouble. Next time I'll be good.

She brushed away a tear with the back of her hand. *Honey, you're always good.* She just wished others could see the same light in him that she did.

Chapter Three

Lisa's coffee grew cold beside her as she focused on the sketch she was working on.

The sun cracked the horizon, and the large bay window in the kitchen was no longer a black slate to gaze at. She didn't need to see the ocean to recreate it in her art. In fact, she preferred to summon the sea from memory and imagination alone. She drew waves crashing against a lone fishing boat's rickety wooden siding and water spraying up over the bow.

Then she began to work on the creature, conjuring a beast from the pitch-black depths of the ocean where miles of water filtered out any sunlight before the warm rays could ever reach the sand. She outlined its tentacles wrapping around the boat's cabin, and its gaping maw poised in wait above the door.

"You're definitely a Whelan."

She turned at the sound of Eloise's voice to see her great-aunt, still in her nightgown and slippers, moving to put water in the kettle. Roxie padded along faithfully behind her before curling up in the dog bed in the corner.

"Only a Whelan would be up *before* the sun," Eloise continued.

"It's always been my favorite time of day. I like the quiet."

"Believe me, I understand," Eloise said. "I mean, look at that. Who would want to sleep through that sight?"

She looked to where Eloise pointed out the window. The sun was a heavy glowing ball, casting fiery pinks and oranges across the sky. The whitecaps of the waves were embossed in gold.

"It's beautiful." She sat back away from her artwork and taking in the sight. If Eloise hadn't said anything, she might not have noticed, she had been so wrapped up in her sketch.

"Keeps me believing in God. Beauty like that can't just be a coincidence."

Lisa took a sip of her cold coffee. She was less certain than her aunt was that there was a god in the sunrise. If there *was* a god, he had failed her too many times, and she found it preferable to believe she was on her own.

The kettle began to whistle, and Eloise filled a mug with hot water and tossed in a tea bag. Then she placed the mug on the table and left the kitchen, returning a moment later with the newspaper.

Lisa went back to her picture, and Eloise flipped to the crossword puzzle at the back, both of them working together in silence for a long while.

"What's a nine-letter word that means 'bust down reason'?" Eloise asked, breaking the silence.

She thought for a moment. "I have no idea."

Eloise tapped her pencil on the table. "One of these days I have to be able to finish one of these puzzles, right?"

"Surely," she said.

Eloise frowned at the puzzle. "I'll come back to this one," she said after a moment. "See if I can get some of the other letters first."

The silence between them was comfortable as they each worked on their own projects and sipped their morning drinks. Lisa filled in the creature's tentacles with suckers, and shaded each of the small circles to add depth and texture. She enjoyed having company next to her without the pressure of explaining her art. She didn't want to talk about her work. It could speak for itself. The feelings she put to the page were too raw for words. She let her pencil curve along the page, making her grief into a tangible image.

"I meant to thank you for coming by the restaurant yesterday," Eloise said.

She tore her attention from her work. "I knew you worked at a restaurant, but you never told me you were such a revered chef."

Eloise waved a hand dismissively, but the pride lit up her great-aunt's face.

"Cooking is more of a pastime than anything. But the Murrays needed a cook, and so I figured it would give me something to do in my old age. I'm glad you got a chance to meet them. I had been hoping I would get a chance to introduce you to Rachel, Frank, and Declan. They're like family to me out here."

"I could tell." She had enjoyed the window into Eloise's life. The connection between Eloise and Rachel had been obvious. The restaurant was clearly more than just a job to her, and it hadn't been hard to understand why Eloise cared deeply for the Murrays. Rachel was warm and gentle, having the type of magnetic personality that would attract anyone, with a sweet, charming son. But Lisa couldn't think about him without her throat tightening and the air starting to feel thin.

"I think you would really like Rachel," Eloise said. "It might be nice for you to have someone to spend time with around here besides your old aunt."

"Hey now, tea and crossword puzzles sound right up my alley," Lisa argued. She appreciated Eloise wanting her to have friends her own age, but she wasn't sure Rachel was the best choice.

She saw Eloise give her that look she hated—the pitying look she had grown so accustomed to. Lisa turned away.

"I didn't tell her about Mitchell," Eloise said. "I know you like your privacy. You're like your grandfather in that way. I didn't say anything. It's your story to tell."

"Thank you." The admission carried some level of relief, but overall changed nothing. It wasn't pity she was avoiding as much as the reminders, and Rachel's little boy . . . it was too much for her.

Eloise took in the details of Lisa's sketch and changed the subject. "It's so detailed. I could almost believe that one of those actually is lurking out there in the depths of the sea."

"Maybe one is." Lisa looked at the sea monster coiled around the boat, lying in wait for the fishermen inside the cabin. Nothing was ever as calm as it appeared. Like the sailors in the sketch, it seemed as if with one misstep Lisa was about to be consumed by the massive creature lurking beneath the surface. In fact, grief already held her tight in its grasp, and she had no idea how to even begin fighting it.

"You know," Eloise said, "any time you want to talk about him, I'm here."

"I know." But she was too scared to open that door. The beast was waiting to swallow her.

Chapter Four

Declan's giggles filled the air as he ran down the beach, and a flock of seagulls scattered as he raced toward them. Rachel and Declan were enjoying their Saturday morning at the beach away from school, teachers, and the restaurant. Just the two of them. They had a couple of hours until Declan's dad, Joey, would pick him up for the weekend, and she wanted to spend every second with him.

The cool morning air had a uniquely autumn smell, and the trees were a collage of yellows, oranges, and reds. Soon they would be nothing more than skeletal branches, but for the time being the coast was ablaze with the fall colors. A chill had already settled into the air, and Declan ran down the beach, bundled in a warm fleece jacket, with a too-big red toque on his head that kept falling over his eyes.

Rachel pulled her own fleece tighter around herself, taking a seat on a large piece of driftwood in their favorite spot near the trees at the end of the beach, watching as Declan chased after the seagulls with glee. She rolled her shoulders, feeling some of the ever-present stress lift away.

It was rare to see Declan enjoying being a kid. Even on good days, the days where he didn't get sent to the office and his teacher didn't send home a behavior report of the things he'd done wrong, he still came home unhappy. He didn't burst into stories about his classmates or talk about who he had played with at recess. Instead, she would ask about how his day went and he would merely shrug.

"Mom!" he called, running down the beach with his hands cupped in front of him. "Check out what I found!"

She peered into his hands and saw a snail curled up inside of its shell.

"Look at that." Her voice matched his excitement.

"He's hiding." Declan gazed into the tiny shell before returning the snail to the rocks near the water.

It was hard for her to reconcile the gentle boy who carefully cradled a snail in his hands with a boy who was physically violent and angry at school. It didn't make sense that such opposing behavior could come from the same child.

After a few minutes, he returned to where she sat and took a seat, cross-legged, on the sand in front of her. "Let's build a sand castle," he said pushing the sand into a pile.

She slid off the log and took a seat across from him, helping pile the cold, damp sand.

"I'm going to dig a moat," he said once the castle reached a satisfactory height. "That way nobody else can get in."

"Good idea." She patted down the sand.

He nodded, working hard.

A dog barking nearby pulled his attention from the castle he was working on. Down the beach a lady was out with her golden retriever. She had a large stick that she threw and the dog chased after with excitement.

Declan's eyes lit up. "Can I go pet him?" he asked, already scrambling up from the sand. Any time he saw a dog, he wanted to play with it.

Rachel was inclined to tell Declan to let them be, but the excitement radiated off of him, and she found herself consenting. "We can go ask."

The sand castle was forgotten as he grabbed her hand and tugged her down the beach after him.

When they were about halfway down the beach, she recognized Eloise's niece, Lisa, and hesitated. Lisa, while nice enough, had not seemed the most child-friendly. She had been polite enough when Declan approached her table, but she had also not seemed particularly happy to converse with Rachel's son, and she got the sense that Lisa was not particularly interested in chatting with a six-year-old.

Rachel tried to think of how to tell her son that they would have to leave the dog be when he let go of her hand and raced toward the animal.

"That's Roxie," he said with a squeal.

"Declan, wait," she called, but he either didn't hear her or didn't care to listen. She chased after him and grabbed his hand to stop him. "Declan, I asked you to stop! You can't just run up to someone's dog like that. It could bite you. You don't know if it's nice or not."

"But Mom, it's Roxie." His eyes filled with tears as he pointed to the dog.

She looked to see Lisa holding the dog by the collar. Roxie pulled against the restraint, tail wagging, appearing just as eager to play.

"I'm sorry," Rachel began, speaking quickly, needing to explain. "Declan loves dogs, especially your aunt's dog."

"Can I please pet her?" he asked.

Rachel was about to answer, to tell him that he still couldn't run up to dogs, even dogs he knew, in case he scared them. Luckily for Declan, Lisa answered first.

"I bet she'd like that," she said, and let go of Roxie's collar, standing while Roxie bounded over to Declan, licking his cheeks, eliciting giggles.

She met Lisa's hazel eyes. "Thank you."

Declan was already picking up the large stick that Lisa had been throwing and tossing it for the dog, happier than Rachel could remember seeing him in a long time.

"Don't go too far," she called after him.

29

"I won't," he called without even a glance back as he chased after Roxie.

When she turned back to Lisa, she noticed her watching Declan with distant, almost sad, eyes.

"You made his day," Rachel said. "He's always asking for a dog of his own, but I'm not home enough, with the restaurant, to care for one."

Lisa gave a small shrug and turned back to her. "Roxie's in her glory. Hopefully he'll tire her out."

She laughed. "Hard to say who has more energy, kids or dogs, isn't it?"

That wistful look again. Lisa nodded.

Rachel wanted to ask, but she didn't want to pry, so she shifted and gazed out at the ocean.

"He seems like a really sweet kid," Lisa said after a moment.

"He is," she answered. She wished more people saw it.

"You're lucky."

Rachel watched Declan and Roxie, and seeing her little boy so completely happy she *did* feel lucky. This was how she was *supposed* to feel all the time.

"So, how're you liking Cape Breton Island so far?" she asked, changing the subject.

"It feels like home. I grew up in Toronto, but still, out here by the sea . . . this feels like where I'm meant to be." Lisa's hazel eyes warmed while she talked about the ocean. Her face softened and her voice took on a lightness.

"Well, if you're here to work, you've picked a good place," Rachel said. "By the end of October all of the tourists will be gone for the year and the island will be quiet. Many people find it too quiet outside of tourist season, but I love it. And Sydney is not too far a drive if you get desperate for some excitement."

"I love the quiet. I feel like I can breathe out here."

She wanted to ask more, but decided it best not to press.

"Look at him. He's in love," Rachel said, motioning toward Declan who was on his knees, scratching the dog's fur and giggling every time Roxie tried to lick his face. His light, happy giggle warmed her, and she couldn't help but smile.

"They do make quite the pair," Lisa said.

She was looking out at Declan and Roxie, and Rachel couldn't help but notice how pretty she was. Dirty-blond, windblown hair fell lightly just above her shoulders. Her cheeks had a slight reddish tint from the cold. Rachel allowed herself a moment to trace her gaze over Lisa's soft features, the gentle curve of Lisa's jaw, the barest dusting of freckles across her nose, her full lips . . .

"There's a ceilidh happening tonight at a pub down the road. Why don't you come with me?" Rachel blurted, before she had time to filter the thought.

"Who or what's a *kayley*?" Lisa asked.

"Well, now you have to come!" Rachel pressed, trying to maintain the initial burst of confidence. "You can't live here and not know what a ceilidh is. They're Celtic dance parties that happen around the island. They're a huge part of Cape Breton's culture."

The invitation was spontaneous, but she found herself nervously awaiting Lisa's answer, genuinely hoping she would come. After a stressful week worrying about Declan, a night out with a new friend sounded perfect.

Lisa tugged the right side of her lower lip between her teeth in thought, but then nodded. "Sure. Why not? It sounds like fun."

"It will be," Rachel promised. "It's at O'Leary's, just a few blocks down from the restaurant. Why don't we meet there at seven?"

"Works for me."

Rachel glanced at her watch, knowing she had to get going but not wanting to leave.

"Need to be getting somewhere?" Lisa asked, reading her expression.

"Yeah. Declan's dad is coming by to pick him up for the weekend, so I should get him home."

"So you've got the weekend to yourself?"

"I do," she said. "I'm not quite sure what to do with myself."

31

"I think taking me to a Celtic dance party seems like a good start." Lisa bumped her shoulder.

Rachel's cheeks warmed. *Is she flirting?* Surely she wasn't.

Declan was still throwing the stick, and Rachel turned to watch as he threw it into the surf and Roxie pounced over waves after it, returning the stick to his feet.

"I don't want to interrupt them," she said.

"They are inseparable, aren't they?"

"BFFs," Rachel agreed.

She cast another glance at her watch. Time was ticking past faster than she could afford.

"Declan, honey," she called. "Come on over here. It's time to go."

"Five more minutes," he called back, continuing to throw the stick for Roxie.

"We don't have five more minutes." She headed toward him. "Your dad's going to be here."

"I don't want to go!"

She didn't know if he meant away from Roxie or with his dad, but the distinction didn't really matter. They had to leave, and she wanted to avoid a power struggle with her son in front of Lisa.

To Rachel's surprise, Lisa didn't look at her with the expression that others often had—the one that was a combination of sympathy and judgment. Instead, Lisa said, "Well, we knew it was going to be hard to separate the two, right?"

She exhaled in relief. "I'm sorry."

"Don't be." Lisa walked down the beach to where Declan was now on his knees, his arms around Roxie's neck.

"Roxie loves you," Lisa said.

His scowl slowly eased.

"You must be pretty special," she continued.

Declan didn't let go of Roxie, but he did look up at Lisa.

"I need to get Roxie home, but I'm sure Eloise would be happy to let you come by and play with her sometime."

Declan didn't seem to believe her, so he turned to Rachel who was at just as much of a loss.

"Really?" he asked.

"Really," Rachel said. "But only if you listen when I say it's time to leave. We need to get going, and Roxie needs to get home, too."

He frowned and then placed a kiss on Roxie's head. "I'll see you later."

Rachel held Lisa's gaze and mouthed the words *thank you*.

Lisa shrugged it off.

Declan pulled himself up from the sand and reluctantly took her hand to leave.

"What do you say to Lisa for letting you play with Roxie?"

"Thank you, Lisa," he said, though his eyes never left the dog.

"Thanks for keeping Roxie company," Lisa answered.

She's cute and she's nice, Rachel thought. *Even to Declan.* She wondered about the distant expression that crossed Lisa's face when she looked at him. It was hard to read, sad almost. But even so she was kind to him, and Rachel's heart clenched at the sight.

Lisa turned to her. "So, I'll see you tonight."

She warmed at the thought. "I'm looking forward to it. It's been a good morning."

"Yeah," Lisa said, her voice distant. "It has been."

Rachel turned back to Declan, taking his hand and leading him home, but her thoughts were on Lisa for the entire walk.

Chapter Five

Water sluiced beneath the kayak with each long, deep stroke of the oar. Lisa closed her eyes and breathed in the salt air, letting the waves gently rock the small boat. Pulling her paddle out of the water and into her lap, she sat still on the open sea, a dust speck in comparison to the vast openness of the water. Sunlight caressed her skin, and a warm breeze brushed her hair from her face.

She would have been content to spend forever out on the water. She wasn't eager to paddle to shore, back to the realities of life. She could float among the breakers, her and the sea, until her kayak drifted off into oblivion. If she closed her eyes, it was easy to pretend she was slipping away into that great ocean, leaving everything behind. But every time she opened her eyes again, she still saw land, not too far from where she sat rocking in the waves.

"I miss you, Mitchell," she said, the wind a silent messenger taking her words and carrying them away from her. There was no answer other than the caw of a seabird, but she felt her words had not gone unheard.

She'd watched Declan play with Roxie. He would throw the stick with all of his might and it would land only a couple meters from where he stood, but still he would giggle with delight each time the dog returned it to him. She used to imagine the day when she would buy Mitchell a pet. Her apartment was pet-free, but she'd been saving to move them into a house. She wanted a yard, even if just a small one, so he could throw sticks to their dog. *Her* son, *her* dog, *her* family. Her future, which was no longer hers.

Her throat tightened at the thought. She could almost see Mitchell, as though he had gotten a chance to grow and laugh and play, legs pumping as he ran down the beach, sandals slapping against the sand. Of course, the visions were just imaginings. She didn't even get the luxury of memories. Tears burned her eyes and she let them fall.

But only for a moment.

Then, she took a few deep breaths—*in through the nose, out through the mouth*—and wiped her eyes. She dipped the paddle in the water, moving forward. As always.

She had to get back to get ready for the ceilidh that evening. She squeezed her eyes shut, wondering what the hell she'd been thinking, but when she closed them, she could see Rachel's hopeful smile, and she knew exactly why she had agreed to go out for the night. The invitation hadn't been made out of pity. Rachel wasn't trying to *fix* her. The invitation had been genuine, and despite all her fear and reservations, Lisa looked forward to the evening. The thought of an evening out with a beautiful woman made her feel a little bit like herself again for the first time in way too long.

Rachel was warm and sweet and gentle. She was strong and soft all at once.

And she had a son who broke Lisa's heart every time she saw him.

Lisa closed her eyes, as though she could shut out the images of Declan laughing as Roxie licked his cheek.

"I'm just so tired of hurting all the time," she said out loud, as though there were somebody there to listen. "I just want one night to be *me* again."

And it was just a night at the pub. She had to remind herself of that. It didn't need to matter that Rachel had Declan.

She began to ease her kayak back toward shore. She was hesitant to return to reality but she was running out of time to get ready for the night ahead.

"It's okay to have a good time," she told herself. She wasn't sure it was possible, but she would try.

Rachel stood outside of the old familiar pub, waiting for Lisa to arrive. Celtic music permeated the brick walls, filtering out onto the street, muted but still audible. She couldn't even begin to remember when she'd last had a night out, and she was greatly anticipating the evening.

It had been a long afternoon trying to get Declan ready to go with his dad. Joey didn't have the best track record with reliability, which, Rachel assumed, was why Declan dug his heels in and refused to help pack, complaining the entire time. Until Joey rang the doorbell, that is, and then Declan was caught up in a whirlwind of excitement, trying to stuff everything he'd "forgotten" into his backpack to take with him.

A night out was exactly what she needed to stop stewing about Joey and what he did, or more frequently didn't do, for Declan.

When Lisa rounded the corner, Rachel felt the stress of the day slip away and excitement for the evening ahead bloom within her. She waved.

"Hey," Lisa said as she stepped up beside her. "How's it going?"

"Good," she said, and she meant it. "You?"

"Can't complain," Lisa said, but her voice had that distant quality to it. Rachel was curious about the haunted expression that crossed Lisa's face from time to time, but she didn't know how to approach her to ask.

"Shall we?" she asked instead, motioning toward the door.

When Lisa nodded, Rachel held open the door and allowed her to step inside before following.

A live band was crammed into a corner of the bar. One of the band members had his hands in the air, inciting the audience to clap along with him. The drummer kept time on the *bodhran*, steadily increasing the song's tempo with the mallet that flew across the little round drum head. The crowd's clapping quickened along with the rhythm. The fiddle player in the middle had his eyes closed and his head tilted back as his bow flew across the strings.

Rachel watched as Lisa took it all in. She had been to a number of ceilidhs in her lifetime, and each one had been an experience to remember, an evening of upbeat Celtic music, beer, and dancing. O'Leary's pub was small and crowded, and the jovial spirit of the crowd practically spilled out of the place. The smile that slowly spread across Lisa's face as she began to clap along with the music told Rachel that the ceilidh spirit was not lost on her, either.

Rachel warmed at the sight. She couldn't imagine life on Cape Breton Island without the infusion of Celtic music and culture, and she realized in that moment how badly she wanted Lisa to enjoy this glimpse into the Cape Breton Island life that she loved.

"Let's go get drinks," she called over the music, and Lisa followed as they wended their way through the sea of people and made their way toward the bar.

"I had no idea what to expect," Lisa said, leaning in close enough for Rachel to hear her over the music. Close enough for her to catch Lisa's soft scent of honey and shea. "This is fantastic!"

Lisa's excitement was contagious, and Rachel grinned. "What can I get you to drink?"

Lisa bit her lower lip as she studied the offerings behind the bar. "Surprise me."

She didn't hesitate before turning to the bartender. "Two Keith's, please."

A moment later, the bartender slid the two pints of beer across the counter to her and Lisa.

"Thank you," Lisa said.

Rachel held up her glass. "To a night of no worries."

"I'll drink to that!"

They each took a long drink of the cold beer, then set the pints next to them on the bar.

A bagpiper joined the band, and the airy harmonies filled the air in an up-tempo song that had people in the bar stomping their feet in time.

"Rachel Murray!"

She turned to the voice. "Ryan Clarke!"

He pulled her into a bear hug that lifted her off her feet and spun her. She was laughing by the time he set her down.

"Who's this lovely lady standing next to you?"

"This is Lisa," she said. "Eloise's niece. Lisa, this is a friend of mine, Ryan. He and his dad work out on the fishing boats and sell fish to our restaurant."

"Nice to meet you." Lisa extended her hand.

Ryan looked at the extended hand, then up at Lisa, and shook his head as he pulled her into a bear hug as well. Rachel tried, unsuccessfully, not to laugh at the terror on her face by the time Ryan released her.

"Care to dance?" Ryan asked, holding his hand out to Lisa.

She grabbed her beer from the counter and held it up. "Maybe later?"

"C'mon," Ryan urged, his hand still extended. "Live a little."

Lisa met Rachel's eyes as though to ask if it was all right to leave for the dance. She smiled and motioned Lisa forward in encouragement, fighting down the swell of jealousy that threatened.

Determination passed over Lisa's face, and she handed her drink over and followed Ryan out to the dance floor.

Rachel leaned against the bar and watched. Lisa appeared shy at first, but eventually she began to loosen up, getting into the dance, allowing Ryan to swing her around the dance floor. At one point, Ryan dipped her, and Lisa tilted her head back with a laugh. She was beautiful when she lit up like that, her stoic wall crumbling for the moment and giving Rachel a glimpse of the woman behind that wall, bright and carefree. When Lisa gave her a small wave, Rachel felt a pull that she hadn't felt for anyone in years. She took another long drink of her beer, scared by the attraction that tugged at her.

Lisa had not given any indication that she shared that attraction, and she clearly had some ghosts she was running from.

Bad idea, she told herself.

But she saw Lisa laugh again, and her stomach tightened despite the warning.

Live a little. That was why Lisa had agreed to the ceilidh, wasn't it? A night where she could get out of her head and pretend to be like everyone else. She hadn't wanted to dance with Ryan, but he had issued a challenge she couldn't back away from. One dance. One song. She would go through the motions.

The thing was, as she started dancing, she wasn't merely going through the motions anymore. She was dipped and twirled in time with the music, and all the while the man across from her was grinning and enjoying the party. Everyone was enjoying the party. The lyrics that she pulled out of the song were bitter and depressing, but the music was upbeat. Everyone in the room was smiling, and the song was frequently accented with whoops or cheers.

Lisa waved at Rachel who leaned against the bar with a beer in each hand. Warmth spread through her when Rachel's eyes met hers, the unique blend of green and blue making her feel as if she were gazing into the ocean. The strength of the connection forced Lisa to turn away, to lose herself in the dance once more. And she did. She let go and let herself have fun for the first time in too long.

When the song ended, she extricated herself from Ryan's arms, thanking him politely before returning to where Rachel stood.

"Sorry about that." She took the beer Rachel held out to her. "He threw down the gauntlet and I couldn't resist."

"You looked like you were having fun."

"I was, actually," she admitted. "I haven't danced in years."

"Well, you're a natural."

Lisa hoped that the dim light in the bar hid the flush that crept to her cheeks. Rachel's eyes held her with a tenderness she was unaccustomed to, and it tugged at something inside of her she hadn't felt in a long time.

She took a long drink of her beer, then placed her glass on the counter, holding her hand out. "Care to dance?" she asked, lowering her voice in imitation of Ryan earlier, in the hopes that she could play off the invitation as light and casual. She wanted to stay caught up in the energy. While normally she would have preferred to stand next to the bar, drinking and people watching, for this one night she didn't want to be a wallflower.

Rachel tilted her head slightly to the side and regarded her with a curious expression, but then she placed her glass next to Lisa's and took the offered hand.

Lisa led the two of them out to the center of the dance floor amid the crowd of people. The song was quick, and she focused on trying to ensure her feet kept up. Next to her, Rachel twirled, throwing her hands in the air. Lisa was struck by the joy that radiated out of her as she danced—complete exuberance.

Her train of thought was derailed when Rachel grabbed her hands and spun her. She allowed herself to stop thinking, to get lost in the movement and the music.

She felt free. Like a weight had been lifted off of her.

Rachel's hands were soft and warm, and the light touch sent heat through her. She moved in closer, drawn to her. Rachel steadily guided her in the dance, and she gave herself over to Rachel's lead. There were others around them, she knew, but it felt as if it were only the two of them and the music. Nothing else.

And then the song came to an end, and she and Rachel stood facing one another in the momentary silence. Lisa tried to catch her breath, and Rachel pushed her curls away from her face, flushed from the dance.

"Thanks for indulging me," Lisa said.

"My pleasure. That was fun."

Fun. Was that the word for it? Lisa could only nod. She had more than simply enjoyed the dance. For those few minutes, she had felt human. The smile that had hardly left her face all evening wasn't forced. In fact, at times she found herself having been completely unaware of the smile.

Rachel headed back to the bar, taking Lisa's hand as she led the way.

Lisa stepped up to the counter and ordered another two beers, one for each of them.

On the dance floor, people moved into groups of three, starting what appeared to be some sort of Celtic square dance. The people who weren't dancing stood to the side clapping along.

The ceilidh was more than just a dance party. It was a celebration, everyone appearing thoroughly grateful to be alive. She'd lived as a shadow for so long, a ghost, she didn't remember what that felt like.

Live a little.

That was why she'd come to Cape Breton Island, wasn't it? She tried to allow herself to let go. For one night, she wanted to put away the mask she'd kept perfectly in place. One night to genuinely be happy. To be *alive*.

The guilt would come later, as it always did. Happiness and grief, life and loss—the two forever inextricably intertwined.

But she wanted *one* night.

Chapter Six

Lisa woke to sunlight streaming through her window, soft rays of light cascading over her skin. She blinked her eyes and stretched. It had been a long time since she had awoken *after* the sun. Sleeping through the night well rested was something she'd grown unaccustomed to. It was a nice change to wake bathed in light, instead of having grief pull her from her dreams into darkness. She let out a contented sigh, pulling her knitted quilt around herself and sinking down into the warmth of her bed.

The ceilidh had been good for her. She'd danced until she could hardly stand, and her cheeks hurt from smiling by the end of the night. The only obligation she'd had for the evening had been to have a good time, and somehow she'd managed that. Somewhere on the dance floor she had found a glimpse of who she had been before—before the broken future and the broken self. Maybe she *could* get back to being that person again, or at least some version of her.

She slipped from the bed, eager to start the new day. She pulled on a pair of jeans, a white T-shirt, and a soft blue hooded sweatshirt. She tied her blond hair back into a quick ponytail and looked herself over in the bathroom mirror. She appeared light and casual, not brooding or haunted; she saw no ghosts in her hazel eyes. She smiled and turned to head downstairs.

Eloise was already up and sitting at the table. She'd probably been up for a while and would be nearly finished with her cross-word puzzle, only the few challenging words still empty boxes on the page.

"Morning, Auntie Eloise." She made her way to the kitchen to reheat the kettle.

"Good morning, dear. Sleep well?"

"I slept great."

Eloise let out a chuckle. "I suppose so. Tea's already cold."

"Dancing really wore me out, I guess."

"So you had a good time last night, I take it?"

"I *did*," she said. "It was so nice to go out and be me again. It's been way too long."

"That's good. I'm glad. And I'm glad you and Rachel are getting to know one another."

"Yeah, me too." She smiled as she thought of Rachel. Lisa had been pleasantly surprised by how much she enjoyed her company. She replayed the previous night as she waited for the water to boil. Rachel was vibrant and warm, and she could still feel the softness of Rachel's hand in her own.

The kettle whistled, interrupting Lisa's thoughts. She pulled it off the stove and reached into the cupboard for a bag of English breakfast tea. Once she had stirred some honey in, she took a seat across the table from Eloise. She enjoyed their easy mornings of tea and artwork and crossword puzzles, but she stilled when she saw what her aunt had on the table in front of her instead of the daily puzzle.

"What are you doing?"

Eloise glanced up, then back at the open sketchbook on the table in front of her. "Admiring your art. You could sell these even without a book to go with them. They're wonderful."

Her stomach knotted as she saw the sketch. It wasn't one she was working on for her new project. It was a personal piece. One she'd drawn for her eyes only. On the page was a baby gently cradled by a pair of hands—eyes closed, tiny nose, tiny lips, wisps of baby-down hair. In the blank space around the cradled child, she had drawn other images: a chubby toddler being lifted in the air; a child on a swing set, hair blowing back, a smile on his face; a long and lanky teenager with headphones on and a skateboard tucked under his arm. In each of the additional images, the boy had a set of cherub wings that grew along with him.

"The detail in this is amazing," Eloise breathed.

Lisa's blood went cold. She put her tea on the table and snatched up the sketchbook. "I didn't say you could look through these." She hugged the book to her chest, as though by hiding it against her she could make Eloise unsee the image.

"The book was open on the table."

"That wasn't an open invitation to go through it. This isn't yours," she snapped, her voice rising. She frantically searched her memory, trying to recall what other images her aunt might have viewed, but the thought of the other sketches in the book made her stomach twist painfully and she had to stop herself. When had she left it there? How could she have been so careless?

"I'm sorry," Eloise said. "You've never really been private about your art. I mean, you make a living off of your drawings. I didn't think it would be a problem."

"Sorry doesn't give me my privacy back." She knew she was being unfair, but panic gripped her, and she turned from the room cradling her sketchbook, wishing desperately to run from the raw nakedness she felt. She grabbed her coat and shoes and pushed out of the little house. She didn't know where she was going, but she needed to be somewhere, anywhere, else. She walked along the road until she was out of sight of the house, and then she headed over to the rocky shoreline and found a seat underneath a large red oak tree.

She was crying by the time she sat down, her eyes leaking tears down onto her cheeks, which she wiped furiously with the back of her sleeve before hugging the sketchbook to her chest, folding herself around her knees, and giving in to the tears.

When finally, she was able to take a breath and clear her eyes, she unfolded herself and opened the book to see what other images she had inside. *How could I have been so stupid to leave this sitting out on the table? Stupid. Careless.*

She paused on the sketch she had drawn right after Mitchell's funeral, and tore it out. A horrible sense of complete nakedness overcame her, and she wished she could make the image disappear. Make it so that her aunt would never have seen it. She was exposed, and the exposure made her burn with something akin to shame. She crumpled the picture into a ball and wound up to heave it into the ocean. Once she had her arm back by her shoulder, however, she froze as though she was paralyzed. She couldn't bring herself to toss the page.

"Goddamn it." She brought the crumpled ball of paper back into her lap. She couldn't rid herself of the sketch. "Goddamn it," she said again, with less anger and more defeat.

She smoothed the paper and studied the sketch of the woman sitting in a rocking chair, folded over herself, clutching a baby blanket. On her back a giant shadow weighed her down, its weight causing her shoulders and head to crumple inward. She had to resist the urge to turn around. She knew she would see nothing, just as she knew that shadow was still standing over her, pressing down on her, crushing her.

She was a fool to think she'd ever be free.

Lisa made no move to go inside, even long after the cold air settled a chill deep into her skin. Shivers only added to her feeling of agitation as she was unable to sit still. But God, to go inside and face Eloise ... She wasn't ready. Not after everything Eloise had seen. Lisa was laid bare inside of that sketchbook. Maybe if she stayed outside long enough the chill would settle right through her bones, tightening up her muscles and tendons, and turning her soft flesh solid and statuesque. She could stay there by the shore until spring thaw, and maybe by then enough time would have passed for Eloise to have forgotten.

"You're going to catch your death out here."

She turned to find Eloise standing a few yards back, hands folded across her chest, woolen jacket pulled tight around her frail frame.

"I'm fine." She went back to staring out at the sea.

"I can hear your teeth chattering from here. Get inside." It was a gentle order, but an order nonetheless, and left no room for question or argument.

She didn't move right away, but as though she were still a child being disciplined, she eventually stood, obeying her great-aunt.

Eloise said nothing as she led the way back to the house, and Lisa sensed the additional chill in the air around the two of them. Even stepping inside the warm house didn't cut through that chill.

"I'm sorry I went through your sketchbook," Eloise said as she hung up her jacket.

"It's all right, I—"

"I'm not finished," Eloise said, her voice stern as she turned to face her. "I'm sorry I went through your sketchbook, but I didn't deserve the reaction I got from you. If you're going to live here, you need to treat me with more respect. I looked at the artwork *you* left on the kitchen table. I get it, I overstepped your boundaries, and it was an invasion of your privacy. It won't happen again. You could've just said that. There's no need for you to snap at me."

Shame crept up Lisa's neck. "I'm sorry."

Eloise sighed, but said nothing else and headed for the living room.

She held her sketchbook limply beside her and remained rooted in place. She had come to Cape Breton for change, and everything felt the same. There were no answers to be found by the sea. She was still damaged.

She stepped into the living room and sat in the recliner opposite her aunt. "I'm sorry," she said again, this time the words more sincere.

"I know you miss him. None of what I saw in that sketchbook told me anything I didn't already know about you."

She held the book in both hands and stared at its plain black cover while she traced her fingers over the coil binding.

"You can talk to me about him," Eloise said.

She shook her head. "I can't."

"Lisa . . ." Eloise began, then she trailed off, as though unsure what words would come next.

"I don't know how to talk about him. Not without falling apart."

"It's okay to fall apart."

She shook her head, shaking away those words. "It's not. I'm trying to put myself back together."

"By avoiding everything that reminds you of him?" Eloise asked.

"I'm processing." She held up the notebook. "In my own way."

At least she was trying. She apparently was not doing a very good job. She didn't know how to move forward. There was no blueprint, no guidelines to follow. She needed time to grieve. She needed to immerse herself in art, and she needed people to stop seeing her as broken or tiptoeing around her in conversations.

She thought of the way Rachel had looked at her, nothing but warmth in her eyes. Rachel just saw *her*. Lisa needed people to look at her like *that*.

Eventually, she'd be able to talk about Mitchell, and her feelings wouldn't be so raw.

"I shouldn't have snapped at you," she said. "It was my fault for leaving the sketchbook out, but I'd prefer if we don't talk about this anymore."

Eloise nodded, but her jaw was set, and her eyes said the conversation was not over.

Chapter Seven

As soon as the customer waved Rachel over, she knew she had messed up.

"Ma'am," the man began, "I ordered the seafood linguine *without* the shrimp."

Rachel cringed, knowing immediately that the mistake had been on her end, and she had forgotten to relay that alteration to the kitchen staff. Her stomach dropped and her face burned with embarrassment.

"I'm so sorry. This was my fault. I can put in a rush for a new order, and the meal will be on the house."

The man looked down at his pasta, then across the table at his wife who had already begun to eat her fish and chips, and he huffed. "Seeing as I'm allergic to shrimp, I guess I don't have much choice if I want lunch."

"Again, I'm *so* sorry." Rachel took the dish from the table.

Well, there goes another tip, she thought as she pushed her way into the kitchen. *I should've stayed in bed today.*

"What's wrong with *this* one?" Eloise asked.

Rachel exhaled, trying to focus on the breath to keep her steady. "I need a rush on a seafood linguine, *no* shrimp. I'm sorry, Eloise. I messed up his order."

"And he can't eat it anyway?" Eloise quipped.

"Not without an epi pen."

"You're on quite the roll today," her dad interjected.

There was nothing Rachel could say. She was a better server than the day would make her appear. She'd worked at Catherine's Restaurant since the place opened when she was fifteen and in all of those years she'd never had to return so many dishes and drinks to the kitchen. What had started out as a rough day had quickly spiraled downhill into the "day from hell" category. She needed to rally, but each mistake left her more flustered and in turn contributed to more mistakes.

"What's going on?" Frank asked.

"I'm just tired."

Frank looked at her, the concern evident in his eyes, but mercifully said nothing. Rachel didn't want to talk, and she appreciated her dad respecting that.

She took another minute to collect herself, then pushed off the counter and back out to the dining room.

Even outside it was miserable: gray and rainy. The kind of day that made Rachel wish she'd stayed in bed. Instead, she wiped down a table to make herself busy and avoid speaking to anyone while Eloise finished redoing the man's seafood linguine. Her stomach sank when she heard the front door open.

"Two minutes of downtime, that's all I want," she muttered, but her bleak mood lifted when she saw Lisa stepping through the door.

"Hi," Rachel said, moving toward Lisa with her first unforced smile of the morning.

"Hey," Lisa answered, one corner of her mouth tugging upward in a casual half-smile, causing Rachel's stomach to do a small flip.

A blush crept up her neck, and she cursed herself as she turned to grab a menu, hoping Lisa didn't notice. "You've got perfect timing. I've just finished wiping down a table by the window."

"Perfect."

She motioned for Lisa to follow, and led the way, trying not to acknowledge how flustered she was. As they crossed the dining room, Eloise brought out the newly cooked pasta to the man with the shrimp allergy, and shame tightened around her.

She was glad Eloise was handling the table for her. She didn't know that she could bring herself to face the man again. If she could have an hour without somebody seeing her as a failure, that would be wonderful.

"Here you go." She placed the menu on the table for Lisa.

"Thanks," Lisa said, sliding into the booth.

"No problem," she said. She craned her neck, peering over at the other table to ensure the man wasn't reaming out Eloise in her stead. Eloise seemed to be handling the situation well.

"Everything okay?" Lisa asked.

"Long day," she admitted.

"Want to talk about it?"

She met Lisa's eyes, seeing genuine empathy and care in her soft gaze. She considered the offer, finding she did indeed want to talk about it. At least with Lisa. "I don't want to bother you," she said instead. "It's all a long story."

"When you get a break, maybe you could join me and tell me about it," Lisa offered.

"Are you sure?" she asked.

Lisa nodded with a steady certainty.

The restaurant had quieted down, with most of the tables finishing their lunch. And she was doing more harm than good by serving anyway. "I could probably use a lunch break. Why don't I get your order in, and then I'll come join you?"

"I'd like that."

"I'll give you a minute with the menu."

"No need. I'll have the chowder." Lisa picked up the menu and held it out to Rachel who arched an eyebrow but took the menu.

"It's why I'm here," Lisa said. "That stuff's addicting."

"I'll go get that started for you. At least that's an order I shouldn't mess up."

"Be warned, I'm very particular. I expect my soup in a timely manner. Clam chowder, *extra* clams. Hot, but not so hot I burn my mouth. And bottled water, not tap. Sparkling, preferably."

"Yes, your majesty." Rachel laughed as she turned toward the kitchen.

"Why so smiley all of a sudden?" Frank asked.

"What are you talking about?"

"You practically floated into the kitchen grinning like the cat who got the canary."

"I did not." She turned away from her dad's inquisition. She had not been *grinning,* and she most certainly did not *float* anywhere.

"Two chowders, Eloise," she said.

Eloise gave a single nod and set to work. The silence was unusual, and Rachel immediately kicked herself for all of the day's screwups.

"I'm sorry you had to deal with the table," she said. "I promise, no more mix-ups today."

"Don't worry, dear. He didn't give me any trouble. Everything is fine."

She wasn't convinced. There was a detached quality in Eloise's normally cheery voice.

Rachel shifted. "It's slowed down out there. I'm going to take a lunch break if that's okay with you two? Have some chowder with Lisa."

Eloise looked up. "I don't know if now is a good time. We still have a few customers."

"They've all got their food now," Rachel said.

"It's still the lunch hour. Others could come in any minute."

She didn't understand Eloise's sudden resistance. Yeah, she'd made a few mistakes, but nothing too terrible. It was just an off day. She was about to apologize anyway, but her dad spoke up on her behalf.

"She can get up if others come in. A break won't hurt anyone. Hell, it might even do some good."

Eloise said nothing, but her jaw was set as she began warming the bowls of chowder. She watched Eloise for a long moment before she gave up trying to decipher her expression and headed out to the booth where Lisa was sitting, staring out the window.

"Chowder's getting started for us," Rachel said.

"Excellent." Lisa smiled.

Rachel fell into Lisa's gaze. Her hazel eyes shone with gold flecks, and when she looked at her, Rachel felt Lisa really *saw* her.

"So spill," Lisa said. "Why has today been such a long day?"

"You cut right to the chase, don't you?"

"And you evade questions."

"Busted." She let out a sigh, feeling the full weight of the day. "I've been the server from hell today."

"I'm sure that's not true," Lisa countered.

"Oh, believe me, it is. More food has come back than has stayed out. I'm distracted, and it's shown."

"What's got you so distracted?" Lisa asked the million-dollar question.

Lisa was practically a stranger, Rachel reminded herself, but still she found she desperately wanted to open up.

"It was a bad morning. Declan got back from visiting his dad Sunday night. Now there are rules again, and school, and I'm the mean parent who doesn't let him do whatever the hell he wants."

Lisa put a hand on Rachel's arm. She looked down at the soft fingers resting against her. The touch sent warm shivers up her arm, and her stomach tightened pleasantly. It was meant as a comforting gesture and nothing more, but the tenderness felt good regardless.

"Joey's visits *always* cause problems. Declan is either angry at Joey for blowing him off, or he comes back from a visit where Joey lets him get away with murder and then he's angry at me for having to follow rules again. Either way, Declan's angry, and I can expect an unpleasant few days. He's *six*. He needs consistency. He needs *parents*. Not glorified playmates. Today I had to fight him to go to school. I'm so tired of always being the bad guy."

"That must be hard," Lisa said.

Rachel couldn't meet Lisa's eyes, so she studied the whorls in the wooden table. "He's a kid. He's supposed to be happy. *I'm* supposed to be able to make him happy."

"You're a *great* mom."

She raised one eyebrow in challenge.

"You are," Lisa assured. There was a distance in her voice, though, and Rachel wondered if she actually believed what she said. After all, why should she? Lisa didn't exactly have anything to base that assessment on. Declan was not a happy child. His behavior marked him as the "troublemaker" in the class. And she saw the way the other parents looked at her, the single mom who had got pregnant at a young age in a small town. Declan's misbehavior only gave them confirmation of their biases. She was a failure as a parent and a person.

Emotion welled within her. She wished she'd heard conviction in Lisa's voice. She knew what people in Craghurst must think of her, but God, she wanted Lisa to believe differently. Even if she didn't feel like a great mom, she wanted Lisa to believe it. Lisa's opinion mattered more to her than she could even understand.

Eloise saved Rachel from having to put any of that into words by showing up at the table with two bowls of clam chowder.

"Enjoy," she said, putting them in front of Lisa and Rachel.

"Thanks," Lisa said.

Rachel watched as Eloise studied Lisa for a long, hard moment before heading back to the kitchen, and she wondered if maybe she wasn't the one that Eloise was upset with.

If Lisa noticed anything off about Eloise, however, she didn't let on. She took a spoonful of chowder and blew on it to cool it off.

"Is everything okay with Eloise?" Rachel asked.

Lisa looked up with her brows furrowed. "As far as I know. Why?"

"I don't know. She just seems off today," Rachel said. Except that it hadn't been the entire day. Eloise had been her usual self all morning.

Lisa shrugged, and Rachel let it drop, taking her own spoonful of the chowder.

"So," Lisa began after a minute, "I didn't just come here for the chowder."

"You didn't?"

Lisa shook her head. "I was hoping to see you. I wanted to thank you for the other night. I had a really good time at the ceilidh."

"So did I."

For a long moment Lisa didn't say anything else, but she clearly had more to say, so Rachel waited.

"I came to Cape Breton Island to get away from people," Lisa said, her words careful and soft. "I thought I'd take a year, isolate myself from everyone, and work on my art. But it's really nice to have a friend here."

Friend. Disappointment settled within her at the single word solidifying their relationship. Perhaps she'd imagined the flirting.

Lisa stirred her chowder.

"Do you like hiking?" she asked, eventually, turning her focus back to Rachel.

She nodded. "I don't get out hiking nearly often enough, but I enjoy it."

"I've been wanting to get out and explore some of the trails in Highlands National Park before the trees lose all of the color and the snow comes. I don't really want to go hiking unfamiliar trails alone, though. If you have a day off, would you like to join me?"

"I'd love to," she said, unable to hide her excitement. "I'm off work Monday. Maybe we could go while Declan's in school?"

"That sounds wonderful," Lisa said.

And it did. More wonderful than she cared to admit.

The aroma of garlic and basil filled the air as Lisa turned the meatballs for her spaghetti over in the frying pan. Roxie sat at her feet, tail wagging and tongue hanging out, in hopes she might drop one of those meatballs straight from the pan and into the dog's waiting mouth.

"Go away, piggy," she said, nudging her. Roxie didn't move more than a foot, and peered up with mournful eyes, too sad and hungry to ignore. She picked one of the smaller, already-cooked meatballs out of the pan and dropped it to the floor.

"Don't tell Eloise," she whispered.

Roxie quickly lapped up the little meatball, chewing less than three times before swallowing and returning her gaze to Lisa as though to say, "I won't say a word. Can I have another?"

"If only we could all be so easy to please." She scratched the dog behind her ears. "Meatballs and tummy rubs, and you're pretty much set for life."

In agreement, Roxie licked her chops and redirected her attention back to the frying pan.

Lisa laughed and shook her head, using the wooden spoon to turn the meatballs, and as she cooked she caught herself whistling. Once she noticed, she quieted, but then she allowed herself to resume whistling. She felt lighter than she had in a long while, and she wanted to savor the moment. So she whistled while she added the sauce to the meatballs, and strained the spaghetti.

"You're in a good mood," Eloise said, stepping into the kitchen.

"I am," she admitted. "It's been a good day." How long had it been since she could say that? "How was your day?"

"Not bad."

Lisa tilted the pasta into the pan with the meatballs and sauce and stirred. "Would you like some?"

"Sure." Eloise took a seat at the table while Lisa spooned some spaghetti onto each plate.

"You know," Eloise began, as Lisa set a plate of spaghetti in front of her, "Rachel hasn't exactly had the easiest time lately."

She sat down with her spaghetti across from her great-aunt and nodded while she took a bite. "I know. She's talked to me a bit about it. Sounds like things have been pretty rough for Declan at school."

"He can be a handful, for sure," Eloise said.

Lisa didn't want to talk about Declan. She pushed the images of him making the card for his mom and playing with Roxie on the beach out of her mind. She had yet to see this troubled side of him. She'd gotten through the conversation with Rachel earlier, mustering as much support as possible. Now she was ready to be done thinking about him.

"Listen," Eloise continued. "I love you. You're family. But so is Rachel. I don't want her to get hurt."

"What's that supposed to mean?" she asked, unsure where this conversation was coming from.

"She told me you invited her hiking."

"We're friends." Lisa ignored the nagging in her gut that told her she wasn't painting an entirely accurate representation of their relationship.

"Maybe I'm wrong," Eloise said, holding up her hands in concession. "But I see the way the two of you look at each other. Just . . . be careful. And know that she comes as a package deal with Declan."

Lisa bristled at the boy's name, and at the same time defensiveness swelled within her at the implication she was somehow too damaged to be around Rachel and her son, even while knowing Eloise was probably right. "I know," was all she said.

"Okay," Eloise responded, and went back to eating her dinner as the conversation dropped.

Lisa *did* know Rachel came with a son. She was painfully aware of that fact the entire time Rachel had talked to her about him. Even when Rachel talked about how hard everything was, she'd felt the envy and grief clutch her.

But Declan wasn't coming on the hike with them. And they were just friends. Lisa didn't need to worry about a package deal because she wasn't *with* Rachel. They could spend time together. It was safe.

She took a bite of her food and tried to convince herself of that.

Chapter Eight

As the elevation increased and the ocean vista spread before them, Lisa felt a world away from the suffocating city of Toronto, with streets haunted by the ghosts of what could've been—the playgrounds Mitchell should have played at, the schools he should have attended, the life he should have had. Out here her prison walls crumbled as the road curved along the coast. She felt as if she was driving along the edge of the earth as the cliffs fell away to the open ocean. She could *breathe* finally, with the vast open space before her.

She drove, and Rachel sat next to her in the passenger seat. Beatles tunes played softly on the car stereo, the sky was vast and blue, and the air felt thick and rich and healing.

"Thanks for coming with me," she said, quickly glancing over at Rachel.

Rachel smiled shyly back. "Thank you for inviting me."

"Hopefully you're not too bored playing tour guide all day," she said, eliciting a laugh from Rachel.

"So that's why you invited me!"

"Well of course," she deadpanned. "That, and I needed somebody to fight off the bears for me."

"I should've known. You brought me along as bear bait. When we get attacked, you're going to take off and hope you can outrun me, aren't you?"

"Now that you mention it . . ." She sent a grin Rachel's way. "I had no idea you could be such a jerk!"

"A jerk? Me?" She played innocent and turned to see Rachel nod, her chin raised defiantly in a gesture Lisa could only describe as incredibly cute.

Eyes on the road, she reminded herself, forcing herself to turn away.

"I'll have you know," Rachel continued. "I'm quite quick."

"We'll see," Lisa challenged.

The road wound upward, and the foliage grew denser. Lisa bobbed her head along with the music as she took in the vibrant autumn colors. The Cape Breton Highlands National Park covered the northern third of the Cabot Trail, and had a number of hiking trails and lookout points throughout, all with views that were supposed to be spectacular. She vaguely remembered driving the route as a child with her family, but the memory was fuzzy and probably an amalgamation of memories from a number of other trips as well. She looked forward to seeing the park again as an adult.

"Hey Jude" came on the stereo, and Lisa turned when she heard Rachel singing along.

"Good song," Rachel said before she went back to singing.

She joined in, getting lost in the music and the moment. She couldn't remember the last time she had sung in the car, but in that moment she vowed to do so more often. As she belted the chorus she was sure that nothing existed beyond the small car on the scenic highway.

"You're quite the vocalist," she said when the song came to an end. "Good job on McCartney's solos at the end."

Rachel gave a small bow. "Thank you. It's just nice to sing along to something other than Disney."

She sobered at the thought of the songs she would much rather be singing along to in the car.

She felt Rachel's eyes on her, but couldn't find the words to break the heavy silence that had settled over them. Thankfully, Rachel took the initiative.

"God, I need to get out here more," Rachel breathed. "I forgot how beautiful the drive is."

Lisa gave a small smile of appreciation before answering. "It's gorgeous."

Rachel reached over and gave her knee a squeeze that sent warmth up the length of Lisa's leg. But the contact was gone far too soon. Lisa didn't want to analyze the empty feeling that followed.

"I can't believe I've been living here nearly a month, and I still haven't gotten out to explore," Lisa said.

"I've been living here for twenty-four years, and I can't remember the last time I came out here."

"You're busy with the restaurant. What excuse do I have?" she asked.

"You needed to wait until you had someone you could bring along as bear bait."

"Well, there's that."

Rachel laughed, and Lisa felt the sound in her chest—a brightness that spread outward, making her whole body lighter.

The two fell silent as the road wended its way further upward into the heart of the highlands. Lisa's gaze was riveted on the scenery unfolding before them. The highway pulled out of the trees, and the coast displayed itself in front of them, waves raging against the cliffs below.

"*Wow.*"

"If you're interested in a good view of the ocean, there's a hike just around the bend. It's a bit steep, but the view makes the climb worth it."

"Let's do it," Lisa said with a smile, excited to be out in nature.

Rachel watched the road, then said, "Here."

She turned onto the small gravel turnoff. "I would have flown right by if I was by myself. You're fulfilling your tour guide duties already."

"In the summer, this road is bumper-to-bumper traffic. Other cars would've been marking this side road. It's a little harder to see in the off-season."

Lisa turned off the ignition and stepped out of the car, taking her knapsack from the backseat. Then she leaned down to tighten her shoelaces for the climb.

"Ready," she said, straightening to find Rachel leaning against the side of the car and watching her with a gaze that felt tender and intimate. Heat shot through her body in response, but she chose to ignore that fact. "Lead on."

Rachel strode off and Lisa followed her, stopping at the foot of the trail to take in the wooden map with details about the route. Lisa was most interested in the cautionary note about wildlife.

"See, it's a good thing I've planned for a bear attack," she pointed out.

"Fair enough. But if we get charged by a moose, I'm using *you* as my human shield."

"Now who's the jerk?"

"You were willing to feed me to the bears. I feel no remorse." Rachel started onto the trail, leaving Lisa standing by the sign.

"Truce?" Lisa asked, jogging to catch up.

Rachel sized Lisa up, but then shook her hand. "Truce."

Things with Rachel were light and natural. Lisa couldn't deny the undercurrent of attraction, but as long as she could continue to ignore it . . . The two walked in companionable silence. She breathed in the rich, clean air as though it could replace the black toxins of grief that weighed heavy inside of her.

"I don't know why I haven't come out here every weekend," Lisa said, as she worked her way up a steep section of the trail.

"Wait until you get to the view," Rachel said as she struggled up a few feet behind her, clearly winded from the climb.

Lisa held out her hand, and Rachel took it, accepting her help up the final stretch. She had only intended to help Rachel balance for the final ascent, but it was impossible not to notice how perfectly their hands fit together.

"Thanks." Rachel took back her hand and brushed herself off. Lisa instantly felt the loss.

"No problem." She turned, the vista before her taking her

breath away. They had reached a clearing at the top, and she felt as though the two of them had reached the edge of the world. A few meters away, the ground gave way to a cliff that fell away to the sea. Her lips parted slightly as she took in the view, the wind whipping her ponytail. Words were inadequate, so she said nothing, simply staring in awe. Beside her, she felt Rachel's eyes on her, but she was too absorbed in the view to meet the gaze.

"I was thirteen the first time I came here," Rachel said. "My mom brought me."

Lisa turned to look at her and this time it was Rachel who didn't meet the gaze, staring out to sea.

"My dad was a fisherman, born and raised on the island. My mom was from Halifax. Sometimes, I think she felt trapped on the island, but when we came out here she seemed so at home. She loved being outdoors on the trails."

"Your dad was a fisherman?" Lisa asked.

"The restaurant was my mom's dream. She was the chef in the family, but right before the place was supposed to open she died. Dad gave up fishing to make a go of it. He always said he couldn't let her dream die, too. He named the place after her, and the rest, as they say, is history."

She let the full weight of that comment sink in. Opening a restaurant couldn't be easy, but especially not for Rachel and her dad who'd had no experience in that field. They'd made it work, completely out of their love for Catherine Murray.

"Good for him, making the place so successful," she said. "Good for *you*." She hoped her voice conveyed how deeply impressed she was with both of them.

"Thanks," Rachel said in earnest. Then her tone shifted, becoming far lighter. "Really, it was all Eloise. I don't know what made us think we had any business opening a restaurant. My dad's a *decent* cook, but he's certainly not great. I'd burn boiling water. Thank God we spend so much time in the restaurant, or I'm pretty sure Declan would either starve or be raised on TV dinners."

Lisa laughed. "I'm sure you're not *that* terrible a cook. You must've picked up a few basic skills at least."

"Oh, believe me, I did not." Rachel shook her head, the breeze and the movement blowing her curls over her shoulder. "I did not get the chef gene from my mom. We lucked out finding Eloise to help us. Without her, the place wouldn't have lasted a week."

"I don't know. There's this cute waitress . . . she's what keeps me coming back." The words were out before Lisa realized what she was saying, and as soon as she said them she wished she could take them back, no matter how true. She didn't wait for Rachel's reaction, scared at whatever it might be. She sat with her legs crossed on the grass, pulling her knapsack into her lap.

"What are you doing?" Rachel asked, sitting beside her.

"I don't know about you, but I could go for some lunch."

"You made lunch?"

"Nothing fancy." Lisa pulled two sandwiches out of her bag. "I hope you like ham and cheese."

"It just so happens ham and cheese *is* my very favorite." Rachel took one of the sandwiches, unwrapping the plastic wrap.

"I figured it was a safe choice."

It was possible, Lisa decided, that the sandwiches were the only safe choice she had made all day.

She reached into her backpack and pulled out the small cooler with the two cold beers inside. She opened one and handed it to Rachel who took the drink. Then she opened the second and took a long pull, hoping it would settle the anxiety that coiled around her stomach.

"Tell me something about you," Rachel said. "What made you decide to pack up and move out to the coast?"

She gazed out at the sea and exhaled. She had the easy answer that she was giving people right on the tip of her tongue. *I needed a change of scenery. My work was getting stale. Stress was getting to me. I thought a change would do me good.* All lies. And she couldn't bring herself to tell Rachel those lies.

But she couldn't bring herself to give her the real answer either.

I hurt all the time. I thought I'd find peace here.

She watched the whitecaps on the waves way down below, lulled by the simple movement of the water.

"Hey." Rachel took Lisa's hand in hers. "Where are you?"

She looked down at their intertwined fingers—Rachel's were so smooth, and her thumb rubbed over the back of Lisa's hand— and met Rachel's sea-green eyes wide with concern, the shades of blue darker than usual.

"I'm here," she said, but she turned her gaze back out to the ocean.

Rachel continued drawing lazy circles on the back of her hand. When she spoke, her words were soft, almost a whisper. "Not just now. In the car too. And a few other times. You get quiet. Where do you go?"

She exhaled a long, slow breath and closed her eyes as though that could close out the warring feelings of wanting to run from Rachel and wanting to sink into her.

"Talk to me," Rachel said, her voice so soft it was barely above a whisper.

Lisa sunk into Rachel's soft gaze, but she couldn't form words to explain. The ones she needed to say were too painful, and the lump that formed in her throat prevented her from being able to utter a word.

She shook her head. "I can't . . ."

"When you feel like you *can* talk about it, I'm here," Rachel said.

She nodded.

But she felt a distance between the two of them that hadn't been there earlier. She wanted to bridge that distance. Rachel was patient and kind, and Lisa didn't want to shut her out.

She wasn't ready to talk about Mitchell, though. Maybe eventually. She wanted to be able to talk to Rachel. But for now, that wall needed to remain in place, or she might break.

Chapter Nine

Rachel sat at her kitchen table, studying the computerized spreadsheet, her dad quietly beside her, worry practically radiating off him as he sat with a downcast gaze. Their lives and livelihood were laid out in the columns and rows of little white cells.

"Are you sure these numbers are right?" she asked.

"I triple-checked 'em," Frank said.

She continued to scrutinize the data. The numbers seemed low. The past month Catherine's had done better than that, she had been sure of it.

"They're not bad numbers," he said. "Not as much of a buffer for the off-season as we were hoping this year, but we've gotten by with worse."

"I know. It's just not what I expected."

Catherine's was one of the only restaurants on the island that stayed open year-round. There wasn't much business in the off-season, as tourists didn't exactly flock to Cape Breton Island in January. Even some of the locals boarded up shop and left the island in the wintertime. It meant any business in the winter went to them, but they relied on the money earned over the summer and fall months to carry them through until tourists began returning in May.

"Festival's coming up," Frank said, "so we still have that last push. Eloise will come up with a special, and we'll market the hell out of it."

Every October the Autumn Air festival brought one last busy push as concerts and cultural events took place all across the island. The festival ran for nine days in various locations, with a weekend stopover in Craghurst. Hotels were booked up with the final tourists of the season planning their travels to coincide with the festival. For the two festival days their restaurant would be slammed, and then there would be an immediate shift to the slow winter lull.

"Joey's going to take Declan for the weekend, so that will help."

Frank uttered a disapproving scoff. "As though anything that boy does could be considered 'help.'"

"Don't start, Dad." She knew how he felt about Joey. She felt the same. But Joey was a part of her and Declan's lives, and it so happened he'd agreed to take Declan that weekend. They were going to be long, busy days, and Declan would be bored and disruptive.

Frank shook his head but said nothing else.

"We should go over the winter menu with Eloise as well," she said. "Cut out as much seafood as possible again to save on costs." The previous year Eloise had come up with a potato bacon chowder to replace the seafood chowder, and the soup had been a hit with the locals during the long cold months.

"Speaking of seafood, Ryan Clarke came by today to drop off our order of cod. Tells me he ran into you at a ceilidh last weekend. Says you had a pretty girl with you."

He had a knowing twinkle in his eye, and she shifted under the gaze. "I took Eloise's niece, Lisa. She'd never even heard of a ceilidh before. I thought it would be a good island experience."

He nodded as if thinking over what to say.

"We went hiking in the highlands today while Declan was in

school," she added, recalling how enjoyable the day had been. "I haven't been out there in way too long. It was a gorgeous afternoon and nice to get away for a couple of hours."

"So, you like this girl," he said. It was a statement, not a question.

"Yeah. It's nice having a friend in town."

"A friend," he repeated. "So, the ceilidh . . .? Not a date then?"

"What?" She asked, heat rushing to her face. "No. Not a date. Where'd you get that idea?"

Frank shrugged and gave a small smirk. "Ryan may have insinuated you had taken a good one from him. That and the way your cheeks are getting all rosy right now . . ."

"My cheeks are not getting all rosy," Rachel said with an embarrassed laugh, despite feeling the heat creep up her neck. "It wasn't a date. We're *friends*. And, anyway, did Ryan ever stop to think that perhaps she just wasn't interested in *him*?"

She knew how overly defensive she sounded and so she bit her tongue. She didn't know why she felt dishonest. They *were* just friends. At least that's what Lisa had called their relationship. Sometimes Rachel felt their banter crossed into flirtatious territory, and she was certain that Lisa felt the spark between them as well. But other times Lisa was distant and hard to read, and Rachel had no idea what was happening between the two of them. In the back of her mind, she wondered if all of the baggage she brought to the table as a single mom was just too much for Lisa, but even as the insecurities echoed inside, she suspected that wasn't the case. Whatever the cause of the distance, Rachel sensed it was something bigger than her.

Her dad continued to watch her, and she wondered if he could read the thoughts racing through her mind.

"It wasn't a date," she repeated, not sure which one of them she was trying to convince.

"Either way," Frank said, "you look happy."

This time she couldn't hide the smile. Their day together had been a ray of sunshine amid the clouds of restaurant stress and

Declan's school troubles. Still, a cautionary knot of nerves tightened in her chest, and she tried to refrain from thinking of the day as anything more than simply a nice day of hiking. She knew in her gut that hoping for more was a surefire way to set herself up for hurt.

Lisa had the potential to hurt her. That much was sure.

Rachel went back to the spreadsheet. Numbers. Menu planning. Tangible concerns she could focus on.

Chapter Ten

Rachel held the open backpack and waited for Declan to pick out three shirts to put inside.

"You're only going to be gone for the weekend," Rachel reminded him as he went through each shirt in his closet. She should have packed for him. "Just pick three."

Finally he pulled three shirts off the plastic hangers and carried them over to Rachel. She folded them and placed them inside the backpack.

"Dad is getting a dog, and he said I could go with him this weekend to help him pick one out."

"That sounds fun." She hoped no hard feelings were apparent to her six-year-old. Of *course*, Joey would get a dog. Anything to win Declan over. It would make him the fun parent. But then he'd probably have to sell the dog in a week when he found he couldn't take care of it with his busy schedule.

"Maybe Dad will even let me name him." Declan smiled as he picked up a stuffed monkey to put in his backpack.

"Maybe," Rachel agreed.

The phone rang, and she put the bag down on the bed. "You finish up packing, and I'll go see who's calling," she instructed.

Declan nodded and she went out to the kitchen, picking up the phone.

"Hello?"

"Rach, how's it going?"

She gripped the phone a little tighter at the sound of Joey's voice. "I'm fine. We're just about packed. How are you?"

"I'm not so bad," Joey said, but the way he drew out the words told Rachel that the bad news was coming.

"The thing is," he continued, "my boss called this morning, and there are a bunch of guys sick. He needs me to work this weekend."

"Tell him you can't," Rachel snapped. God, why was she still surprised to be having this conversation? "You have Declan."

"He didn't *ask* me Rach, he *told* me. I didn't exactly have the option of turning him down."

"How convenient."

"What's that supposed to mean?"

She pinched the bridge of her nose and tried to rub out the tension, but it didn't ease. "Why is it something always comes up on the weekends you're supposed to have Declan?"

"That's not true," Joey protested. "I came to hang out with him last time, didn't I?"

"Yeah, after canceling the time before." And the time before that, and God only knew how many times before that.

"I have a shitty work schedule right now," he said. "I've told you, I have to put in a couple of hard years if I want the opportunity for advancement. My schedule interferes with a lot of things. Not just my time with Declan."

"I have work, too, Joey." She swallowed the desperation trying to crack through. "I have the festival this weekend, and you *promised* you could take Declan for me. This is one of our busiest weekends of the year, and we need it to go well to make enough money to pull us through the winter season."

"I told you, if you need money, let me know. I'm going to make sure my son is taken care of."

"It's not about the money, Joey. I'm just saying we've all got responsibilities. I need you to follow through on your promises, and I don't want to go back in that room and tell Declan that he's *not* going to see his dad this weekend after all."

"Let me talk to him then."

She didn't want to give in; she wanted him to *understand,* but that was clearly not about to happen. She was in a losing battle. She couldn't make Joey get in his truck and come pick Declan up.

"Hang on," she said.

She went back to Declan's room and stood in the doorway for a minute, watching him pack stuffed animals into his backpack. He was going to be crushed.

"Declan," she began. "Your dad's on the phone."

He looked up, and the weariness in his eyes told Rachel that he already knew what was coming. His shoulders were slumped, and she could read the defeat written in his entire body.

"He wants to talk to you for a minute," Rachel said.

Declan nodded once, a somber nod that was far beyond his years, and he sulked to the kitchen, picking up the phone. Rachel wished she could say *something* that would get through to Joey and get him to come pick up his son for the weekend.

"But, Daddy, you promised." Declan's voice broke.

Rachel stepped over and put a hand on Declan's shoulder, but he shrugged it off. She could only watch as Declan's emotions built up within him. His tiny body tensed, from his fist that gripped the phone up to his shoulders and down his back. His brow pulled into a scowl and his lips pursed together tightly before his words finally burst from him.

"You're a liar!"

And then the tears started. All the tension fell away, his shoulders slumped, his head dropped, and he looked so impossibly small. Too small to ever have to be so sad.

And there was nothing Rachel could do to make it better.

Finally, he handed the phone to Rachel, and fled the room in tears.

"Happy now?" Rachel asked, putting the phone back to her ear.

"Of course, I'm not happy! I don't want to see him upset any more than you do."

"Yeah, well as soon as you hang up the phone you get to forget about how upset you've made him, and I get to go try to calm him down." She knew she should stop, but the anger boiled over, so palpable she could taste the bitterness, and she was powerless to stop the words.

"I don't need to listen to this. You want to make me feel bad? I *already* feel bad. You think I'm going to put down the phone and forget about this? I wish. It's going to haunt me. I don't have a choice. I'm done explaining."

"You *did* have a choice." She hung up the phone.

For a minute, she just stared at the phone in its cradle, but then she headed toward Declan's room, where he was ripping things out of his backpack and throwing them at his bed as hard as he could manage.

"Declan, honey, I'm so sorry," she said, not sure what else she could say.

"I hate him!" Declan said under his breath.

"We don't say 'hate' here," she said instinctively, immediately regretting the words. She took a breath and then added, "But I guess it's all right for you to hate that he's not coming to pick you up for the weekend."

"He's a liar. He *promised*."

"I know." He had broken the promise to Declan, but he had also broken a promise to her. And now she had a devastated son to comfort, one who was not likely to enjoy spending a weekend hanging quietly around Catherine's during the Autumn Air festival rush.

She wasn't about to say so out loud, but at the moment she hated Joey, too.

Lisa looked at the sketchbook in front of her. The blank page stared unwaveringly back at her, as it had for hours. The problem wasn't that she didn't know what she should sketch. The problem was that the image in her mind caused her chest to constrict, and when she went to lower her pencil to the page, she felt the vice grip tighten until she could no longer breathe. All she could see was Mitchell's face with his delicate newborn features. But all the sketches in the world would never be enough. They'd never bring him back. The empty page said nothing and everything at once.

Finally, she set her pencil down, tore the blank page from the sketchbook, and went to the closet. She reached up and carefully pulled the wooden box from the top shelf. She set it on the bed, unlatched the lid, and opened the box. She breathed in the cedar scent of the box, folded the blank page, and set it on top of the other papers inside. Mitchell's birth certificate. His tiny hand and footprints. She was careful not to look at the set of photos. She couldn't. It would be too much. She set the paper inside, closed the box, and gently returned it to its place in the closest, next to the small urn.

Then she picked up the sketchbook, made herself comfortable on the bed, and allowed herself to think of the other image that had been predominant in her mind recently. The happier image.

This time her pencil flew across the page with ease. She pressed hard to create dark rocks and lightly to add whitecaps to the waves in the ocean below. She kept the picture simple, a cute cartoonish sketch, but still she traced her fingers lovingly over the finished product as though it were a photograph. A light, happy sketch of her and Rachel gazing out at the ocean from their vantage point in the highlands. It captured the two of them from behind, and to an outsider it might not have been obvious who was in the sketch, but it was enough that Lisa knew.

Lisa could still close her eyes and see the tender way that Rachel looked at her with those beautiful green eyes swirled with various shades of blue. Rachel had the prettiest eyes she'd ever seen.

Guilt coiled around Lisa's stomach, but she shook the feeling away. There was no reason to feel guilty. She hadn't done anything. She had not ever insinuated that she and Rachel could be more than friends. She could feel attraction without acting on it. And, sure, she could acknowledge she was attracted to Rachel.

She also knew Rachel deserved more than she could give. She couldn't be in a relationship, she wasn't ready, and so friendship was all she could offer.

But she didn't have to completely avoid Rachel, who made her feel something other than the ever-present grief. She wondered if the guilt would go away if she kept telling herself that.

Lisa nodded resolutely. *It's the song of freedom,* she thought. She had not come to the coast to burrow away like a hermit crab. She'd done that in her apartment.

She picked up her phone and dialed Rachel's number for no other reason than she wanted to talk to her. She allowed a small smile to cross her lips as she listened to the ringing on the other end.

"Hello?"

Warmth spread through Lisa's chest and her smile widened. "Rachel, hi. It's Lisa."

"Oh hi!" Rachel exclaimed. She sounded slightly winded.

"Did I catch you at a bad time?" Lisa asked.

"Yeah," Rachel breathed. "I wish I could chat. Declan's dad was supposed to pick him up, but he canceled, and I'm trying to get him ready so I can get to the restaurant. This is the last busy weekend before winter, and Declan is fighting me, of course. Can I call you tonight when I'm done with work?"

"Yeah sure," Lisa said. The exasperation was clear in Rachel's voice, and something tugged inside of Lisa.

She heard Rachel add, speaking away from the phone, "Why are you still in your pajamas? Go get dressed. You have five minutes until we leave. No *buts*. Let's go!"

She said her next words before thinking. She heard the desperation in Rachel's voice and responded in kind.

"Do you need someone to watch him?"

There was a beat of silence, and Lisa wished to God that she could take the words back. Or that perhaps, mercifully, Rachel had been distracted by Declan and not heard her. She could absolutely *not* babysit Rachel's child. Of all the bad ideas she'd ever had, this one was perhaps the worst. Followed closely by calling Rachel in the first place. This was why she was supposed to keep her distance.

"You'd do that?" Rachel asked. Her voice sounded like it was about to break, and Lisa knew she couldn't take back the offer.

"Of course," she said, already planning in her head how she might be able to survive the day. "I could bring Roxie to play with him, if that's okay, of course." A distraction for him. That would be a start.

"He would love that."

Despite her fear, she softened at the gratitude in Rachel's voice.

"He can be a handful," Rachel warned.

"We'll have fun. I promise." She was almost certain it was a promise she couldn't keep on her end, but the kid would be okay.

"I wouldn't normally ask you to do this, but I really need this weekend to go smoothly," Rachel said.

"You didn't ask. I'm offering," she pointed out. She had nobody but herself to blame. "We'll be fine. I'll be right over."

"You're a lifesaver," Rachel said.

She quickly jotted down the address Rachel gave her, then hung up the phone and slumped down on her bed, wondering what she had gotten herself into.

Chapter Eleven

Lisa steeled herself for an evening of heartache as she loaded Roxie into the car and headed over to Rachel's house, cursing her impulsivity the entire way. It was a too-short drive to the small blue bungalow. She double-checked the address and then sat parked in front for a moment, breathing in through her nose and out through her mouth.

As if sensing her discomfort, Roxie leaned forward from the backseat and rested her chin on Lisa's shoulder, brushing her cheek with her wet nose.

"I'm hoping you do most of the work for me," she said to the dog.

She took a moment to meet Roxie's soulful, understanding eyes and then unbuckled her seatbelt, grabbed the bag of belongings she'd brought, and forced herself from the safety of the car.

Lisa held Roxie's leash like a lifeline as she stepped up to the front door and rang the doorbell.

For a moment she forgot all of her trepidation. Rachel stood in the doorway, the relief evident in her entire body, which softened at the sight of Lisa. Her hair was pulled back, and she was dressed for work in black pants that perfectly hugged the curve of her long legs. She wore a soft green button-down shirt, with the top buttons left undone around her throat, hinting at her perfect skin underneath.

"Thank God you're here," Rachel said. "I don't know what I would've done."

Rachel pulled her into a hug before she could say anything, and she squeezed her eyes at the soft scent of vanilla.

My God. They fit together perfectly, Rachel's body soft against her own. Lisa let the hug linger, not wanting to step out of the comfortable embrace.

But then Roxie tugged hard on the leash, nearly pulling Lisa off balance. She stepped back to see that Declan had appeared at the start of the hall and that Roxie was pulling toward the boy, tail wagging furiously. Lisa bent down to unclip the dog from her leash, and Roxie instantly bounded over to Declan and started licking his face.

Declan sat on the floor giggling, his eyes squeezed shut, hands in front of his face to protect himself from Roxie's eager affection.

"Declan, come say 'hi' to Lisa," Rachel prodded.

Declan had to stand to get Roxie away from his face, but even then he barely forced his gaze up from the dog to say a quick "hi."

"Do you remember me?" Lisa asked, stepping over and kneeling to his level. "We've met a few times. I saw you at the beach with Roxie."

He nodded, but didn't appear any more comfortable with Lisa than she was with him. He kept Roxie in between the two of them, and avoided meeting Lisa's gaze, his attention on the dog instead—a good shield.

That makes things easy enough, she thought.

"Come give me a hug good-bye," Rachel said to Declan, and bent down to squeeze her son.

Lisa turned away, and tried not to hear the exchange between mother and son. She was unsuccessful and each word hit her like a wave, knocking her off balance.

"You be good," Rachel said. "I love you."

"Love you too, Mommy," he said, but then he pushed out of her arms and took Roxie toward the living room.

"And just like that I'm forgotten," Rachel said with a small laugh.

Lisa laughed as well, but the sound was fake and hollow. She'd never hug Mitchell good-bye before leaving him with a sitter. She'd spent the last year and a half thinking about all of the little moments that she had lost, and still she could be blindsided by the realization of losses that she *hadn't* thought of already.

"Thank you again," Rachel said. "I'll be home as soon as I can, but it probably won't be until late. He's had lunch already and there is leftover lasagna in the fridge you can warm up for dinner. He'll tell you where all the snacks are, I'm sure. If possible, he usually goes to sleep around eight, but if he won't go to sleep with me gone, that's fine. You can put on a movie for him, and he'll at least quiet down. If you need anything, I'll have my phone on me the entire time and I can be here within five minutes. The restaurant number is—"

Lisa cut her off by reaching out and resting her hand on Rachel's arm.

"We'll be fine," she promised, but her nerves increased with the realization that Rachel was about to leave and she was going to be alone with Declan.

"Thank you," Rachel breathed. Then she grabbed her in another quick hug and was out the door.

She took a minute to steady herself, running her fingers through her shoulder-length hair and taking a couple of deep breaths. Then she headed into the living room where Declan knelt on the floor, with Roxie pouncing around him and on him.

Lisa pulled Roxie's frayed toy rope out of her bag. "I brought her toy if you'd like," she suggested, holding out the chewed-up dog toy.

Declan came over and grabbed the rope, and soon the boy and the dog were engaged in an intense game of tug-of-war. For a few moments she watched, unsure of what to do with herself, before pulling her sketchbook out of her bag and settling into the couch. If the kid was happy, she might as well try to get some work done. She flipped open to a blank page and began to draw.

She drew a cliff, with waves raging down below, and positioned at the edge of the cliff was a twisted and barren old tree, reaching out toward the ocean, toward freedom. Her pencil pulled the branches away from the confines of the shore, the tree bent away from land. She shaded knots into the weathered bark. Then perched on the very edge of the tree she drew a hawk, head stretched forward, wings back, ready to take off.

She was adding the details to the wing feathers when she felt Declan crawl up onto the couch beside her. She put her pencil down and turned to him.

"Wow," he breathed. He stood beside her, looking down at the page and taking in the image with awe on his face.

Lisa found herself touched by Declan's earnest enthusiasm for the project.

"Can I have it when you're done?" he asked, looking up at her with his big eyes.

"You want this picture?"

"Uh huh."

Lisa watched the way Declan studied the drawing. His eyes—the same sea-green as Rachel's—were wide and focused on the image. His lips were slightly parted, and his brow furrowed as he took in certain details. His focus made him appear so much like Rachel. Other than his eyes, Lisa assumed Declan got his features from his dad. His light-brown hair fell across his forehead without the slightest hint of curl, and his jaw was wider set than his mom's. But looking at him, there was no doubt that he was Rachel's son. He had her expression of concentration down perfectly. The look endeared her to Declan a little, and she smiled at the visual of Rachel making the same face.

What parts of her would Mitchell have inherited? As soon as the thought came to her, she pushed it away. If she let herself wonder about that, she would get sucked in and the thought would become quicksand, pulling her under.

"I'll tell you what." Lisa forced herself back to the conversation with Declan. "Why don't you draw a picture, too, and we'll trade."

Declan smiled and nodded at the idea, and she pulled a blank sheet of paper from her sketchbook and set it on the coffee table in front of him. Then she fished her pencil crayons from her bag.

Declan knelt in front of the coffee table and selected a color to begin his picture.

She caught herself smile as she watched him for a minute before she flipped back to her drawing, now finishing it up for Declan.

She added feathers to the hawk, giving each one texture and detail. She focused carefully on each line. Then she used her pencil to shade gray wisps of clouds above the shore. There was a storm brewing, but out over the ocean the sun shone bright, reflecting off the water down below. She sat back looking at the finished drawing, satisfied. Then she wrote *To Declan* in the top left corner and *From Lisa* in the bottom right. She swirled his name into the clouds, and wrote hers in the reflection on the water.

"What do you think?" she asked, holding up the picture for Declan to examine.

"Whoa . . ." He scooted closer, taking the picture and holding it out in front of him with care. "It says my name!" He giggled as he traced the letters in the clouds.

"That's because it's for you."

"I'm going to hang it over my bed," he said.

Lisa's chest expanded with pride in her work at his earnest enthusiasm. She was used to people praising her art, to the point that the opinions of others rarely mattered. But somehow the fact that Declan liked her picture felt important.

"How's your picture coming along?" she asked, leaning in toward the coffee table to see his art.

"I'm not a good drawer like you."

Anxiety was etched into Declan's little features.

"How long have you been drawing?" Lisa asked.

He shrugged. "I don't know. Probably since I was three."

"So you've been drawing for about three years?"

Declan nodded.

"Can you guess how long I've been drawing?"

Declan shook his head.

"Probably about twenty-eight years."

Declan said nothing. He just continued to look up at Lisa.

"I bet you draw better than I ever did when I was six. I've just had a few more years of practice."

He bit his lip, but he picked up his piece of paper and handed it to Lisa.

She held it in front of her and studied the picture. He had drawn two stick people, one with brown curly hair who Lisa assumed to be Rachel, and a man with a mustache. Each of them had a wide grin. Stick-figure Rachel wore a yellow sundress with blue spots, and the man had blue pants and a red shirt. "Is that your mom and grandpa?"

"Yeah," he said.

"Declan, this picture is great. I love the colors you picked for your mom's dress."

A smile spread across his face. "Thanks."

"Does your mom have a dress like that?"

"Yeah. She wears it in the summertime. The blue dots are flowers."

"It sounds pretty." She suddenly wanted nothing more than to see Rachel in the yellow sundress with the blue flowers, her dark curls falling loose over her shoulders.

Declan nodded.

"Your mom and grandpa both look really happy in the picture."

"That's 'cause I'm dead," Declan said. He said it matter-of-factly, no change in emotion, but Lisa froze.

"What?"

"They're happy because I'm dead."

She sat there dumbfounded for a moment, wondering what she could possibly say to that.

"Do you know what dead means?"

Declan nodded. "My grandma died. It means she's gone to Heaven. I didn't get to meet her because she went to Heaven before I was born."

"If you went to Heaven, your mom and grandpa would miss you a lot."

"No, they wouldn't. They'd be smiling like in the picture. I

80

make my mom frown all the time. Like when I get in trouble at school. I try to be good, but still I get in trouble. My dad didn't want me this weekend, and that made my mom sad because she didn't want me this weekend, either. If I died and went to Heaven, my mom wouldn't have to yell at me anymore and then she could be happy all the time."

Lisa looked at the picture because she didn't trust her emotions if she looked at Declan. She tried to remind herself that he was a child who did not fully understand what dead meant, but still her heart ached for the boy who now seemed even smaller than before. He was barely more than a baby. He shouldn't ever think about how his mom would feel if he died.

Lisa flashed to an awful, heartbreaking moment. She could still feel that feeling of falling as the foundation of her entire life crumbled beneath her—an earthquake only she felt.

She could guarantee that Rachel wouldn't be smiling.

"You don't like the picture, do you?" he asked.

"I love the picture," she promised, looking up from the picture to Declan. "I'm going to hang it over *my* bed."

He beamed, and then he took the picture she'd given him and raced off to place it in his room. When he returned, he slid down onto the floor and called Roxie over, going back to playing as though the day were as normal as ever.

She continued to look at the picture Declan had made for her. She had no idea what she was going to say to Rachel at the end of the day. She knew she had to say *something*.

They're happy because I'm dead.

There were no other words left in her vocabulary. Those five consumed her thoughts. The ache of her own loss was amplified tenfold, and it was all she could do to remain in the room and not run from it.

Catherine's Restaurant was small, with tables close together that made the place loud and congested when full. By the end of the night, Rachel's legs hurt and she ached to sit down, but she was abuzz with the excitement from the day. She loved days when Catherine's came alive with customers. When the place was crowded, she pictured her mom enthusiastically cooking for all of the guests. Her mom would have loved the place. In the rush of people, Rachel often felt her mom there with her. It saddened her to think it was their last busy day, before the crowd would thin to nearly nothing over the winter.

Two men entered the restaurant, checking their watches as they entered.

"We're not too late, are we?" one asked.

Rachel shook her head. "I think we can fit you in. Follow me." She picked up two menus and led the men to a table, watching with a smile as she saw one take the other's hand as they walked. Then she went to the door and flipped the "open" sign to "closed." They'd be the last patrons of the evening.

Rachel was ready for a good night's sleep, but still found it bittersweet.

"And what can I get for the two of you tonight?" she asked, pulling out her little notebook.

"I think I'll have the clam chowder," one said.

"And I'll go for the fish and chips," said the other.

"Excellent choices," Rachel said. "I'll get those started for you. Feel free to wave me over if you need anything."

She took the men's orders back to the kitchen.

"Well, Eloise, this is it. One clam chowder and one fish and chips."

"They're the last customers?" Eloise asked.

"The very last."

Eloise let out a sigh. "I'll miss this."

Rachel watched as Eloise heated oil in a pan over the stove. Eloise worked in a way that made it obvious cooking was her passion. She moved through the kitchen with ease, knowing by heart where to find every pan, ladle, and knife.

Eloise caught Rachel watching her. "What?" she asked with a laugh.

Rachel shook her head. "Nothing. It's just . . . you remind me a lot of my mom sometimes." As a child, she had frequently sat on a stool to watch her mom cook. She hadn't learned anything, but she had enjoyed watching the graceful way her mom moved while she cooked. Often, they would have a record on in the background, and she and her mom would sing together while her mom made dinner.

"She'd be proud of you, hon,'" Eloise said.

"Days like today I can *feel* how proud she is. This place is everything she ever dreamed of. You've helped us make her dream a reality."

"You're going to make me cry. And I've still got work to do. Your dad has been in the dining room for awhile now. You should get out there and make sure he's not scaring away our final guests for the evening."

She laughed. "Will do." She turned and headed for the door to the dining room, but she hesitated and added, "I love you, Eloise. You know that, right?"

"Love you, too, Rachel. You and Frank are my family."

This time she was going to start to cry, so she pushed her way back into the dining room before that happened. The end of the season always made her emotional, but everything with Joey and Declan had her feeling more raw than usual.

She watched as her dad talked cheerily to a young woman and her mother who were sitting in the far corner finishing up their meal. The restaurant was home. She hadn't exactly planned for the restaurant to become her career, but she loved the life that she'd fallen into.

She noticed that the young gay couple held hands across the table as they talked to one another while waiting for their food. A pang of jealousy hit her. She didn't normally dwell on the fact that she was single. She liked her life on the island. She had watched as her friends from high school got married, and it didn't normally bother her. She had long since resigned herself to staying single. She had Declan, and he required her entire focus. She had no interest in going on dates with women she hardly knew in hopes of finding a connection. She'd made peace with being single, but seeing the two men together reminded her of what she didn't have.

Her mind flashed to Lisa, which just made the pang of jealousy stronger, because for a split second she *could* imagine a relationship like that, which was stupid. There was a chemistry between her and Lisa. She could feel it, but that didn't mean Lisa wanted a relationship.

There were the flirty comments Lisa had made on their hike in the highlands though . . . She might be rusty and out of practice, but she could swear that had been flirting. But then there were the moments when Lisa distanced herself . . . she didn't know how to read her.

A man waved Rachel over and asked for another glass of wine, which pulled her from her thoughts. The restaurant was winding down for the night, but there were still customers. She had to focus.

Eventually the young gay couple left, the last customers for the evening. The door shut behind them, and she went over to flick the lock, leaning against it once the restaurant was secured.

"Well, we survived another summer," Frank said with a grin.

Eloise stepped out of the kitchen. "We managed to use up most of the seafood. We shouldn't have too much waste this year."

"Perfect," Frank said.

Rachel said nothing. She just took it all in. Then, somberly, the three of them set about closing the kitchen. They would stay open through the winter. It wasn't like they were closing completely, but it wouldn't be the same. Winters never were.

"I'd better go get Declan," she said. "He's probably making Lisa crazy by now."

"I'm sure she's doing fine," Eloise said, but an unreadable expression passed over her face.

Rachel hoped Lisa was doing all right. God, she hoped so. As with school pickup, though, her stomach knotted at the thought of what Lisa might have to tell her about the day. "Do you mind if I leave the two of you to lock up so I can get home to him?"

"Not at all," Eloise said. "We'll finish up here."

"Thanks," she added. Then, on a whim, she pulled Eloise into a hug. "See you Tuesday."

"See you Tuesday," Eloise echoed, giving her a squeeze before releasing her.

She got in her truck and drove down the dark side streets toward her house.

"Please let it have been a good day," she said into the empty truck as she drove up to her house. Lisa had turned the porch light on for her, and that simple gesture warmed her and helped set her mind at ease.

She turned the key in the door and stepped inside. Music was coming from the living room, and she followed the sound. The sight that awaited her stopped her in her tracks and took the breath from her lungs.

Lisa was asleep on the couch, with Declan in his robot pajamas asleep against her side. The end credits of a movie were rolling on the television screen with the movie's most notable song overlying the list of names.

Roxie padded over sleepily and licked Rachel's hand. She reached out to pat the dog, hoping she would stay quiet and not wake the two for a minute. She was enjoying the sight.

Roxie shook her head, though, her collar jingling. Lisa stirred before opening her sleep-lidded eyes and peering up at Rachel.

"Hi," Rachel said softly enough to not wake Declan.

Lisa rubbed a hand over her face and smiled. "You're home."

She nodded and headed over to the couch. "I'll get him to bed, and then I want to hear all about your day." She reached down and lifted her son, who shifted to wrap his arms around her neck and his legs around her waist, and she carried him to his bedroom, setting him down in his bed where he quickly rolled over and fell back into a deep sleep.

When she got back to the living room, Lisa was taking the DVD from the machine and placing it back in its case.

"Sit," Rachel offered, but Lisa shook her head.

"I should be getting home."

She helped Lisa straighten the living room and then walked her to the door.

"How was he?" she asked. "Did he behave?"

"He's a good kid," Lisa said, buttoning her coat, and clipping Roxie to her leash.

"Thank you. For everything today."

"How was everything at the restaurant?" Lisa asked.

She wanted to tell her to sit, stay awhile, maybe tell each other about their days or maybe just *be* in silence. Anything. She just didn't want her to leave. But asking her to stay felt too vulnerable.

"Busy," Rachel answered instead. "My everything hurts, but it was the perfect way to end the season. It might just get us through winter."

Lisa seemed genuinely happy for Rachel when she smiled back. Her hair was still slightly messy in the back from sleep. God she was cute.

Rachel shifted closer to Lisa. She wanted to close the distance between the two of them. She wanted to rest her hands on Lisa's hips and press her mouth to Lisa's. She wanted to feel Lisa, soft and warm against her.

But Lisa spoke first.

"Before I go I need to talk to you about something."

She felt the distance widen between them, though they remained standing in place. Concern was etched across Lisa's features, and Rachel was scared to ask but formed the words anyway. "What happened? Did he do something?"

"No," Lisa assured her, shaking her head. "He's a great kid."

Still, she waited for the other shoe to drop.

"It's just . . ."

Rachel watched Lisa search for the right words.

"He made a comment," she said at last, "about people being happier if he were gone."

"What?" Rachel asked. She heard the words, but they didn't make sense. "What did he say?"

Lisa seemed to war with herself about how much to say.

She took Lisa's hand. "Lisa, please."

Lisa met her eyes, and Rachel saw her resolve break. "He drew a picture of you and your dad. He said the two of you were smiling because he was dead."

The words were a knife to her stomach. She could feel them, the physical pain of them, but still she couldn't understand or process the words.

"What?" she asked, as though there was some magic clarification to be found. "He wouldn't say that."

"He doesn't understand what it means," Lisa said. "He's a kid. But it does seem like he's hurting. I'm sorry. I just . . . I had to say something to you about it, right?"

Tears burned the back of Rachel's eyes. She took a breath and stated, "He wouldn't say that."

"Rachel—" Lisa began, but Rachel cut her off.

"He wouldn't say that."

She reached past Lisa and opened the door. She caught a glimpse of the hurt on Lisa's face and avoided Lisa's eyes. If she did, her resolve would crumble, and she didn't want that. Not until she was alone.

Lisa took the hint and stepped from the house, giving her arm a squeeze on her way out.

Rachel leaned against the door and let the tears come.

Chapter Twelve

It was early morning. Declan was still asleep, and Rachel was still awake. She'd tried to go to sleep the night before, but every time she lay down, she thought of her son, and her heart clutched painfully in her chest. In the end, she'd called Joey and railed on him as though she could pass off the blame. After all, if he'd just picked up Declan as he'd said he would. She didn't know why she bothered, though. He'd given her the same tired excuses, and she'd hung up the phone more enraged than when she'd called. That rage quickly burned out, though, replaced with a deep ache of guilt. She was the one there every day, after all. She was failing Declan.

Rachel remembered when she found out she was pregnant. She was nineteen, still practically a child, and terrified. Joey had been a mistake. She'd known that the first time she'd kissed him, but she'd had no idea what that meant for her life, and no other lesbians as an example, so she had slept with Joey in a desperate attempt to make herself not be gay. For a while, she'd thought maybe it could be different if she didn't live in such a small town. Maybe if she moved to the city . . . But she hadn't wanted to leave her dad and the restaurant. Then she got pregnant, and everything changed. She had known she couldn't stay with Joey, but he wanted to still be involved in Declan's life, and she had known she would need all the help she could get. She was still more or less a teenager, and she hadn't known what to do with a baby. She had gone to sleep each night praying she wouldn't completely ruin her child's life.

And now he thinks I'd be happier without him, she thought, bitterly. She wasn't even meeting the bar of "good enough" parenting. She was a complete failure.

"Mommy?"

The small voice pulled her from her thoughts, and she turned to see Declan standing in the hallway, his auburn hair tousled from sleep, poking up in random directions. His pajamas were a rumpled mess with one pant leg bunched up around his knee. She wanted to scoop him up, hold him, and never let him go.

"Can I watch cartoons?" he asked.

She nodded and patted the couch beside her. She wrapped the two of them in a large blanket and turned on the television to the cartoon network. She didn't often allow television in the mornings, but she needed the time cuddled up next to her son.

She listened to him giggle at a joke, and watched the way his eyes were wide and rapt. He looked so small, and sweet, and happy.

Rachel wished she saw that look on his face more often and vowed to make it happen. She couldn't make Joey be more involved, but she could be better herself.

Whatever it took. She would do anything for Declan.

Lisa didn't want to think about Declan.

She ran, one foot in front of the other, trying to direct her mind to her breath, watching as it puffed in front of her in white clouds from the cold.

But still she thought about the little boy.

She ran faster, pushing herself harder, as though she could kill the thoughts with exhaustion. Still, she replayed the previous evening in her mind—a film reel on repeat.

Declan was charming, and sweet, and sad, and dammit if her heart didn't go out to him. But her heart didn't have the strength to break for another little boy.

She ran down the street to the beach, along the frozen sand of the shore until she reached the rocks down by the end of the beach. Then she rested her hands on her knees and sucked in air.

"Dammit," she said out loud, once her breathing had steadied enough to talk.

She kept seeing Declan's face, the hurt so clearly etched across it. He was just a baby, and already he felt as though there was no place for him. The thought made her chest tighten.

But, goddamn it, she didn't want to care.

She should never have offered to babysit. She should never have gotten involved. It was better when Declan was just a ghost of the future she could have had with Mitchell. Now she had to see Declan as his own little person with his own hopes and fears and hurts, and somehow that only hurt her more.

Waves crashed along the frozen shore, the water as turbulent as Lisa's thoughts. She watched the water and found nothing— not God, not her grandfather, not Mitchell.

There were no answers to be found, no comfort. Just salt water rubbing in her wounded heart.

"I should never have come here," she said, not sure if she meant to the beach or to Cape Breton in general. All she knew was that she couldn't keep standing still with her thoughts, so she turned to continue her run.

She ran along the coast until she was exhausted, and then she turned and ran home. By the time she reached Eloise's small cottage, her limbs were heavy, her body spent. The buzz of anxious energy had burned itself out.

Until she saw Rachel sitting on the front step.

"I was starting to think you'd never get back," she said.

Lisa walked over, the grief for both Declan and Mitchell returning full force. She didn't trust her voice to say anything.

"I'm a shitty parent, aren't I?" Rachel looked up from where she sat, arms wrapped around herself, pain heavy in her voice.

Lisa shook her head. "You're not."

Rachel rolled her eyes and cast her gaze down to her feet.

Lisa took a seat next to Rachel and took one of her hands

in her own. Rachel interlocked her fingers with Lisa's, and Lisa traced her thumb over the incredibly soft skin on the back of her hand.

"You're a great mom," Lisa said. She meant the words, but she was sure they must have sounded hollow.

Lisa leaned against Rachel who was tense but softened against her. She turned, kissed Rachel on the side of her head, and then whispered against her ear, "A shitty mom wouldn't be worried. I know you want to protect him from hurt, but that's just not possible. It doesn't make it your fault."

Rachel pulled her hand from Lisa's grasp and rested her head in both her hands, letting the tears come. Lisa smoothed a hand over Rachel's hair and back.

After a long minute, Rachel straightened and wiped her eyes.

"Sorry," she said, steadying herself.

"You have nothing to be sorry for."

"I wanted to find you to apologize," Rachel said. "For how I spoke to you last night. You were worried about Declan, and I was cold in response."

"You were hurting, too. I got that."

"Still," Rachel said.

"We're fine," she promised.

Rachel gave a nod and a small smile. "Thank you. For everything."

Lisa just shrugged. She wanted to pull Rachel in for another hug. She looked sad, and Lisa wanted to ease that hurt, but Rachel spoke instead.

"I have to get back home, but I just wanted to make sure I thanked you and apologized in person."

And with that she left. Lisa watched her walk away.

She sank forward and ran her hands through her hair, before resting her head in her hands.

She couldn't care about Rachel and Declan.

But dammit, she did.

Chapter Thirteen

Halloween had always been Lisa's favorite holiday. Ghost stories, eerie decorations, horror movies, and candy. There was nothing not to love about the holiday. This year, however, she wished she could sleep through it. She watched the town change from a gorgeous autumn seascape to a haunted port. Trees lost the last of their leaves until only skeletal branches remained, reaching out like bony hands. Plastic tombstones protruded from lawns now more brown than green and transformed front yards into grave-yards. Cloth ghosts hung from neighborhood trees, though it wasn't the cloth ghosts that haunted her.

Even before she was pregnant, Lisa would look at the little infant Halloween costumes and imagine celebrating the holiday with her baby. It was probably the holiday she looked forward to spending with him the most. She had been so excited for trick-or-treating, pumpkin carving, costumes, and spooky stories.

He would have been walking this year—fifteen months old, not quite a toddler, but not a baby anymore either. She'd have found him a costume and taken him trick-or-treating along with Andrew, Sarah, and the twins. Even with him being too young to fully understand what was going on and too young to eat most of the candy, she would've enjoyed the start of their yearly tradition. Lisa's stomach ached at the thought of what would never be.

She had lost track of the number of times people had told her time would heal her grief. She wanted to shout at every one of those people and tell them how wrong they were. Time didn't heal anything. She hurt more this year than the previous year. Missing the first Halloween had been hard, but this year Mitchell would have been able to participate to an extent, and losing that hurt so much more. She imagined that pain would only continue to increase as she continued to realize the person she was missing out on.

She sat, gazing out at the water, with her sketchbook in her lap and allowed herself to feel the grief as she pulled the pencil over the page.

She sketched a store sales rack with various Halloween costumes, each with a label. She sketched a white robe for the ghost costume, a series of monster masks, furry creature costumes, and a few creepy clown getups. Then in the middle, she sketched a pair of jeans and a T-shirt, identical to the outfit she was currently wearing. And she began sketching the mask that held an intentional resemblance to herself.

If only the mask she now wore was only for Halloween, and not an everyday facade.

The buzz of her cell phone pulled her from her artwork. She saw Rachel's name across the screen, and a smile crossed her face.

"Hello?" she answered, finding her stomach tightening at the thought of speaking to Rachel.

"Hi, Lisa!" The voice that greeted her wasn't Rachel.

"Declan? How are you?" The familiar ache clutched at her, and yet a part of her was glad to hear his voice. She'd forged a tentative connection with him while babysitting, and she'd been worried about him. Still, a child's voice on the line elicited a visceral grief response.

"I'm good. In school today, I drew a picture just like yours, and Mrs. Harvey hung it on the art board outside of our classroom for everyone to see."

"Wow, Declan," she said, wondering how she came to be having a telephone conversation with a six-year-old. "Good for you."

"Thanks. I've been practicing lots."

"Does your mom know you're calling?"

"Yeah, she's right here," Declan answered. "She said I could invite you trick-or-treating with us. Wanna come?"

She squeezed her eyes shut. His voice was so hopeful. She tried to find the words to let him down gently, but she could practically see his face with his wide hopeful eyes so like Rachel's, and she didn't want to disappoint him. She tried to think of words that would let him down easy.

"That sounds fun," Lisa began, "but—"

"Yeah," Declan interrupted. "I'm gonna be Spiderman! I'll show you my costume. I have a mask and everything."

"I bet you're going to look fantastic."

"Uh huh," he said. "So, will you come?"

Her brain shouted at her to say *no*. To stay home and forget all about the holiday. But each time she tried to form words she thought of the sad look on his face when he had explained his drawing the other night, and she just couldn't.

They're happy because I'm dead.

She thought of Declan feeling like he didn't belong, and she didn't have the heart to say *no* to the invitation. Not when Declan sounded so eager for her to join.

"Sure." There was no other answer she could give.

"*Mom! She said she'd come,*" Lisa heard in the background.

Soon Rachel was on the line.

"He's been talking about you nonstop," Rachel said with a laugh.

"Really?"

"All the time," Rachel stressed. "You're his new favorite person."

Lisa was hit with unexpected warmth. "He's a sweet kid."

"Thanks."

A swollen silence rested between the two of them.

"Everything okay?" Lisa asked.

"It's been a rough week, but yeah. I made an appointment for Declan with a counselor in Sydney. I take him in next week."

"I think that it will really help," Lisa said, unsure what else to say.

"Yeah," Rachel said, trailing off. "I think so too. I don't really know what to expect. But if it helps Declan . . ."

She heard the hurt in Rachel's voice and wished she could

94

reach out and touch her. Words felt inadequate. She wanted to be there to rest a hand on her shoulder, or pull her into a hug.

"So, you're going to join us for trick-or-treating Wednesday?" Rachel changed the subject.

"I am." Lisa hoped she didn't sound as terrified as she felt. "I guess I'd better find a costume."

Rachel laughed, and the warmth of the sound eased some of Lisa's fear. "You don't have to worry about dressing up."

"Hey now, that's half the fun."

"All right then, I look forward to seeing your costume," Rachel answered. "Want to meet at our place around seven?"

"I'll be there," she promised.

The call ended, and she sat back, wondering what the hell she had gotten herself into. She registered the glimmer of excitement, but it was faint and surrounded by a massive chasm of ache. She was supposed to be taking *Mitchell* trick-or-treating.

Lisa looked down at her sketchbook, and put the finishing touches on the mask. Above it, she wrote the label *HAPPY* in big block letters.

She would put the mask on for the night, and then she could come home and fall apart.

"Pshw!" Declan dashed out from behind the couch and shot an imaginary web from his fingertips as Rachel walked into the room.

"Declan, settle down. You're going to break something running around like that."

He hadn't even had any sugar yet, and already he was hyperactive, overly excited about the costume and the candy.

"Is Lisa gonna be here soon?" he asked through his Spiderman mask.

"Soon," she promised. As if on cue the doorbell rang, and Declan dashed past her to open the door.

She shook her head with a laugh and tried to keep up.

"Hi, Spiderman!" Lisa smiled down at Declan and caught Rachel's gaze. "Happy Halloween."

"What are you supposed to be?" Declan asked.

Lisa stood at the door with a black cape on. She held out one finger and reached into her pocket for the black mask, which she pulled on.

Declan giggled. "But you're a *girl*."

"Not tonight," Lisa answered. She deepened her voice and added, "Tonight, I'm Batman."

Declan giggled harder at her Batman impression.

"I thought us superheroes should stick together."

Rachel watched the exchange. Lisa crouched down and held out a fist, which Declan bumped, sealing their superhero pact.

"And what about you?" Lisa asked, standing and turning her attention to Rachel. "Who are you supposed to be?"

Rachel had not spent much time or money on her own costume, and she pulled the cowboy hat onto her head almost sheepishly.

"Very cute." Lisa gave her a wink.

Rachel flushed and looked away, hoping that Lisa wouldn't pick up on her skin's betrayal.

Declan ignored the exchange, already tugging his shoes on.

"You need a jacket, too." Rachel pulled his blue fleece out of the closet and handed it to him. The nights were hovering around the freezing mark, and it threatened to snow any day.

"But Mom," he complained, "I can't wear a jacket or nobody will be able to see my costume!"

"They'll see your costume. You've got your mask."

He shook his head.

"You can leave it open if you want," she compromised. "Everyone will still see your costume, but that way you won't get cold."

He stared at the jacket with a scowl for a moment, but pulled it on, leaving it open in the front.

Rachel grabbed his toque from the closet as well. She wouldn't try to convince him to wear it, but she would carry it along with her in case his ears got cold.

He grabbed his candy bag, and she pulled on her own jacket before heading out to collect candy.

The sun had just set, and trick-or-treaters were starting to filter out into the streets. It was a small town, so it wouldn't get *too* busy, but still there were quite a number of children out with their parents.

"I'm going to get a whole bag full of candy," Declan told Lisa, taking her hand as they headed down the sidewalk.

"That's a lot of candy," Lisa affirmed. "I'm thinking we split it fifty-fifty. What do you say? You get half and I get half?"

Declan shook his head. "It's all mine!"

"What?" Lisa cried, the mock horror sending Declan into a fit of giggles.

Rachel watched the two of them with a smile. Lisa was great with Declan, which only endeared her to Rachel more. She couldn't remember the last time she felt so strongly for another woman. She was attracted to women, yes, but there was more to it than that. Lisa *saw* her. She saw Declan. There was no need for façade or pretenses. There was a comfortable bond between them. Rachel was terrified at the strength of the attraction she was feeling.

At the first house, Declan let go of Lisa's hand and headed up the front walk, ringing the doorbell while the adults stood at the bottom of the driveway waiting.

"He's so cute all dressed up," Lisa said.

Rachel nodded. "He's pretty excited about that costume. He's been tearing up the house fighting 'bad guys' all day."

Lisa laughed, a light, relaxed sound.

Rachel watched Declan hold open his little bag for a lady who dropped a couple of candies inside.

"You're pretty cute as a superhero yourself," she chanced.

"Thanks. The comic book nerd in me is loving this."

Rachel laughed, and Declan ran back to them and then up the driveway to the next house.

"He'll slow down soon, I'm sure," she said as they followed him. "He's not going to be able to run to every single house."

"Hey," Lisa said, "candy is a powerful motivator. You never know."

"This is true."

The two of them followed Declan to the next house, watching

him again dash up to the door and hold out his bag for the candy to be dropped inside. Though her eyes were fixed on her son, Rachel's attention was focused on Lisa standing next to her.

Lisa who dressed as Batman. Lisa who sealed a superhero pact with her son. Lisa who liked comic books and science fiction and dressed up for Halloween.

She took a deep breath and reached down, taking Lisa's hand.

For a split second, Lisa tensed, and Rachel expected her to pull away, but then Lisa's fingers closed around hers.

She chanced a quick glance at Lisa, who smiled at her in return.

Warmth flooded her, despite the biting October wind. Declan was the happiest she had seen him in a long time, and so was she. She couldn't imagine a more perfect evening.

Lisa couldn't convince herself to let go of Rachel's hand, despite every rational thought telling her that that was exactly what she should do. Rachel's skin was soft, and she traced her thumb over the back of Rachel's hand, sending shivers up her spine. The smallest, simplest contact with Rachel had a hugely physical effect on her. Warmth carried from her hand up her arm and pooled low in her stomach. She might regret the contact later, and everything it carried with it, but for the meantime she let herself enjoy the touch. Besides, it grounded her amid the storm of emotions from watching Declan race house to house collecting candy.

"That guy is giving out the *big* chocolate bars," he exclaimed, skipping up to them. "He even let me pick which kind I got."

"And which kind did you pick?" Rachel asked.

"A Kit Kat," he answered with a grin.

"Are those your favorite?" Lisa asked.

Declan thought for a moment before nodding.

He held up his bag. "Look how much candy I have. My bag is getting heavy."

"Are you just about ready to head home?" Rachel asked. "We can cross the street and hit all the houses on the other side on the way back."

He frowned at his bag, clearly torn. "Okay," he assented.

Once the three of them had crossed to the other side of the road, Declan dashed up the next walk to a house with three jack-o'-lanterns on the front porch, fake cobwebs strewn all over the porch railings, and myriad plastic graves littering the lawn. Plastic talking gargoyles even chatted from the railings of the porch.

"This is my kind of house," Lisa said, as she listened in on the gargoyles' sinister conversation.

Rachel laughed. "Really?"

"The spookier the better."

"If you weren't out here trick-or-treating with us, you'd be watching some god-awful slasher flick, wouldn't you?"

Lisa turned to Rachel. She seemed so light and happy. The cowboy hat was so ridiculously cute, and she had to resist reaching out to tuck Rachel's hair behind her ear. She liked it down, falling around Rachel's face. In that moment, she didn't want to think of how she had planned to spend Halloween.

"The scarier the better," she said, not about to admit that she would have been hiding upstairs with her sketchbook and some music to drown out the sounds of the children trick-or-treating. She had planned to hide away and wait out the holiday, emerging once it was November.

"You know," Rachel began, "if the candy doesn't keep Declan up all night, we could always watch a scary movie of some sort once he's asleep."

So much about the evening already terrified Lisa. She didn't need the knife-wielding psychopath, but Rachel's eyes were soft, her gaze sweet and hopeful.

Goddamn it, Lisa was weak. "Sure."

Rachel lightly squeezed her hand, and the two of them followed Declan down the street to collect candy from the remaining homes.

As soon as they returned home, he dumped his bag of candy onto the floor and began taking inventory of his collection. His eyes shone with pure, unadulterated joy.

"You can pick two candies before bed," Rachel said.

He riffled through his stash, looking over each and every

choice. Picking just two was a big decision the kid clearly didn't take lightly. Lisa smiled in amusement as she watched him sort through the candy to make the exact right decision. Eventually gummy vampire fangs and a chocolate bar won out.

Rachel helped him put the rest back in the bag before it was time for him to head off to bed.

"You go get changed and I'll come read you a story," Rachel said.

"Can Lisa read me a story?"

Rachel looked at her. "If she wants to."

"Can you?" he asked.

Lisa wanted—no, needed—to escape. The small house was a coffin, and she was buried alive, trying to breathe at the thought of having to read a bedtime story.

"Please?" he bounced on his heels as he looked up at her.

There was definitely only one answer, but her brain screamed at her. She didn't know how she managed to stay outwardly composed.

"Sure," she said. "Once you're all ready for bed."

He raced off and she turned to find Rachel smiling at her.

"You've completely won him over," Rachel said. "I expected bedtime to be a big fight. I should get you to come read him his bedtime story every night."

Panic welled within her. She had never wanted to get involved, and somehow she now found herself about to read Declan a bedtime story. It was too much. She couldn't do it.

Before she could run, he appeared in flannel alien pajamas with a storybook in hand.

"Go on," Rachel said. "I'll wait here."

She swore she could hear her heartbeat as she took the book and followed Declan into his room, where he crawled into bed.

Lisa sat beside him with the storybook and began to read. She didn't know how she managed words—she was not even sure she was breathing—but she made it through the story, and when she was done she closed the book and set it on the nightstand.

"Good night," she said. "Thanks for inviting me. I had a lot of fun."

The words brought a smile to Declan's face, but they weren't empty platitudes for him. She had meant it. She wasn't sure how to feel about that fact, but the evening had been surprisingly enjoyable.

"Will I see you tomorrow?" he asked.

"I don't know." *Probably not.* "Maybe."

"I hope so."

Declan pulled Lisa into a hug, and she tensed as his arms wrapped around her. She forced herself to wrap one arm around him quickly in response before pulling away.

"Get some sleep," she suggested. She stood and left the room.

Rachel was waiting in the living room. "He let you get away with just one story?"

She nodded.

"Amazing," Rachel said. "You're hired."

Lisa dismissed the comment. "It was all the walking. It tired him out."

"It tired *me* out," Rachel agreed. "I'm going to go say goodnight, and I'll be right back."

"'Kay."

Rachel headed toward Declan's room, and Lisa leaned back against the wall. She ran a hand through her hair, wondering what the hell she was doing. She couldn't stay for the movie. It was a bad idea. In fact, everything about the evening had been a bad idea. Panic rose within her, a thick knot in her stomach. Her chest was tight. She needed air.

She headed for the door to get her shoes and coat, nearly colliding with Rachel as she came out of Declan's room, closing the door behind her.

"You scared me," Rachel said, steadying herself with a hand on Lisa's shoulder. "Ready for that movie?"

"Rachel." She tried to think up an excuse to leave. Instead she fell into the depths of those sea-green eyes.

Rachel arched an eyebrow, as she waited for her to finish what she had begun to say. Lisa couldn't find any words.

A curl had fallen across Rachel's forehead, and without thought

Lisa reached out and brushed it away. Somehow, even over the sound of her own pounding heart she could hear Rachel's intake of breath. The thoughts screaming at her to leave, however, were drowned out by the thrum of desire coursing through her.

Rachel's hands rested on Lisa's hips, and her thighs burned from the contact, despite the denim barrier.

It was Lisa who closed the distance between them, Lisa who captured Rachel's lips with her own. As soon as their lips met, the spark that had been flickering between them ignited a fire that consumed her.

Rachel let out a soft moan and her lips parted slightly, an invitation Lisa couldn't refuse.

She pressed closer, pinning Rachel to the wall, their bodies flush against one another. Her fingers knotted into Rachel's hair, which was even softer than she'd imagined. There were no coherent thoughts left, only Rachel, and her body reacted of its own accord. She ached to be closer, to feel more of her . . . all of her . . .

"Lisa."

The word cut through everything, tearing her violently back to reality.

It took all of her effort, but she stepped back.

Rachel's eyes were heavy with desire, and she reached for Lisa.

"I can't," she managed. "Shouldn't have . . . I'm sorry."

Then, before Rachel could react, she fled, turning to grab her coat and shoes.

"Lisa, talk to me," Rachel begged as she hurriedly pulled on her shoes.

"I have to go." She pushed her way out into the dark Hallow's Eve.

Chapter Fourteen

The restaurant was empty. It didn't open until noon, but Rachel had gone in early for a quiet place to sit. She'd been there since dropping Declan off at school at 8:30 a.m., setting up camp in a little booth by the window. Halloween decorations still lined the street, gaudy remembrances. She didn't need the reminders. As it was, she kept replaying Halloween over in her mind. She still couldn't say where the night had gone wrong.

It had all been so perfect . . . until all of a sudden it wasn't.

She still felt Lisa's lips on hers, and her stomach tightened at the memory. The heat had sparked between them, hot and bright. And it burned itself out almost as quickly as it ignited. Lisa had left her in the ashes, wondering what the hell had happened.

She turned when she heard the sound of the door opening.

"Good afternoon," Eloise called in a singsong voice as she stepped into the restaurant, wind gusting in behind her.

Rachel checked her watch, surprised to see she had been sitting in the booth for nearly three hours already.

"Hi, Eloise. How's your day?" She hoped she sounded reasonably cheery.

"Oh, can't complain. How was trick-or-treating?"

"Not bad." That was the best she could do.

Eloise pulled off her heavy coat and hung it on the coat rack next to Rachel's booth before sliding into the booth across from her. It was clear neither of them felt any huge rush to get things started in the kitchen.

"Was Declan on a sugar high this morning?"

She groaned. "He's going to be on a sugar high for the next month. Halloween should be outlawed."

Eloise laughed. "So then Halloween was a huge success! What's the fun of being a kid if you can't binge-eat candy once a year?"

"Yeah," she agreed. Clearly the wrong answer, because Eloise sent a curious glance her way. Rachel shifted uncomfortably under the gaze.

"What's wrong?" Eloise asked finally. "And don't tell me nothing."

She met and held Eloise's gaze. "There's nothing wrong."

Eloise raised an eyebrow. "I didn't meet you yesterday, darling. You're acting all quiet and distant. It's not like you."

She sighed. "Can I tell you I don't want to talk about it?"

"You could. But I'm a good listener, and I've heard it's not healthy to keep things bottled up." The concern on Eloise's face was clear.

She wavered. Eloise was her friend. Almost a parent to her. She'd been able to confide in Eloise about everything before. She was exactly the type of confidante Rachel needed at the moment. But Eloise was Lisa's aunt. She had loyalties in the Lisa and Rachel equation. Rachel couldn't just go dragging her in, no matter how much she wished she could process all of her hurt and confusion with someone.

"I'm fine," she promised.

Eloise reached across the table and took both of her hands. She looked at Rachel for a long moment, clearly working over the words she wanted to say.

"You should talk to Lisa," Eloise said at last.

"Why?" Her chest tightened. "Did she say something?"

Eloise shook her head. "I haven't seen her since she left to go trick-or-treating with you and Declan yesterday. But I can see the sadness in your eyes, and I've got a pretty good idea something happened involving my niece. You should know she's family, but so are you."

She exhaled a long breath, surprised at the strength of the emotion that hit her at Eloise's gentle statement. "She kissed me," she said finally, so quiet that it was as though she was speaking to herself rather than Eloise.

Eloise squeezed her hand.

"It was a mistake. It was nothing. It shouldn't have happened." Rachel didn't know why she was dismissing the kiss, just as Lisa had. She heard the words and she hated them. "At least, that's what she called it. It didn't *feel* like nothing, though. And it certainly didn't feel like a mistake. But then she took off, and I don't know where exactly that leaves me. I don't know *why* it was so wrong. She clearly *wanted* to be kissing me. It wasn't a one-sided thing."

She was rambling, but once she'd started to speak, the words poured out of her, all the turmoil she'd been feeling for the past two days. "I'm sorry. She's your niece. I should shut up now. I'm just . . . confused."

Silence hung heavy in the air.

"I love my niece," Eloise said slowly, "and it's not my place to tell you what's going on with her, but you should talk to her. She'll try to get out of saying anything, most likely, but make her tell you what's going on. You deserve to know."

"Do *you* think it was a mistake?"

The pause before Eloise answered told Rachel everything she needed to know, and yet she needed to hear Eloise say the words.

"I think Lisa isn't in a place to be kissing anyone," Eloise admitted. It was clear she had chosen her words carefully. "But you deserve to know why."

She didn't *want* to hear the reason why. Mostly, she wanted to lie in bed and have a good cry. She hadn't experienced such a mutual attraction and connection before. She didn't care to know why it was wrong. Her mind conjured a million scenarios, and she didn't care to find out if any single one of them were accurate. If the kiss was a mistake, she wanted to forget it ever happened and go on with her life.

"Thanks," she managed and Eloise nodded, sliding from the booth and heading for the kitchen.

"Make her tell you," Eloise said again.

She nodded and turned to look out the window. She touched a finger to her lips, and tried unsuccessfully to shut out the memory of the kiss. She didn't know how a kiss so perfect could possibly be a mistake.

She'd talk to Lisa, despite the fear telling her she didn't want to hear the reason they needed to stay apart.

Lisa felt shackled.

She lay on the bed, limbs heavy, unable to move. Her arms were wrapped around Roxie, who lay against her chest, and she focused on the dog's breathing as though it were a reminder to push air in and out of her own lungs.

The depression was an old, familiar friend. It had been a few months since she'd had a day like this, a day where she had no strength to get out of bed. But it wasn't the first and wouldn't be the last. She didn't try to fight it. She let the pain settle in and pulled the blankets around herself. The best thing she could do was simply stay curled up and wait for the pain to pass.

And so she waited although she was unsure for how long. She had slept off and on since she returned from Rachel's—short, fitful bouts of sleep that left her feeling more exhausted. Daylight had long since flooded the room, but she had no idea how well into the day it was. She only knew she was physically incapable of pulling herself from the bed. She had no appetite for breakfast, or lunch, or whatever meal it was supposed to be time for. She had no energy or ability to get up and force herself to eat.

She was imprisoned. Chained down. Trapped inside her body and her mind.

At some point, the phone rang, cutting through the silence. She didn't answer. She didn't even check to see who was calling.

Probably Rachel, she acknowledged, feeling as though another link attached itself to her chain, the links all weighing heavily upon her. The guilt stacked upon her, but she had no way to remove those links. She couldn't make things right.

She'd so wanted to have a good time the night before. And she *had*. She'd enjoyed walking through Craghurst, watching Declan's excitement for candy, holding Rachel's hand, talking and laughing. She'd had *fun*. She had let go of her grief and apparently forgotten all of her boundaries in the process.

Lisa replayed the previous evening in her mind over and over again, unable to stop the torturous film reel. Trick-or-treating, the kiss, Rachel, the kiss, running away, the kiss . . . It all came back to the kiss. The kiss that *never* should have happened.

She and Rachel could never happen. She didn't know what the hell she'd been thinking, practically playing house, tucking Declan into bed, getting all familiar and cozy with a family that *wasn't her own*. Would *never* be her own. She cared about Declan, sure. But the *only* child she wanted was Mitchell.

The memory film reel in her mind was overlaid with an older, but no less torturous, reel. The doctor's somber expression as he told her the awful news, the photographer saying nothing as she took newborn photos of Lisa's baby, the small funeral with her family and friends.

The short couple of hours had become the entirety of Lisa's life. Her new reality. A reality with no room for Rachel and Declan. She didn't have anything to give. As it was, she barely made it through each day.

And now she had hurt Rachel.

Another shackle of grief.

Lisa had left Toronto. She'd fled. But she wasn't free. She was never going to be free of the grief.

The phone rang again.

She turned over and closed her eyes, wishing that sleep would claim her for another merciful couple of hours.

Despite Eloise's insistence, Rachel had wavered all day about whether or not it was a good idea to go speak with Lisa. A large part of her felt Lisa should seek her out to explain, and another large part of her simply did not want to know whatever was going on if it meant they couldn't be together. But eventually Rachel set aside both her pride and her fears, deciding she needed answers.

Still, her heart pounded in her chest as she walked up to the Whelan home.

She carried two cups of coffee, one in each hand, and a bag of fudge draped over her wrist. When she got to the door, she stacked the coffee cups atop one another in her left hand so she could knock with her right. And then she waited.

There was no answer right away, so she knocked again. Eloise had assured her Lisa was home, and after all the courage it had taken to come here, she wasn't about to leave and return later.

Finally, Lisa opened the door.

Everything about her appearance was tired and sad. Her usually put-together clothes were wrinkled, her hair had not been combed neatly into place, and her eyes had dark circles under them as though she had either been awake all night or crying.

Rachel had gone over charged with determination and a shade of anger, but when she saw the state Lisa was in, that all dissipated, and she wanted nothing more than to reach out and comfort her.

"I brought a peace offering." She took the top cup of coffee and extended it toward Lisa. "Maple blueberry coffee and some homemade fudge from Peabody's Candy."

"Thank you." Lisa accepted the coffee and held it close to her chest with both hands.

"Can I come in?"

Lisa stepped back and held open the door, and Rachel stepped past her into the home, practically feeling the heaviness of the atmosphere settle over her as she entered.

Lisa led the way to the living room, and she followed nervously. She took a seat next to Lisa on the chesterfield positioned in front of the big bay window with an expansive view of the ocean. Rachel sat facing her, but Lisa fixed her gaze on the view. Rachel watched her take a long sip of the coffee that she held almost protectively in both hands.

"I came here ready to demand that you speak to me. But now ..." she trailed off, searching for the words. "I would like it if you'd talk to me. I care about you. And I'm worried."

Lisa didn't meet her eyes when she answered. "The kiss was a mistake." Her voice was quiet and flat. There was no emotion in the way she spoke that single sentence.

And yet it hit Rachel like a punch to the stomach. She could feel the physical impact of those words, and she had to try to ignore the pain they elicited. "Why?" she asked gently. "Talk to me."

Lisa continued to stare out the window. The silence was thick and heavy between them. Rachel said nothing, waiting, but eventually she began to believe Lisa wasn't going to answer.

"You have a son," Lisa said, finally.

She furrowed her brow, not understanding the connection.

"I like you," Lisa said, turning to her for the first time since taking a seat in the living room. "Really, I do. But you have a son, and the two of you are a package deal, and I just ... can't."

"Okay." Disappointment rose to a lump in her throat, but she swallowed it down. Lisa was right. She and Declan were a package deal. She couldn't pretend to understand, not after seeing how great Lisa was with Declan, but she wasn't about to argue. If Lisa didn't want the package deal, that was that.

Rachel took a steadying breath, smoothed her hands over her jeans, and started to stand.

Then Lisa spoke again.

"I had a son."

Rachel sat down and tried to process the words, but they were as foreign as though spoken in a different language. She was certain she had misheard. The words didn't make sense.

"He'd be fifteen months old now," Lisa said. "Had he lived."

Rachel saw the pain etched across Lisa's face, and then she knew. The full impact of the words hit her, and she felt tears mist in her eyes. She tried to think of words, but she was at a complete loss. All she could do was reach out to rest her hand on Lisa's knee. And even then, she wasn't sure if the touch was meant to steady Lisa or herself.

Rachel looked up into Lisa's eyes and was met with an ocean of grief.

"What happened?" Rachel asked, tentatively.

Lisa looked back out the window. "About a month before his birth, the doctors did an ultrasound. They discovered he had an inoperable tumor on his heart. They knew he wouldn't live long. I got two hours and fifty-three minutes with him in my arms, and then he was gone." The words were repeated as facts, but she could tell Lisa was keeping to the CliffsNotes to keep from crying. She could hear the emotion threatening to break free.

"I'm so sorry," Rachel said. The words felt empty and stale. The words, she knew, were not enough. She thought of Declan and the pure joy she had felt when she held him for the first time. She could not imagine what it would have been like to lose him hours later. There were no words to convey the truly deep sympathy she felt for Lisa in that moment.

"Me too," Lisa said. She looked at Rachel with equal parts grief and longing. "You and Declan deserve the world, and I can't give it to you. Declan's wonderful really, but every time I see him I'm reminded of the fact that *my* son died. I know that's not a fair thing to say, but I need you to know *why* we can't be together. And that it has nothing to do with you."

Rachel nodded and turned away to keep from crying at the injustice of it all. The last thing Lisa needed was her tears over a crush that would never become anything.

"We can be friends," Lisa offered. "I'd really like to be friends. The time I spend with you makes me happy, and I haven't been happy much this past year and a half. I just can't commit to anything more than friends. I wish I could, but I can't."

Rachel nodded. She understood. The disappointment was a tidal wave, but she'd have to deal with her feelings later. There was no room for her own selfish sadness. She chose her words carefully when she answered. "I would like for us to be friends."

It wasn't everything she wanted, but it would have to be enough.

Rachel got in her truck and allowed the tears to fall. Tears for Lisa and tears for herself. She had gone to Lisa's for answers, and based on Eloise's assessment that the kiss was, in fact, a mistake, she had expected to come away disappointed. But she'd been completely unprepared for the answer she had been given.

Lisa's son had *died*.

Rachel understood the weight of that fact. She couldn't imagine losing Declan. She had been young and scared when she found out she was pregnant, but she had also been completely in love with him from the start. Even on the days when parenting was hard, when she was sure she was doing everything wrong, when he drove her absolutely crazy, he was her little boy and she loved him more than life itself. Since that first moment, looking into her son's eyes, losing him had been her greatest fear in life. If she lost Declan, there'd be no coming back from that grief, she was certain. How Lisa got up in the morning and still functioned seemed a miracle to Rachel.

Lisa had stuck to the facts. She'd told Rachel the bare bones. Rachel had wanted to ask more, but she had seen the grief etched across Lisa's features, seen her struggling to keep herself together, and she'd decided it was best not to push. Lisa could open up and tell her everything, but it wouldn't make the pain any less. She wished she could make things better, but there was no better in this situation. She understood why she and Lisa couldn't work. But that didn't make it easier to accept.

She still felt sorry for herself as she drove toward the restaurant. *This isn't about me.* She chastised herself for being selfish, but that didn't take away the hurt and disappointment. She had *finally* met somebody she could picture building a future with, and it turned out to be an impossible dream.

She wiped her eyes as she got closer to the restaurant and tried to pull herself together. The last thing she wanted was to go into work looking like she'd been crying. It was bad enough that she had to work at all. She was drained and wanted nothing more than to go home and spend the afternoon curled up under some blankets feeling sorry for herself and even worse for Lisa. Knowing she couldn't shirk her responsibilities, however much she wished she could, she parked behind the restaurant and took a few minutes to breathe before getting out of her truck and heading inside.

Eloise and Frank awaited Rachel when she stepped into the kitchen, and she felt their eyes on her as she entered. She purposefully avoided Eloise's knowing gaze. She didn't want to talk about the conversation with Lisa. She didn't want Eloise to further elucidate the reasons why she and Lisa couldn't be together, but the truth weighed heavy in the air between them.

Her dad, for his part, was thankfully ignorant to the heaviness in the air.

"We've got a couple of diners," he said. "Gonna be a quiet day, though, I suspect."

She wasn't opposed to a quiet day. A quiet day sounded wonderful in fact.

"I'll be out front then." She could keep an eye on the diners, but even better, she could have some quiet time away from Eloise's knowing gaze.

She slipped into the dining room and saw a pair of diners sitting at a booth by the window, meals already in front of them. Rachel took a seat near the kitchen, and looked around. The place was home as much as her house. She'd grown up here. It had always been a place of comfort for her. After her mom had passed away, the restaurant became her touchstone to her mom, and she had sat out in the dining room any time she needed to feel her mom with her.

This time, however, as she sat in the dining room, all she thought about was Lisa. She thought of her warm smile on the first day they'd met. Then she recalled the sadness that sometimes crossed Lisa's gentle features, and her heart broke, knowing the depth of pain lying beneath that expression. It was a pain that she could never help ease.

She thought back to that first day, to Declan approaching Lisa's table for help with his card. To Declan throwing the Frisbee on the beach for Roxie. To Declan and Lisa dressed as superheroes for Halloween.

Rachel was hit with the knowledge that all of those little moments she'd found so endearing had hurt Lisa. All of the memories took on a different light, and guilt coiled around her stomach. She'd had Lisa babysit, allowed Declan to invite her trick-or-treating . . . How hard had those things been for Lisa? Sure, Rachel hadn't known, but now she did, and all she could think of was the pain she'd unintentionally caused.

And yet, Lisa had been there for them. She'd agreed to go trick-or-treating. She'd *offered* to babysit. Rachel could only imagine how incredibly painful that had been, and still Lisa had been there for her and Declan.

She sighed, wishing things were different. Declan idolized Lisa. In so many ways they fit together so well, but those moments that had been so special for her had further wounded Lisa.

The idea of them being together was a dream never grounded in reality.

She noticed that the diners had finished their meals. She got up to clear their plates and get them their cheques, thankful for the brief distraction work provided.

Then the diners left, and it was just Rachel and the empty restaurant and her thoughts.

Eloise slipped into the booth across from her. "I gather she told you."

She nodded.

Eloise said nothing else for a long time. She just reached out and took her hand. "Give her time. I can see that the two of you make each other happy, but she needs to grieve first. She's not ready, but she'll get there."

She shook her head. Some things were too big to move past, and this was one of them. If she didn't have Declan, then maybe that would have been true, but her son would always be a reminder to Lisa of the son she had lost.

Chapter Fifteen

The depression gradually began to lift from intense storm to dark, low-lying cloud, but Lisa stayed in her room to weather the remains. She sat on her bed, alternating between napping, sketching, and scrolling her phone aimlessly. She was doing the latter, flipping through social media, when she saw the post that made her heart catch in her chest.

The photo of her nieces displayed itself mercilessly across the screen—Kara and Susie, each wearing a shirt that said "Big Sister," big smiles on both of their little faces. Lisa stared numbly at the photo, then flipped to the next image: a grainy sonogram photo. Andrew and Sarah were proud to announce that their family was going to be growing in April.

She couldn't breathe.

She'd posted a similar pregnancy announcement. A photo of a tiny pair of baby shoes. She'd never gotten to post a photo of Mitchell wearing those little sneakers. There'd been no joyous birth announcement. She'd made Andrew announce Mitchell's death. She hadn't been able to face the idea of putting the words into writing. Of course she'd received an outpouring of condolences, comfort for a time. Then she was left alone with a grief too huge for anyone in her life to fully comprehend. Nobody could be with her in her grief, even if they tried.

She turned her phone off and set it on her nightstand, wishing she could unsee the images. Not that it mattered. There would be other posts. Birth announcements. Newborn photos. Birthday pictures. Life went on for everyone around her, and there'd always be visual reminders of that fact.

Tears burned behind her eyes, but she refused to let herself cry. She had left Toronto to escape the grief. She didn't want to cry anymore. She had cried too much as it was. She didn't know how she could have any tears left in her.

She had not come to the coast to wallow. God, she was supposed to be moving forward, not sitting on her bed crying over social media posts. She could have done that in Toronto.

With renewed determination, she pulled out her sketchbook and flipped through the pages, looking over the artwork she'd created since she'd come to the coast. The sketchbook was nearly full of images inspired by her grief, but there were a number of images distant enough that Lisa thought they could be worked into a project. She had told her agent she wanted time off, but maybe productivity was exactly what she needed now. Lisa ran her fingers over her most recent sketch as she toyed with the idea of sending the drawings off to her agent. Something akin to hope fluttered in her chest.

She scanned her finished images and emailed them to Natalie with a brief explanation, and then she sat back on the bed and began to sketch. She drew a woman, sitting in the center of the page, folded in on herself, a tiny urn clutched to her. The rest of the page was filled with phone screens. On the screens she sketched baby shoes, women displaying their pregnant bellies, blurry sonogram images, positive pregnancy tests, and T-shirts announcing a new baby. The constant inundation of everyone else celebrating what she would never have.

She was adding the finishing touches to the sketch a couple of hours later when her phone rang, interrupting her work. She set her pencil down and reached for the phone, smiling when she saw Natalie's name on the screen. Her work had been cathartic, and she felt certain that progress was what she needed. *Purpose.* It would be a distraction from the chasm inside of her.

"Natalie, hi," Lisa said.

"Lisa, I got your work," Natalie answered.

"And?"

The long pause told Lisa everything she needed to know. She felt her stomach drop, and was surprised at the intensity of the rejection she felt.

"You don't like it."

"No, it's not that," Natalie interjected. "It's good work. Some of your best. I'm just not sure how I can sell this as it is. You sent some wonderfully detailed work of sea monsters and creatures climbing up lighthouses. But there's no context. They're just monster pictures."

Lisa burned with a sense of embarrassment and exposure. She'd laid herself out bare in those pictures, and to hear them reduced to "just monster pictures" stung more than she cared to admit.

"I need to work," she said. "Isn't there something we could use these pictures for? Can't we add context?"

"We could pair them with your story," Natalie suggested. "Let the readers know about Mitchell. Tell the reader where these pictures are coming from."

"No," Lisa said without hesitation.

"Lisa, you have a beautiful images here. They could help thousands of women who share your grief."

"I'm not bringing him into this. I can't. He's my baby. He's not some tool to sell books."

"Lisa," Natalie began, gentle but serious, "you and I both know he wouldn't be a tool to sell books. You've never done work simply for profit. It's one of the things I respect most about you. But your work could have an impact. Mitchell's story could have an impact. Think about it."

Lisa had no intention of thinking about it. They ended the call and Lisa closed her sketchbook. Mitchell didn't belong in a book. He was her *son*, and she needed to keep him close, tucked safely inside of her heart.

Suddenly the room felt small. She needed to get out. She was tired of being trapped in the loft bedroom alone with her

116

pain. She realized as she was putting her coat on that she was just continuing to run, but that didn't stop her. There was nothing else to do but run from the pain. If she didn't, it would swallow her.

Still, she suspected that it was going to catch her eventually.

Lisa was bundled up in her jacket and walked down the road toward O'Leary's, the pub where she'd met Rachel for the ceilidh. Snow came down in fat flakes, the first real snow of the year, a heavy, wet snow that clung to her eyelashes. She usually made it a point to not drown her sorrows out of fear she'd never resurface, but for one night she wanted the escape that a few beers could offer.

She pulled open the door to the brick building, instantly greeted with warmth and upbeat Celtic music—a recording this time, not a live band. The bar was mostly empty, with a few patrons playing pool in the corner or sitting at the bar sipping on drinks.

"I'll have a Guinness," she said. The dark, frothy brew was exactly the type of liquid comfort she wanted.

"Coming right up." The bartender poured the beer into a mug from the tap. He set the beer in front of her, and she pulled the mug toward herself with both hands.

She closed her eyes as she took the first sip.

She had worked so hard on those sketches. Anger bubbled inside of her, which she tempered with another sip of the beer. She didn't understand how Natalie could tell her the work wasn't personal enough. She had poured her heart into each of those images. It was the most personal work she'd ever done.

She took another sip—longer this time.

She wanted to drink as much as it took to fill the void in her chest. She knew there was no amount of alcohol that could fill it, but she was determined to try.

As she neared the bottom of her first beer, she heard the door open and she instinctively glanced over, meeting Rachel's eyes.

"Lisa?" She saw, rather than heard, Rachel ask.

She lifted her hand in greeting.

Rachel stood for a minute as if unsure what to do before coming over to where she sat.

"Is it all right if I join you?" Rachel asked.

She nodded and signaled for the bartender to pour another round—one for each of them this time.

Rachel took off her coat and hung it on the back of the bar stool. Lisa tried not to notice the snug fit of the white knit sweater that clung perfectly to all of her curves.

"Is Declan with his dad this weekend?" she asked.

Rachel nodded. "He actually showed up this time."

"That's good, right?" She was uncertain, given Rachel's tone, which held more bitterness than relief.

Rachel shrugged. "Declan's happy. But when he comes home, I'll be the mean parent and it'll be a few rough days. And next time, most likely, he won't show up, and Declan will be crushed. It would be easier if he'd just stay gone, you know?"

"I'm sorry. Declan deserves so much more."

"Yeah," Rachel said, her voice small.

She watched as Rachel stared down into the dark beer, curls falling forward around her face. Lisa wanted to tuck those curls back behind Rachel's ear, brush her hand across Rachel's cheek, and somehow make the ocean in her eyes less stormy. But she sat in place and took another drink of her own beer.

"Thanks for the drink." Rachel held up her glass, clinking it against Lisa's. "I needed this."

Lisa gazed down at her beer as well and nodded. "Me too."

"Does it make me a terrible person?" Rachel asked after a long moment. "Wishing Declan's dad would stay out of his life?"

Lisa took a moment to search for the right words before she answered with a question. "If Joey was a responsible parent, would you want him gone?"

Rachel shook her head. "Of course not. He's not a bad guy, and it wasn't his fault that we broke up. The fact that he wasn't female was a bit of a deal breaker for me. We were young, but he was always nice enough."

"There you go. You're *not* a bad person. You're wanting to protect your son."

Rachel sat still for a long moment. "I feel like a bad parent," she said, her voice small. "I see the way his teacher looks at me every time I have to pick Declan up from school and he's in trouble. I see the way the other parents look at me. Hell, I see the way *Declan* looks at me half the time."

"He's six. No matter what you do, he's going to decide that you're the *worst* some of the time. Like when you make him eat his vegetables or finish his homework. God forbid."

The smallest smile formed on Rachel's lips.

Lisa bumped Rachel with her arm. "You're not supposed to be his friend all of the time. It's your job to teach him all of the rules and be the bad guy sometimes." Emotion caught her off guard as she finished the sentence, and she tried to swallow it down with her beer, but her throat was tight.

"I'm sorry," Rachel said. "You don't want to hear all of this. I shouldn't have said anything. God, I'm so insensitive."

"I asked. I care about you. *And* I care about Declan. Just because I can't be more to the two of you doesn't mean I want to forget he exists."

The bar was loud with music and background chatter, but the silence between the two of them stretched thick and tight. She knew that Rachel heard her, though, because she fell silent, her gaze fixed steadily on Lisa.

"What was his name?" Rachel asked gently after a long moment.

She didn't want to answer, her familiar defenses falling into place around her. And at the same time she felt a deep pull to tell Rachel everything. She wanted Rachel to know her, and that meant wanting Rachel to know about him. She took a long drink of her beer and shook her head.

She could feel Rachel's eyes on her, a safe, caring gaze. Not the look of pity that she was used to.

"Mitchell," she answered at last. "Mitchell Adam Whelan."

Rachel rested her hand on Lisa's forearm. "Tell me about him?"

Lisa focused on the warmth of Rachel's fingers. The gentle

touch was grounding. "I don't know how to talk about him without falling apart."

"It's okay to fall apart."

She shook her head. She finished off her beer and slid her credit card across the bar to pay for the drinks. The bar was suffocating. There were too many people. Too much noise. Too much expectation.

She didn't want to leave Rachel, though; her warmth was calming. "Walk with me?"

Rachel pulled on her coat, and Lisa led the way outside. As soon as she pushed through the doors, she sucked the dense, cold air in greedily in a long deep breath, tilting her head back to the night sky as she took in the air.

Rachel rested a hand on the small of her back.

Lisa pulled her toque on and zipped her coat, but she didn't mind the cold. She could *feel* the cold, which was a welcome change from the emptiness.

She began walking toward the cliffs overlooking the harbor, and Rachel wordlessly fell into step beside her. She could feel the alcohol—she wasn't drunk, but the jagged edges of the world were all lightly blurred.

When they reached the cliffs, Lisa spoke. "My grandpa once said that the song of the sea was the song of freedom, but it's bullshit. I'm just as trapped here."

"Talk to me," Rachel urged. "Tell me about Mitchell."

She shook her head. "I can't."

"Why not?"

Lisa thought for a long moment, trying to find the words to describe her hesitation.

"I feel like . . . like I'm at sea, and it's storming, and I'm in a rickety wooden boat, and all I can do is hold onto Mitchell. I can't let him go. Talking about him feels like letting him go. I need to keep him close. Safe. With me."

Rachel put her hands on Lisa's shoulders and turned her so that she was looking at Rachel. Rachel's eyes were warm and beautiful and grounding. Rachel was a lighthouse.

"Talking about him isn't letting him go," Rachel said.

Her chest was tight. Her heart hurt, an ache that spread from the middle of her chest outward all the way through her limbs. "I'm not ready to talk about him. I'm not ready to move forward. I don't want to stop hurting, not if it means I'm letting him go."

At the admission the tears came. She felt the sob rip its way from her chest. This time she couldn't stop it.

Rachel pulled her in close, holding her tight.

She fell into Rachel, resting her head on Rachel's chest and wrapping her arms around Rachel's waist to anchor her as the sobs coursed through her. In the first month after losing Mitchell, she had done little else other than cry, hard sobs as though her heart had been trying to break free of her chest. She had cried enough saltwater tears to form a sea. And then she had swallowed her tears down. She had cried since, but she hadn't fully let go, hadn't let the tears take over since. Now the floodgate was open, and there was no stopping them.

"Shh," Rachel breathed against her ear. "It's okay. I've got you."

Lisa held Rachel closer, needing her solid, steady warmth. And she stood like that, crying, until she was sure there could be no tears left, and her eyes were sore and swollen from the tears.

"I'm sorry," she said, stepping back, embarrassment hitting her.

"Don't," Rachel said. "Please don't apologize. It's okay to cry."

She saw nothing but compassion in Rachel's gaze. There was no pity, no judgment.

"One day I'll tell you about him," she said, and she believed it. She *wanted* to open up to her. It felt important that Rachel know about Mitchell. But not yet. She wasn't ready to let go.

"I'll walk you home," Rachel said.

Lisa took her hand as they walked and was sad to let go of Rachel once they'd reached Aunt Eloises's house.

Chapter Sixteen

Rachel sat on the chesterfield, remote in hand, mindlessly flipping channels, not really searching for a show to watch. She checked her watch every few minutes, even though knowing the time did nothing other than fuel her anger. It was nearly 8:30 p.m., and Joey was supposed to have dropped Declan off over an hour earlier. She knew better than to worry the two were dead in a car accident. She had learned the simplest answer was usually that Joey was just an irresponsible screwup who was unbelievably bad at time management. She'd already spent many an evening wondering if she should call highway patrol only for Joey to saunter up, Declan in tow, as though he had done nothing wrong. She had even expected Declan to be dropped off late. But expecting the late arrival did nothing to quell Rachel's anger. Eight p.m. was Declan's bedtime, and he would be irritable enough after his dad leaving without sleep deprivation being added into the mix.

Rachel's cell phone buzzed, and she picked it up, expecting to see a message from Joey, preparing herself for a fight. Instead, she saw Lisa's name, and a smile lit up her face despite everything.

Thanks for helping me through my emotional wreckage last night, the message read. *I didn't think two beers would turn me into such a mess, but I appreciate having a friend there to listen.*

Rachel didn't hesitate with her response. *I'll always listen. You can trust me.*

A long couple of minutes passed before Lisa's response came. *I believe that.* Followed by a heart emoticon.

She stared at the little red heart on her screen. She didn't want to read anything into it. She *really* didn't. But the message and the little heart brought a tightness to her chest.

She held the phone in her hand and tried to think of what to say to extend the conversation, but before she could send off another text, the doorbell rang.

A glance at her watch told her it was 8:43 p.m. One hour and forty-three minutes late. The anger was still present, but luckily for Joey's sake it burned less intensely after the distraction of Lisa's messages.

Rachel opened the door. Joey stood on the step, holding a sleeping Declan in his arms.

"Sorry I'm late," he whispered, having sense enough at least to look ashamed.

Rachel gave him a hard glare, but said nothing, not wanting to wake Declan with an argument. She reached out to take Declan from Joey.

"Can I?" Joey asked. "I'll just lay him in his bed and then I'll be out of here."

Rachel saw the longing etched across his face—which suddenly no longer looked like the boy she'd once dated, but now a man, worn out and tired. She softened and stepped aside to hold the door open for him.

Joey kicked off his shoes, and Rachel showed him to Declan's room. She stood in the doorway as Joey carefully set Declan down on the bed and took Declan's little backpack off his shoulder, setting it on the end of the bed.

Joey leaned in and placed a kiss on Declan's forehead.

When Joey went to stand, Declan stirred and woke.

"Daddy," he said sleepily.

"Shh," Joey said. "It's bedtime, buddy."

"Are you leaving?" Declan rubbed his eyes and sat up in bed.

"Yeah, bud. I am. But I'll see you again in a couple of weeks."

"I don't want you to go." He started to cry.

Rachel ached to go to Declan, scoop him up and hold him, but she stayed back, giving Joey and Declan their space to say good-bye. As much as she wanted to take away all of Declan's pain, she could never take away the hurt of having to say good-bye to his dad, and it was good that Joey see the hurt.

"I don't want to go either," Joey said, "but I have to work. I'm sorry. I love you so much."

"I love you too," Declan said, but the words had not placated him because he started to cry harder. "Don't leave."

"Declan, I have to," Joey said, his voice slightly sterner. "And you need to get some sleep."

"I don't want to sleep. I want to play with you," Declan sobbed.

Rachel knew Declan was too exhausted for play; otherwise, he'd have been climbing out of bed and trying to find something for him and his dad to do together. As it was, he clutched his dad's hand and cried, but made no move to get up.

"I have to go." Joey kissed Declan again. "I love you."

Joey pulled his hand from Declan's and stepped back, making him cry harder.

"Just a couple of weeks," Joey repeated. He stepped out into the hallway beside Rachel, pulling the door closed behind him.

Joey leaned back against the wall and ran a hand through his messy auburn hair. His eyes glistened with tears. Rachel decided not to say anything about the time.

"It's not like I *want* to leave all the time," he said aloud, not seeming to speak to her, but just putting the words out there.

"I know."

"I hate this," Joey said, looking at her this time. "But this is the best I've got. At least right now. I need to work. I need to make a life for myself. Or else I'm going to be stuck forever."

"I know." Joey would have been miserable if he'd stayed in Craghurst, worked on the boats, and grown old never having had a chance to experience anything else. That was the difference between them. She was willing to sacrifice everything for Declan. He *was* everything.

"I'll do better about being on time next time," he said. "I promise."

"Okay." She showed Joey to the door.

Then she went to Declan's room where her son was already asleep. She stood in the doorway and watched him for a long time. When she'd gotten pregnant, Joey had seen a barrier to the big future he'd dreamed of, and he'd been treating Declan as such ever since. When she'd gotten pregnant, she'd seen her future for the first time. Declan became her whole world.

Joey was trying, but Declan deserved so much better than half-commitments and playing second best to an unreliable work schedule.

She sighed and closed the door halfway. Declan deserved to come first, and there was no point wasting time with anyone who couldn't commit to that.

Chapter Seventeen

Lisa sipped her coffee while she sat at the dining-room table gazing out at the morning. A few streaks of color still spread across the sky from the sunrise, but beyond that the world was in gray scale: gray rocks, gray water, and white snow blanketing everything else. She enjoyed the calm of the winter scene. Bright colors only mocked her. The gray was a comfortable fit.

"You should get out of the house today," Eloise said, as she hand-washed the mug she'd used for her tea. "You've sat home for two days now. You haven't even been working on your art. You just sit and stare out the window. I'm worried about you."

She gave a small shrug. "My agent doesn't want my art. What's the point?"

"Yes, I'm sure she said it exactly like that. That she didn't want your art and you shouldn't bother."

She rolled her eyes, feeling like a child. "You know what I mean. I *was* working, but the project didn't go anywhere. I'm not ready to jump into something else."

"I'm not telling you to start a new project. I'm merely suggesting that maybe you get out of the house. Take Roxie for a walk. Go out for a coffee. Come by the restaurant and let me feed you some actual food for lunch. Do something. Anything."

"I'll think about it." That was the best she could offer.

Eloise looked at her for a long moment, and then said, "That's all I ask."

Eloise pulled on her coat and left for work, and Lisa went back to looking out at the cold, gray morning. That was about all she had the energy for. She had tried to run from her grief, and it had caught up with her. Any initial rest she had felt out by the coast was gone.

She didn't know how long she sat staring out the window, limbs heavy, unable to move, before her phone pulled her back into the present. She saw that Andrew was calling and considered ignoring the call, but a sense of obligation took over and she answered.

"Hi," Lisa said.

"So you *are* alive." He said it in a lighthearted manner, but she could hear the underlying concern. She almost felt guilty for her radio silence, but then she thought about hearing details about Sarah's pregnancy and listening to her parents speculate on what Andrew and Sarah might name the baby, and the guilt dissipated. She was functioning out of sheer self-preservation.

"I know. I've been a bit elusive. I've needed some time to myself."

"A bit elusive is an understatement," he said. "I considered Google-searching your name to make sure it didn't come up in the obituaries, but Auntie Eloise kept assuring us all you're alive."

She breathed out slowly. "I'm sorry."

Silence answered.

"I'm worried about you," he said at last. "I knew telling you about the baby was going to be hard for you, but I didn't realize it would be so hard."

"It's not that," she lied. "I'm happy for you." A part of her *was* happy for them. She loved her brother and her nieces. Before she'd lost Mitchell, watching Andrew grow up from her annoying little brother into a pretty great dad had been one of her greatest joys. The part of her that was happy for them, though, was now buried deep beneath her own grief. It was there, but there was so much heaviness over it.

"It's okay not to be," Andrew said. "I know how much you wanted to be a mom, and I know how much you miss Mitchell."

"Please don't." Her voice broke.

"Don't what?"

"I don't want to talk about him."

There was a long beat of silence, and then Andrew asked, "Don't you think maybe we *should* talk about him?" His voice was gentle, but Lisa still tensed against the words as if they were an attack. "Hell, I want to talk about him. He was my nephew. *I* miss him."

Lisa's throat closed, and she shook her head as though he could see the movement. "I can't," she breathed. "Please."

"Okay," he conceded. "But I hope one day we can talk about him."

She didn't answer. She just looked out at the gray seascape and tried to steady her breathing.

At first, when Mitchell died, she wanted to speak his name in every conversation as though she could keep him alive that way. But she only ever saw pity in others' eyes. His name wasn't being repeated back. They didn't help keep Mitchell alive. They turned him into a ghost that haunted the room, and Lisa stopped talking about her baby, keeping him tucked away safely in her heart.

"I love you, Lisa," he said. "And I need my big sister back."

Whoever Andrew wanted back was gone. She was a different person than she'd been before. Losing Mitchell had irrevocably changed her. Why didn't he see that? She couldn't just move on, couldn't be his sister like before, couldn't be Kara and Susie's aunt like before. Everything was different now.

"I just need some time," she said, not sure time would help anything at all.

"Okay. But maybe call me once in awhile and let me know you're alive, so I don't have to send search and rescue."

"Will do."

She hung up the phone, guilt swirling in her stomach. She wanted to be there for Kara and Susie. She wanted to be able to love her new niece or nephew. And, as much as it terrified her, she wanted room in her heart for Declan. She had always enjoyed being around children, seeing the world through their eyes, filled with magic and wonder. She hated that losing Mitchell meant she had to shut out the other children in her life, but the loss took up too much space. And letting go of that loss felt like letting go of Mitchell.

All she could do was hide inside of her pain, and try to act like her heart still beat while she was around others.

God, the facade hurt.

She looked out the window and decided that she should follow Eloise's advice and get out of the house, or else she was going to make herself crazy. Especially after the call from Andrew. Besides, her stomach had started to growl, and she was fairly certain she couldn't remember the last time she'd had real food.

She pulled her coat and hat on to walk the few blocks to Catherine's Restaurant. She tried not to think about the fact that Rachel would be there or to question the warmth that spread through her at the thought of seeing her. It was the middle of the day, so Declan would be in school. She felt guilty for taking that fact into consideration. It wasn't that she was avoiding him. Not exactly. It was just that her emotions felt raw, and it felt safer to not be around him for the moment. Safer for both of them. The last thing she wanted to do was to add to Declan's hurt when she inevitably couldn't stick around.

The snow crunched under her feet, and she breathed in the refreshingly cold air as she walked. She had never particularly cared for winter, but this year she found that the quiet streets provided the serenity she needed. She was almost tempted to keep walking, to skip lunch and having to interact with people, and enjoy the outdoors, but her hunger won her over as she neared the diner.

She stepped inside, taking off her toque, which she tucked into her jacket pocket.

"Well, look what the cat dragged in," Eloise said happily, approaching Lisa and pulling her into a hug. "I'm glad to see you out of the house."

"You were right," she admitted. "Fresh air is doing me some good."

"Fresh air and a proper meal," Eloise said.

Without conscious thought, Lisa scanned the room, disappointment sinking into her chest when she realized that Rachel wasn't there.

"She went to pick up Declan from school," Eloise said knowingly. "It's their half day today."

She wasn't sure if she was blushing about her transparency or if her cheeks felt warmer than usual simply because she'd come in from the cold. At the same time, she realized that Declan would be there shortly, and she tried to push down her fears and prepare herself for conversation with the child as if she could easily compartmentalize her grief.

Eloise grabbed a menu and led her over to a booth.

"I'll go get you some water," Eloise said, leaving her with the menu.

Lisa hadn't been to Catherine's since the winter menu changes, and she read it over, impressed with the selections. She decided to try the beef and cabbage stew. Then she sat back and looked around the diner, taking in the photos on the walls. Rachel at various ages was in a number of them. There was a picture of a young Frank Murray, proudly holding up a giant fish, surrounded by a number of other men who had their arms thrown over him. And another of Frank and Rachel with a woman who Lisa realized must have been Rachel's mom, Catherine, for whom the restaurant was named.

They hadn't hidden all reminders of her after she passed away. Frank and Rachel had opened her restaurant, and her dream had become a fixture in Craghurst. Lisa simultaneously admired and envied that ability to grieve without hiding.

She heard the jingle of bells and turned to see Rachel and Declan enter the restaurant. More specifically, she watched Declan stomp in and Rachel follow him, looking helpless.

"Hey you," Eloise said, stepping up to Declan. "Bad day?"

"I *hate* school."

Rachel looked tired, and Lisa wanted to go up to her and hug her, but she stayed seated, not wanting to interfere.

"Let's go have a seat," Rachel said to Declan. "I'll make you a grilled cheese."

He turned toward the tables and brightened when he saw Lisa, giving a little half smile and a wave.

Rachel followed Declan's gaze and waved shyly as well.

"I want to sit with Lisa," Declan said.

"Lisa's having lunch. You can pick a different table."

He looked impossibly small, standing in front of his mom with a defeated expression on his face. Lisa's heart tugged, and she spoke before she could think the words through.

"I don't mind," Lisa said.

Her own fears were silenced by the happiness that spread across Declan's face.

Rachel shot her a questioning glance, as if to confirm that Lisa was, in fact, okay with the company. "If I wanted to eat alone, I could have stayed home," she said with a shrug. She liked being able to ease his sadness. She could care enough to want him to be happy, couldn't she? It didn't feel right to let him sit by himself while he was clearly upset.

He scooted into the booth beside Lisa, and she was caught off guard, moving over to accommodate him. She watched Rachel stifle a laugh.

Eloise came over to ask Lisa what she wanted for lunch and then headed to the kitchen to make the stew and a grilled cheese for Declan.

"I'm going to go say hi to my dad and help out in the kitchen for a few minutes, but I'll be back out shortly," Rachel said.

"We're good," Lisa promised.

Rachel left and she turned to Declan, who pulled paper and crayons out of his backpack, making himself right at home.

"I've been practicing drawing," he announced. "I want to be good at it like you are."

He pulled out a picture that was an obvious attempt to re-create the eagle picture she'd drawn. There was a scraggly brown tree and a shape atop the tree that appeared to be the bird, with a bright yellow beak.

"I love the colors you used," Lisa said, and Declan smiled wide.

"I showed Mrs. Harvey, and she said I'm really talented." He lifted his chin a little higher.

"Is she your teacher?" she asked.

Declan nodded. He flipped to a blank page and pulled out a yellow crayon.

Lisa looked at him. He didn't look like the sullen boy who had stormed into the restaurant just minutes earlier. His anger seemed to have faded. She felt as if she was on thin ice, and that later she'd fall through and into a grief worse than earlier, but she skated forward anyway, her concern for Declan overpowering that grief. "What happened at school today?"

"Sam and Patrick are stupid," he answered, as though she should know who Sam and Patrick were, and just why exactly they were "stupid."

"Are they in your class?"

"Uh huh. They wouldn't let me play with them at recess, and then when I got mad and called them stupid they tattled on me and I had to sit on the bench."

"That sounds really frustrating."

"The other kids never want to play with me." The heartbreak was evident.

Lisa leaned over and looked Declan in the eye when she promised him, "Those guys are missing out."

As if the conversation had never happened, Declan began drawing a bright yellow circle at the top of his page with yellow lines extending, which Lisa knew immediately to be the sun.

"Want to come tobogganing with me and mom?" he asked as he colored in the yellow sun. "She said she'd take me after lunch."

It was at that moment that Rachel stepped up to the table, carrying Lisa's stew and a plate with two grilled cheese sandwiches.

"Declan, Lisa's probably busy. We'll go the two of us, and maybe we can invite Lisa another time."

Rachel looked at her, and Lisa could see she was trying to give her an out. She should take it. But she thought of Declan feeling like the other kids didn't want to play with him, and the last thing she wanted to do was add to that feeling. "I'd love to come tobogganing. That is, if it's all right with your mom."

Rachel's gaze was so tender that butterflies swirled in her stomach. She slid into the booth across from them.

"You sure?" she asked.

Lisa nodded even though she did not feel sure about anything. "It will be fun."

She couldn't remember the last time she'd gone tobogganing. She had probably been a kid herself. She could let herself enjoy the afternoon.

"All right then," Rachel said, taking a bite of her grilled cheese. "Tobogganing it is."

"Sit down." Declan tugged excitedly on Lisa's coat and pointed one mittened hand at the little red saucer that sat at the top of the hill.

"Declan, ask nicely," Rachel scolded. She wasn't sure when her son had become quite so bossy, but as much as she wanted him to not be so demanding, she was glad to see him confident and happy for a change.

Lisa didn't seem to mind. She was already sitting down on the little red saucer and Declan was climbing into her lap.

Rachel shook her head with a laugh. She smiled as she watched Lisa use her hands to propel them over the top of the hill.

Declan squealed in delight the entire way down the hill. The sound broke Rachel's heart wide open and filled it up with so much happiness.

She wasn't entirely sure how this afternoon had come to be, but Declan had woken up sad that his dad was gone, and he'd come home from school angry about something he wouldn't talk about, and so she was beyond thrilled to see him having a good time. It almost felt like a dream, and she reminded herself that she was bound to wake up. She didn't know how the three of them ended up on the toboggan hill, but surely it was a one-time event.

Lisa and Declan slid to a stop at the bottom of the big hill. Lisa didn't have a chance to catch a breath. They'd hardly stopped before Declan grabbed her hand and started excitedly racing back up for another saucer ride down. Lisa scrambled to pick up the little saucer and follow Declan back up the hill, hardly able to keep up with him.

Rachel couldn't help the smile that formed as she watched them, but the smile was replaced by the memory of Lisa crying on her shoulder in the snow just a few nights earlier. She wanted to enjoy the afternoon, but fear echoed in her chest, reminding her that spending time with Declan hurt Lisa, and the afternoon could easily end in more pain than happiness.

Declan and Lisa reached the top of the hill, and he immediately began pushing her back onto the saucer.

"What about me?" Rachel asked with a laugh.

Declan frowned as he looked from Rachel to Lisa. "All three of us can ride," he decided.

"I don't think we're all going to fit on that little saucer," she said, looking at the small round sled.

Lisa hesitated for only a moment, sitting down on the sled. "We could give it a try."

Rachel looked down at her, hesitant, and she saw the moment the full extent of the suggestion dawned on Lisa.

"It's just a sled ride," Lisa said softly.

She nodded once and sat down on Lisa's lap. Declan climbed on top of them. She wrapped her arms around Declan, and Lisa's arms wrapped around her. Lisa was soft and strong, and Rachel had to close her eyes as she breathed in her floral scent.

Just a sled ride, she reminded herself. None of the afternoon felt all that innocent.

Then Lisa dug her feet into the ground, pulling them forward an inch at a time, until eventually they slipped over the crest of the hill and gravity began pulling them downward. As they picked up speed, Lisa lifted her feet onto the saucer and tightened her grip around Rachel.

The little sled spun down the hill, moving through the thick, powdery snow, faster and faster. As they neared the bottom of the hill, they hit an uneven patch of snow and the three of them were tipped off the sled, landing in a pile.

Declan got up quickly, laughing and dashing up the hill.

Rachel was on her back and used the back of her mitten to brush snow away from her eyes, peering up from where she lay in the snow. Lisa was sprawled half on top of her, half beside her. She was pushing herself up, adjusting her toque, and brushing her blond hair back from her face.

Without thinking, Rachel reached out and helped brush a strand of hair away from Lisa's eyes.

Lisa froze. Her cheeks had turned a rosy tint from the cold, and clumps of snow clung to her eyelashes. Rachel's breath caught.

She'd known it was going to be hard to be just friends, but she never would have imagined just *how* hard. The air between them hummed with electricity. She physically ached to sit up slightly and close the distance between the two of them, but the boundaries of their relationship were clear.

Damn it.

She swallowed hard and forced herself to extricate her legs from beneath Lisa. Standing, she picked up the saucer.

Declan was halfway up the hill, chugging forward, seemingly unaware that neither adult was right behind him. She started after him, not waiting for Lisa, not wanting to prolong whatever had just transpired between them. Surely Lisa felt it too.

"Let's do that again," Declan said excitedly, when Rachel caught up to him at the top of the hill.

Lisa was on her way up as well.

"Let's go just the two of us this time," Rachel said, sitting in the saucer and motioning for Declan to crawl into her lap. He looked at her uncertainly at first, but then sat down and she propelled the two of them down the hill.

Declan waved at Lisa as they passed her walking up the side.

Everything would have been easier if Declan didn't adore Lisa so much, Rachel thought. Not only was Lisa gorgeous, smart, and funny, but she was great with Declan. The last part made it nearly impossible to ignore the attraction. If only Lisa could have adored Declan just as much in return.

No, she amended, *Lisa does adore Declan.* That was the problem. Lisa didn't want to adore him. Didn't want to have a role in his life.

She carried the saucer up the hill once more as Declan dashed up ahead of her, shouting up at Lisa to go down the hill with him next.

Don't fall for her, Rachel thought. She wasn't sure if the thought was directed toward her son or herself.

Lisa stomped the snow from her shoes before stepping inside. Her jeans were heavy and wet from the snow, and her legs were chilled from the cold.

"Come with me," Rachel said. "I'll get you a pair of dry pants."

She nodded and followed Rachel to her bedroom where she pulled a pair of sweatpants out of the dresser and held them up.

"Try these," Rachel said. "They may be an inch or so too short, but otherwise they should fit."

"Thank you." She took the offered garment.

Rachel's gaze was warm, and she wanted to move in and close the distance between them. She wanted to pull Rachel against her.

"Mommy," a voice called, cutting through the thick silence. "Can I watch a movie?"

"I'll be right out," Rachel called, then turned back to her. "I'll let you change, and I'll help him set up the movie," she said, resting her hand on Lisa's forearm before heading back out to the living room, closing the bedroom door behind her.

Lisa sat back on the bed and pulled the sweatpants into her lap. She was exhausted. Physically. Emotionally.

She hadn't been able to stop smiling as she spun down the toboggan hill. The laughter had been completely unbidden. She'd been silly and spontaneous and enjoyed herself more than any other time in recent memory. Even now, she could still feel her arms around Rachel and see the look on Rachel's face as she'd gazed up at her from the snow. It had been a look of naked attraction, and if Rachel hadn't moved, Lisa would have leaned in and kissed her right there, at the bottom of the toboggan hill, to hell with the boundaries she'd set or the reasons she'd set them. And, damn it, she'd had fun sledding with Declan, and listening to him laugh each time they reached the bottom of the slope. It had been a good day, and she'd enjoyed every minute. She hadn't thought of Mitchell once.

That realization hit her like a tidal wave, and she felt nauseated from the force of the guilt.

Not even once. Not even the most fleeting thought.

Tears burned at the back of her eyes and thickened in her throat.

She hugged the sweatpants to her and let the tears come.

"I'm sorry, Mitchell," she said through her tears, over and over. Eventually the tears choked out the words.

He was her son. *He* was the one that she should've been tobogganing with. She should've at least *thought* about him.

She thought of the sweet, perfect little boy the doctor had handed her and how he'd squirmed in her arms as she tucked him close to her chest, knowing their time together was limited. His face was wet and wrinkled, but somehow when she saw him, she knew exactly what he would have looked like as a boy.

He was her boy.

And she hadn't even thought of him.

A knock interrupted her spiral, and she glanced up at the door, furiously wiping her eyes.

"Everything okay?" Rachel asked.

She couldn't answer. She knew her voice would betray that she had been crying, and she took a few deep breaths in an attempt to steady herself.

"Can I come in?" Rachel asked.

"Yeah," she managed.

Rachel opened the door, saw her, and instantly moved to the bed, taking a seat next to Lisa and putting a hand on her back.

"What's wrong? Talk to me."

She wiped her eyes and met Rachel's warm, empathetic gaze. She wanted to open up to her. She was so used to keeping Mitchell safe, tucked away inside of her own heart and mind, but suddenly she *wanted* Rachel to know about him. Rachel was so tender and caring, and she wanted to allow herself the luxury of the comfort Rachel could offer.

"I miss Mitchell," she said. "And I feel guilty having fun without him. I had such a great afternoon, and then it hit me that I'd enjoyed the afternoon so much I hadn't even thought about him."

Rachel's hand rubbed slow circles on her back, and she fell into the comforting touch, closing her eyes against the emotion that continued to threaten.

"I feel like a bad mom," she continued. "Like I forgot him."

"You didn't forget him," Rachel said. "I bet you remember every last detail."

She nodded. "I see him every time I close my eyes."

"You know," Rachel began, "it doesn't have to be him or us. You can enjoy tobogganing and still love and care about Mitchell. You can *talk* to me about him. He doesn't have to be absent when you're with me."

"When I talk about him, people shut down." She'd seen it so many times. A good mood would instantly dampen the minute she spoke Mitchell's name. Nobody wanted to be reminded of the baby who died.

"I won't shut down," Rachel promised. The hand she'd had on Lisa's back moved to her thigh. "You can talk to me about him anytime. Whether it's to happily tell me something about him, or because you need to cry about the injustice of it all. I'm here for all of it."

She looked at Rachel, unsure if she dared to open up. Unsure if she could *trust* opening up. But she *wanted* to. She wanted Rachel to know about him. She wanted Rachel to know about *her*.

"Before I even got pregnant, I dreamed about Mitchell," Lisa said. "Maybe once every month or so. More frequently once I

138

actually began the process of deciding how I was going to get pregnant on my own. Every time I dreamed about my baby, I'd see his face so perfectly. I just *knew* I needed to be a mom. It was the only thing I've ever truly known that I wanted for my life.

"I'd watch friends get pregnant, and I'd be so jealous each time. It seemed like it would never be my turn, and I wanted it so desperately. By my late twenties, I started thinking about how I was going to make it happen. I was happy single. I had a good career and I was able to work from home. I stopped seeing the need to wait. When I turned thirty, the time just felt *right*. I researched fertility law and pored over websites and forums and blogs. I carefully chose my donor. Mitchell was my *dream*."

Rachel continued to rub her leg. She said nothing, but Lisa could feel her in the silence. It wasn't a withdrawn silence. Rachel was giving her the space to talk about her son. Lisa could feel the compassion in the air around her. She felt safe. And heard.

"You know, I never used to cry much, but then I got pregnant," Lisa said. "I wept when the pregnancy test showed the plus sign. I wept again when I found out I was having a son. When he was born, the doctor handed him to me, and I held him against my chest and cried happy, exhausted, tears. When I held him for the first time, all the bad was forgotten, and those moments were the most perfect, most gloriously happy, moments of my life."

"He's lucky you're his mom," Rachel said. "That's a huge love you have for him."

Lisa turned to meet Rachel's eyes. They were misty, but still held every bit of their usual warmth.

"You didn't use past tense," she whispered.

Rachel's face softened—as if that was possible—and said, "He's not past tense. Mitchell's very much still with you. He'll always be your son."

This time she couldn't stop the tears. She fell against Rachel, who took her in her arms and held her as she cried. Rachel's hands smoothed over Lisa's back, slowly and gently. She rubbed her hair, brushing it away from her forehead. She kissed Lisa's head. And she held Lisa. Tender and patient.

When the tears subsided, Lisa wiped her eyes and sat up, feeling lighter, the burden of guilt lifted off of her.

"Shall we join Declan for the movie?" she asked.

Rachel smiled. "Why don't you change into those warm dry pants and I'll make us all some hot chocolate, and then we can join him."

"That sounds perfect."

And it did. She wanted nothing more than an afternoon with Rachel and Declan.

Maybe Rachel was right. Maybe being with them didn't have to mean setting Mitchell aside.

Chapter Eighteen

Rachel drove Declan to school and headed home for a relaxing day. She had the day off work and no pressing plans other than to change back into her pajamas and laze on the couch, binge-watching movies. It was her favorite type of self-care and something she didn't get to do nearly as often as she would have liked.

She kicked off her boots and let her jacket fall to the floor, leaving it there while she went to her bedroom to get her pajama pants. She stopped at the dresser, her mind flashing back to Lisa sitting on the bed, clutching the worn pair of sweatpants to her as though they were a comfort object. She'd looked so heart-wrenchingly sad. Rachel's heart still ached for her. She thought of all of the things Lisa had told her about Mitchell. She wished she could have met him. She wished she could have met Lisa and her son. It was clear from the patient way that Lisa interacted with Declan that she was *meant* to be a mom. It was so god-damned unfair.

She had rested her hand on Lisa and tried to remain quiet to give her the space to talk. She wasn't entirely sure how to respond, but she hoped Lisa knew she was there listening. She hoped that Lisa had felt how she hung on every word. How much she cherished every memory that Lisa was willing to share.

It had only been a couple of weeks earlier that Lisa had told her she was unable to talk to her about Mitchell. Rachel had wanted so desperately for Lisa to open up, to trust her with her pain. She hoped that now that Lisa *had* trusted her she had proved worthy of that trust.

Afterward, Lisa had changed and stayed for hot chocolate and a movie. She'd let Declan crawl up beside her and snuggle in against her. She'd been quieter and more pensive than earlier in the day, but she had not seemed sad exactly. Certainly, there had been a lightness to Lisa after sharing. But that didn't mean she hadn't gone home and regretted being so vulnerable.

Rachel had not heard from Lisa since, and she desperately hoped Lisa wasn't shutting down in response to that vulnerability. She was giving her the space she needed. She ached to hear Lisa's voice and to know things were all right between the two of them, but she forced herself to be patient and let it be on Lisa's time.

Rachel selected her most comfortable pair of pajama pants, changed, and left the bedroom and her worries. She could do nothing more than wait and trust she'd hear from Lisa when she was ready.

She was halfway into her first movie when her phone buzzed.

She picked it up and smiled with relief when she saw the text message from Lisa light up her screen. *Are you free today?*

Maybe, Rachel messaged back. *What did you have in mind?*

She waited, smiling at her phone like a teenager, until Lisa's message came through.

I can't tell you that or it would ruin the surprise. Pick you up in half an hour?

Rachel's curiosity was definitely piqued. *I suppose I could be ready by then.*

Dress warm.

Rachel read the last text a few times, wondering what the hell they were going to be doing. She wasn't much of an outdoorsy person in the winter. She was much more of a pajama pants, fireplace, and all things cozy type of woman. But she realized she had become much more of an up-for-anything woman if Lisa was involved.

Rachel squeezed her eyes shut, chastising herself for having such a huge crush on someone so unavailable.

Then she got up from the couch, realizing that dressing warm probably did not mean warm pajamas, and went to change into some winter clothes. She wished she had an idea of what they were doing so she would know exactly *how* warmly she was supposed to dress.

She was busy laying out her jacket, toque, and gloves when the doorbell rang.

The smile returned to her face. Her heart quickened. Butterflies in her stomach. Yeah, she definitely had it bad. She shook her head at herself as she opened the door.

As soon as she saw Lisa, she forgot all the reasons why she was chastising herself. Lisa stood on her front step, her blond hair falling lightly around her face, her hazel eyes shining, and she didn't even have to say anything. Rachel just melted into her easy smile.

"Hi," Lisa said.

Dammit, was she blushing? "Hi yourself." God, she sounded twelve.

"Are you ready to go?" Lisa asked, smiling and looking so impossibly perfect.

"That depends. Are you ready to tell me where we're going?"

Lisa shook her head. "It's a short drive. You'll find out soon enough."

She looked at Lisa and tried to judge whether she needed all of her winter clothes.

As if reading her mind, Lisa answered, "You're going to want the hat and mitts. Mine are in the car."

"It's a good thing I like you," she said and then cringed to herself as she picked up her hat and mitts. Did she really just say that?

She didn't make eye contact with Lisa as she stepped out the door and locked it behind her.

"It's a good thing I like you, too." Lisa bumped her shoulder before heading to the car.

Rachel slid into the passenger seat and searched the car for clues as to what they were going to be doing, but she found none.

Lisa headed down the street. The two of them sat in companionable silence until they reached the edge of town, and Lisa drove up to the parking lot near the beach access.

"It's a little cold for a beach day, don't you think?" Rachel asked.

Lisa turned off the car. "First of all, it's never too cold for a beach day. The ocean is perfect year-round. And second of all, we aren't going to be building sandcastles or going swimming, so you don't have to worry." Lisa went to the trunk, and Rachel followed suit. She laughed when Lisa pulled out the set of snowshoes.

"I'm going to fall flat on my face," Rachel said.

Lisa looked at her in mock horror. "You've never been snowshoeing before?"

She shook her head. She could honestly say the opportunity had never arisen.

"What kind of Canadian are you?"

"The kind who stays warm indoors throughout the winter. Also known as the smart kind."

Lisa laughed. Rachel couldn't help but notice how much lighter and happier she looked today. Not just in comparison to the last time she'd seen her, either. She looked happier than Rachel had ever seen her.

"It's really not that hard," Lisa promised. "It's not that different from walking in boots. It will just help keep us from sinking into the deep snow. I thought we could check out the trails along the water. It's a nice sunny day. We ought to be outside enjoying it. I was going to come out on my own, but as I was getting ready, I noticed that Eloise had a second set of snowshoes and thought it would be more enjoyable with your company."

"Now you're just sucking up to get me to strap those to my feet," Rachel said, still uncertain about this idea.

Lisa laughed again and handed her a pair of the snowshoes. "Busted. Now put these on."

She might have been uncertain about the snowshoes, but she was quite enjoying Lisa's warm, uninhibited laughter. She wanted to hear more of it. She wanted to see more of this carefree, happy Lisa. And so, without further comment, she stepped into the snowshoes and strapped them up around her boots.

Lisa strapped her snowshoes on as well and pulled a set of poles out of the trunk for each of them. Rachel was pretty sure that if you needed sticks to walk, it was too hard, but she said nothing. She would give this snowshoeing thing a shot.

"If I break an ankle, you're coming over to help around the house while I watch movies all day."

Lisa laughed and handed Rachel a set of the poles. "Deal."

Rachel took a few trepidatious steps, surprised to find it was in fact much easier than she expected. She quickly fell into a stride with Lisa walking beside her. They followed the little walking trail that was etched along the coast and that had clearly not been used since the summer time. Their poles sank deeply into the snow, giving perspective to how thick the snow had fallen over the past month, but their snowshoes kept them from sinking up to their knees. Their breath puffed out in front of them in little clouds. The sky was a bright expanse of blue, not a cloud in sight, and the sun shone brightly with sun dogs on either side.

"You're right," Rachel said. "It is a gorgeous day to be outside."

Lisa lightly elbowed her. "Say that again? The part about me being right?"

"No way. You'll get a big head. I clearly don't need to feed that ego of yours."

"I hardly have a big ego. I just happen to know when I'm wonderful and clever."

"Nope, not a big ego at all."

The trail cut right next to the rising cliff that lifted above the ocean. Rachel gazed out at the sea. The breakers crashing against the rock and ice along the shore looked new to her as she stood beside Lisa. It was no longer the same stale winter seascape she saw every day. The salt and brine were not as palpable on the crisp winter air, but the scent carried lightly on the cold breeze. She stopped and walked over to the edge, gazing out at the water and really breathing it all in for the first time in as long as she could remember.

"I think I've come to take the ocean for granted," she said. "I never come out and just enjoy it like this. It's so beautiful."

Rachel turned to meet Lisa's gaze and found her hanging on each word. "Thank you for bringing me."

Lisa planted her poles in the snow and took Rachel's to do the same while they looked out at the water.

Eventually, Lisa reached out and slid her arm around Rachel's. Even with the thick jackets between the two of them, Rachel could feel her warmth.

"I've been drawing again," Lisa said.

She watched Lisa as she gazed out at the sea. She traced the subtle slope of her nose and the gentle line of Lisa's jaw with her eyes. The sun brought out the natural highlights in Lisa's blond hair.

"I felt so stuck after my agent told me my work wasn't personal enough. I didn't want to share the details about Mitchell. I still don't. At least not publicly. But after opening up to you the other day . . . I feel a little unstuck. In my work, and in my life."

Emotion rose in Rachel's chest and pooled in the back of her throat. She couldn't talk around the lump. She simply stared at Lisa through her own misty eyes.

"I guess I just wanted to say 'thank you.'" Lisa turned and met her gaze. Her hazel eyes were warm, the sunlight capturing flecks of gold. *How had she not noticed them before?*

"You're the strongest woman I've ever known," Rachel said softly.

Lisa's head cocked to the side slightly, and her eyebrows pulled together in confusion. She shook her head. "I'm not strong. I'm a mess."

Rachel leaned in closer ever so slightly, her body moving of its own accord. "That's how you know you're strong. When things are easy, when they don't feel like a mess, then it doesn't take strength."

"Then I wish I wasn't strong," Lisa said.

She nodded. Lisa's eyes had darkened a shade. "Yeah, me too."

The air was thick with emotion around the two of them. She rested her hands on Lisa's hips. She couldn't help but notice that somehow she managed to have the perfect curves, even with a thick winter coat and sweater on. Despite the cold, Rachel wished she didn't have her gloves on. She wanted to pull Lisa closer.

Lisa's gaze fell to her lips, and Rachel swallowed hard.

Lisa shifted her weight to close more of the distance between the two of them. They stood there by the sea, so close, and yet the inches between them were too much . . . too far. Rachel needed them to close that gap.

"What are we doing?" Rachel interjected, not wanting to stop but needing to know where they stood. Lisa had made it clear they couldn't be more than friends, but, God, if they weren't both about to break that boundary they'd set in place . . .

"I don't know," Lisa answered, her eyes still focused on Rachel's mouth. "All I know is I really like you. I feel safe with you. I don't feel so broken."

Rachel's breath caught, and before she could answer, Lisa's lips were on hers.

This kiss was different from their kiss on Halloween. It wasn't hurried or desperate. It was slow and languid. Rachel melted in against Lisa's body. Her hands which had been on Lisa's hips snaked around and pulled Lisa closer, anchoring her.

Rachel's lips parted, and she heard herself moan softly at the first touch of Lisa's tongue.

She met Lisa's pace, light and unhurried, and she breathed in Lisa's soft scent of honey and shea.

Eventually the kiss ended, and Lisa rested her forehead against Rachel's. She listened to the sound of Lisa's breathing, lulled by the gentle rhythm.

"I have Declan," she said after a long moment of silence.

"I know," Lisa said, and she pulled away from Rachel, who felt the loss instantly. The air chilled her as it replaced Lisa's warm breath against her skin.

Lisa reached for the ski poles and handed a set to her. "I like Declan, too. I can't make any promises, but I *can* tell you that much. I care about both of you."

Rachel met Lisa's gaze, seeing the honesty there. She knew Lisa cared. She'd always known. But the fact that Lisa was willing to admit it now, that was big.

With a grin, Lisa broke their gaze and took off down the path in a jog, shouting that the last person up the hill was going to buy them both a coffee on the way home.

Rachel didn't try to race off after her. She took a minute to watch Lisa. She didn't know where they were going to go, but hope swelled within her. Lisa was open in a way that hadn't even been possible a week earlier. She would tread slowly and carefully, but maybe they weren't impossible after all.

Chapter Nineteen

By December Rachel started to hate the long, lazy days of winter in the diner. November was a welcome break after the summer rush, but after about a month of few to no customers, she was beginning to go stir crazy. There was very little for her to do to pass the day. She scrubbed tables that were already clean, organized and reorganized the fridge, went over finance spreadsheets, and spent the day mostly sitting around idly. She watched the door for customers, and she watched the clock. The days passed by agonizingly slow, and she was grateful for the break when it came time to pick Declan up from school.

This particular day was seeming to go slower than usual. She had started the day with sanguine thoughts of Lisa, and for a slow, perfect moment she'd allowed herself to imagine the warm embrace of her quilt was really the warmth of Lisa's body tucked up against hers. She'd imagined the feel of Lisa's arms around her waist, Lisa's soft breath against her neck. Then her alarm went off, and since that moment all she'd wanted was to be back curled up in bed, able to lazily daydream about Lisa. She didn't want responsibilities, and work, and errands. But, as it was, she found herself keeping busy in Catherine's Restaurant with menial tasks. She didn't get a day of relaxation and daydreaming.

The best break she was going to get was her drive to the elementary school, which was better than sitting bored in the diner.

Rachel pulled up in front of the elementary school, but she didn't get out. She sat and waited in the truck until she heard the school bell ring. She had stopped waiting in the hall outside of Declan's classroom. She saw the looks other parents gave her. She felt their judgment. She knew everyone's perception of Declan. Parents, teachers, other kids. They all thought Declan was the "bad kid," and it broke her heart every time she saw a parent guide her kid away from Declan at the playground. She saw the way the other kids quieted as Declan approached. She saw the way the other parents looked at her, placing just as much blame on her shoulders as they placed on Declan's. They were the "bad family." So she waited until class let out before going inside to pick up Declan.

Finally, she stepped into the elementary school and made her way down the hallway to Declan's classroom. The school always smelled faintly of peanut butter and apples. The hallways were decorated with children's artwork. Rachel no longer ever felt cheery in these halls. She suspected Declan didn't, either.

When she reached Declan's classroom, she saw Mrs. Harvey, and the single gaze told her everything. Rachel showed herself back down the hallway to the office, where Declan sat in the waiting room across from the secretary's desk.

At first she assumed that meant he was free to go home, and she started to help him collect his belongings, but then she heard her name and turned to see the principal standing at the door to her office, motioning for Rachel to join her.

She wanted to say *no*. She wanted to tell Joanna Steward she didn't care what Declan had done this time. That she didn't need to be told every time he talked back or got into an argument. That it was their job and that sometimes she wanted to hear *good* things about her child. But she held her tongue. She simply glanced over at Declan, who looked as defeated as she felt, and stepped into the small office.

"Ms. Murray," Joanna Steward began, "please have a seat."

Rachel did as instructed and asked in a voice so small she almost didn't recognize it as her own, "What did he do today?"

"He punched one of the other boys in the stomach," Mrs. Steward said. The words were delivered gently, but Rachel could still hear the judgment. She was being judged. Declan was being judged. The office grew smaller around her. He was a *good* kid. He didn't go around hitting people. She felt the desperation rise in her, though, as she saw the school principal sit back in expectation of an apology, an explanation, a promise to fix things. She wondered if Declan felt that same desperation as he tried to get his school to understand.

"Why'd he punch the other boy?" Rachel heard herself ask.

"Excuse me?" Mrs. Steward asked, seeming shocked by the question.

Rachel took a deep breath, knowing she was pushing a boundary. "What's Declan's side of the story?"

Joanna Steward gave Rachel a hard look before answering tersely. "He claims the other boy was making fun of him. The other boy denies this. It really doesn't matter, Ms. Murray. Our school has a zero-tolerance policy for violence. Declan had no right or reason to punch another child."

"I understand that," Rachel continued, "but Declan comes home unhappy a *lot*. Is anyone looking out for him? What exactly is going on in that classroom?"

"Ms. Murray, I understand you're looking out for the best interests of your son, but I have full confidence that his teacher would deal with any name-calling or bullying in the classroom. The fact remains that Declan has been the only child to be physically violent with others, and that behavior has consequences."

Rachel ran her hands through her hair in frustration. She wanted to cry but wouldn't give the principal the benefit of tears. They could come later once she was alone.

"I'm trying," Rachel said, the frustration welling within her. "I'm getting him counseling. I'm talking to him about his behavior. I'm doing everything I can. I don't have some magic quick-fix."

"I understand that, and I can empathize, really," Mrs. Steward said, softening slightly. "I know there's no easy answer, but his teacher and I have spoken and we're beginning to wonder if perhaps this school is not the right fit for Declan. If his behavior continues, I'm afraid we'll be forced to expel him. His behavioral concerns are beyond the capacity of what we're able to manage while maintaining the safety of all of the children."

"Declan is hardly a safety concern," she protested, her voice rising with fear.

"He punched another child today."

This time tears did burn at the edges of her eyes, and when she spoke she was embarrassed at the way her voice broke around the lump at the back of her throat.

"Where would he go?"

"The nearest elementary school is in Ingonish."

"That's nearly an hour's drive. I can't. I have work here. I—"

"There are buses that could take him," Mrs. Steward interjected. "I know it would not be ideal. It's not what we would like to see either. I'm just telling you that if his behavior continues like this we would have no other choice."

She stood, feeling like she should speak, but unable to form any words. Instead, she left the office, picked up Declan's coat and backpack, and motioned for him to follow her.

Once she got into her truck, she let the tears fall, careful to sit up straight and not let Declan see them from the backseat.

Chapter Twenty

"Oh my God, it smells amazing in here," Lisa said as she stepped downstairs and into the kitchen, waking up to the smells of coffee, bacon, and French toast. Easily three of her favorite things.

"I was beginning to think you were going to sleep through breakfast," Eloise said. "You never sleep this late. At least you haven't in the time you've been staying here."

"Oh, I'd have smelled this amazing food and woken up, if I hadn't already been awake," Lisa said. In truth, she was as surprised as Eloise that she'd slept in. It was nearly 9:00 a.m. By Lisa's guess, it had been her longest and most restful sleep in about two years. She'd had no nightmares, and she hadn't woken up searching for Mitchell, only to then be hit with his loss once more.

She'd slept and gradually eased into consciousness, relaxed and well rested.

Eloise brought two plates of food to the table and returned to the kitchen, bringing back two mugs of coffee.

"You're the best." Lisa took a seat and breathed in the rich, robust aroma of the coffee. She blew on the hot liquid and took a small sip, closing her eyes with pleasure as the flavor hit her tongue.

"I've been meaning to ask what your plans for the holidays are."

Lisa opened her eyes and frowned at the reminder of the upcoming family celebrations.

"Mom called yesterday morning to ask me that exact same thing," she said. "She wanted to make sure I knew I was invited to Christmas dinner back in Toronto." It had been less of an invitation, and more of a reminder that they expected her there. The question "will you be there?" carried all sorts of guilt-riddled overtones. And when she politely declined the invitation, there was the less subtle guilt trip. *Kara and Susie miss their Auntie Lisa. The family misses you. You can't run away from everything, you know. Life goes on. It has to.*

"I know," Eloise said, guilt etched across her face. "She called me yesterday afternoon."

Anger welled up inside of Lisa. Her mom couldn't just accept her answer. She had to call Eloise and ask her to give Lisa a second lecture.

"And?" she asked, preparing for an argument.

Eloise shrugged as she finished chewing a piece of bacon, which she chased with a long sip of coffee. "I'm pretty sure she wanted me to convince you to spend Christmas with them, but selfishly I'm hoping to have your company here. So, you do what you need to do."

Relief washed over her, and she had to refrain from throwing her arms around her aunt. She looked over at her in hopes that her eyes could convey the gratitude she didn't have the words to express.

"She doesn't understand how hard it is on me. Seeing them all, one big happy family, doting on the twins and getting ready for the new baby . . . it's all too much. Christmas especially."

Life went on for Andrew and Sarah, who enrolled the twins in preschool and decorated the nursery for the arrival of their newborn. Life went on for Kara and Susie, who were now more children than toddlers, and who were about to be big sisters. Life didn't go on for Mitchell. And it didn't go on for Lisa. A big part of her had died that day with him. They didn't understand.

Eloise cast Lisa a look of empathy. "And yet," she began gently, "you've been spending a lot of time with Rachel and Declan."

Lisa thought about how she could possibly explain the difference to her aunt. First of all, it hurt more to see her *family* so excited and happy without Mitchell. She knew it was selfish and petty, and they loved and missed Mitchell, too, but she wanted to *see* how much they missed him. She was tired of seeing such a postcard family, with no evidence of the huge hole in the picture. Second, there was something about Rachel and Declan. Lisa didn't feel broken around them. And things hadn't been easy for them, either. There was a sort of camaraderie between the three of them. They understood better than anyone how hard it was to try to appear okay when things really weren't okay. She didn't have to pretend around them. She could just *be*. But she couldn't explain any of that. It wouldn't make sense. A couple of weeks earlier, Lisa had been sure she couldn't spend time around them, either.

"It's just different."

Eloise looked at Lisa as though she had more to say, but instead all she said was, "It's good to see you happy again is all, dear. They seem to make you happy."

Lisa felt her cheeks warm. She thought about Rachel and Declan, and happy was the word that fit. The grief was still there, but happiness was as well. She didn't know where things would lead—she wasn't sure where things *could* lead—but she enjoyed their company.

And it had been too long since she'd felt anything even close to happy.

Chapter Twenty-One

"This much?" Declan held up a heaping measuring cup of sugar.

Rachel leveled the top of the sugar with a knife. "There, now you can add it to the bowl."

He furrowed his brow in concentration as he added the sugar to the rest of the ingredients.

In moments like these he still looked so little. He stood on a step stool and poured all of his concentration into adding just the right amount of sugar into the bowl. She needed to talk to him about school, but, dammit, it was the weekend. She wanted him to enjoy the break. And also she didn't know where to start.

She handed him a large wooden spoon. "Do you want to stir it?"

He nodded and took the spoon, putting all of his energy into mixing the thick flour, sugar, milk, eggs, and butter. Flour puffed out of the bowl, and she watched him focus hard on keeping all the ingredients inside it, his tongue poking out of the side of his mouth, and his nose crinkled up as he worked.

"This is hard," he groaned as the dough thickened with the mixture of wet and dry ingredients.

He tried to hand the spoon to Rachel, but she waved it off. "Why don't you try mixing it with your hands?"

He stared at her as if she had just made the world's most ridiculous suggestion.

She took the spoon out of the dough. "Like this," she said, kneading the dough slowly.

Declan cautiously reached his hands into the bowl. "Eww." He giggled as his fingers tentatively touched the dough.

Rachel wiped her hands on a dish towel and smiled as she watched Declan mix the dough for the Christmas sugar cookies with his tiny hands.

"Can we talk about what happened the other day at school?" she asked finally as he worked.

Declan frowned, but kept working. He shook his head.

"Mrs. Steward said that the other boy was making fun of you. Can you tell me what he said?"

He once again shook his head and began working the dough harder.

She sighed. She didn't want to tell Declan how much trouble he was in, but she *needed* him to understand. "Declan, your principal said that you only have one more chance. If you hit someone again, they have to expel you."

This time he stopped and looked up at her, tears welling in his eyes. "Mom, it's not fair. They're mean to me, and they make me so mad. I didn't *mean* to!"

"What did they do that was mean?" Rachel asked, wanting desperately to understand.

"Patrick called me bad."

Rachel sighed. She could see the hurt on Declan's face, and she wished so much that she could take it away. She wanted to tell him that Patrick was wrong, that he was great, that the other children were at fault here. And at the same time he was on the verge of expulsion. She had to talk to him about *his* behavior.

"I know that must have been hurtful," Rachel said. "But honey, if they're mean to you, I need you to tell the teacher and not hit them. If you get expelled, you'll have to take the bus an hour away to Ingonish."

He nodded. All the fear and hurt she felt echoed across his face. "'Kay."

Rachel took the dough out of the bowl and placed it on the table, which was covered with lightly floured wax paper.

"Now we're going to roll the dough until it's flat," she said to

Declan as she showed him how to use the rolling pin. She wanted them to have a good afternoon baking cookies. They were both tired of hurting so damn much.

"Let me do it," he said, eagerly taking the rolling pin from Rachel's hands and rolling out the dough.

He wasn't able to put the same weight behind the rolling pin that she was, so it took him awhile to get the dough even remotely flat, but he kept at it. She finished it up, flattening the dough until it was about a quarter of an inch thick all the way around.

Declan had already figured out the next step, and he had picked up a snowman-shaped cookie cutter. At Rachel's nod of permission, he pressed the cookie cutter into the dough. Rachel picked up a cookie cutter shaped like a Christmas tree and showed Declan how to wiggle the shape a little so that the dough separated enough for the cookie to be lifted out without ripping.

They filled two trays with their sugar cookies.

While the cookies were in the oven, she had him help her mix the icing. They made three separate bowls, each with a different color. She also laid out a bowl of Smarties, which he tried to snack on, and various sprinkle shakers to decorate the cookies with.

"Can we take some to Lisa?" he asked as he shook a sprinkle container over a bell-shaped cookie.

"We could do that," she affirmed, admittedly excited to have an excuse to see Lisa. They hadn't talked much since their snowshoeing adventure. Just a few casual texts back and forth. They hadn't had a chance to talk about the kiss and what it had meant, and they hadn't had the chance for a repeat of that kiss. She hoped there would be a repeat.

She all but said she couldn't commit to anything, Rachel reminded herself. The last thing she needed was to develop unrequited feelings for someone who was emotionally unavailable. And yet things had shifted between them. Lisa had been more open, more *able* to be open. The wall of grief between the two of them was still there, but it had crumbled a little, and it no longer seemed like an insurmountable barrier. The feelings were there for both of them, but she had to hold back and let Lisa set the pace. Maybe they would never grow into anything, but if there was any hope for them, it was in Lisa being able to take things at a pace that was comfortable for her.

"I'm going to invite her to my Christmas concert!" he exclaimed as he smeared icing messily over a cookie.

The statement was said so cheerily, but it instantly dampened Rachel's daydreaming. It wasn't only her developing feelings for Lisa. She could tell herself to be patient and take things slow all she wanted. But it was her *and* Declan. She could handle heartbreak, but she wasn't so sure he could.

She also knew the school Christmas concert would be too tough for Lisa. It would be a room full of parents all proudly videotaping their children as they displayed their rehearsed songs with their classmates.

"Declan, honey," she began, unsure of what words should follow to let her son down easy. "The school Christmas concert is really just for family only."

He frowned as he thought about that statement.

"Oh," he said at last, his voice impossibly small, making her want to take back the comment and force Lisa to come out to the Christmas concert. But as disappointed as Declan was, it was better he faced that now, rather than get in too deep and have the disappointment turn to devastation. It was hard enough watching Joey constantly let him down. Lisa would do the same thing. She'd told them that she couldn't be there. Rachel needed to listen to her and not let them get their hearts broken. Her heart ached at the thought, but she needed to set that boundary between them and Lisa. If not for her, then for her son.

She wondered if she hadn't already crossed that line.

Lisa ran her fingers over the ceramic Santa, trying to find a spot for it on the Christmas tree among all the other million ornaments. Christmas was hard, and she'd initially had every intention of ignoring the holiday altogether, but in the end she had agreed to help Eloise with the Christmas tree. She didn't want to be immersed in the holiday, but she could dip her toe in, so to speak. She and Eloise had gone together to pick a short, squat pine tree from the Christmas tree farm, and she had volunteered to help decorate the tree once they got it set up in the living room. It seemed like a safe enough activity to participate in.

She had not anticipated the sheer volume of ornaments that Eloise had, however, overwhelming the ornament-to-branch ratio.

"I'm not sure you have enough ornaments," she quipped, frowning as she hung the Santa on the same branch as a snowboarding snowman. The tree branch sunk under the weight of both ornaments, practically resting on top of the branch below it.

"They may have gotten a little out of hand."

"A little? The tree can barely hold them. I'm surprised the branches aren't weighted right to the ground."

Lisa watched in horror as Eloise pulled out a gaudy candy cane ornament, made of pipe cleaner and plastic beads, from the ornament box.

"Where on earth did you get that thing? And does this really need to go on the tree?" she asked, looking at the misshapen ornament.

"You don't remember?"

Lisa shook her head.

"You made this. I bet you were five. Maybe six."

She eyed the ornament in horror. "I didn't."

"You did. Everyone got one of these from you that year. Your parents were so proud."

"And you kept it?"

"Of course I kept it," Eloise answered, as though the question had been the strangest question ever asked.

She groaned. "Well, let's keep it between us that I created something that hideous."

Eloise laughed. "It's cute."

"It's . . . something."

She shook her head at the thought of the candy cane and pulled a wooden angel out of the bin, turning it over in her hands. Eloise took it from her.

"This one is a favorite of mine," Eloise said. "It goes near the top, right near the star. It's the angel that my mom gave me after my dad died. She said that she wanted him to have a place in my new home." Eloise smiled at the small ornament before setting it near the top of the tree.

Lisa looked up at the little wooden ornament, wondering how many other ornaments on the tree had sentimental value attached.

"I have one for your grandfather as well." Eloise reached down to point to a little lighthouse ornament—a tourist trinket with the words "Peggy's Cove" etched into the base. "He was my lighthouse growing up," Eloise said.

"I wish I'd gotten to spend more time with him."

"He loved you," Eloise answered. "I remember him always getting excited for you and your brother to visit. When you went off to college, he'd brag about his brilliant granddaughter to anyone on the island who would listen."

She laughed. Despite growing up in Toronto, she'd always been close with her grandfather. They'd both been the quiet internal processors in a family of boisterous, big personalities.

Eloise looked at her with a long, gentle gaze for a moment, and then she left the room without a word. Lisa was about to call out and ask what was going on, but Eloise returned a moment later with an ornament that had not been in the box cradled in her hand—a small, glass infant.

"I bought this one for Mitchell," Eloise said. "I wanted to make sure it was all right with you before putting it on the tree."

Lisa took the small glass ornament and turned it over in her hands. The glass infant was curled on his side, eyes closed, sweet smile on his cherubic face. The little ornament baby even had light wisps of hair, reminding her of the little tufts Mitchell had been born with. Her throat tightened, and she wasn't sure she could say anything, so she simply reached up and placed the ornament near the top, next to the wooden angel.

"He looks good there," Eloise said. "We'll be able to see him and feel him with us from anywhere in the room."

She turned to her aunt, tears misting in her eyes. "Thank you."

Eloise reached out and squeezed her hand.

The doorbell rang, and Lisa wiped the mist from her eyes as she turned toward the sound.

"Are you expecting someone, dear?" Eloise asked.

She shook her head. "No. But I'll see who it is."

She smiled to find Rachel and Declan standing on the front step.

"Hi," she said, genuinely happy to see both of them.

"I hope it's not a bad time."

"We brought you cookies!" Declan cut in.

"There is never a bad time for cookies," Lisa said, looking at the holiday tin he clutched between both hands.

"They're for you and Eloise," Rachel amended.

"I don't know that I want to share these." She took the tin from Declan. "I might have to sneak inside and hide them from Eloise."

"Hide what from me?" Eloise asked, stepping up beside her.

"Busted," she grumbled, and Declan giggled.

"I mixed the dough with my hands," he said. "Isn't that silly?"

"Don't worry, I made sure he washed them first," Rachel whispered with a wink.

Lisa took the lid off of the tin. "They look delicious," she said, looking over the cookies with multicolored icing, sprinkles, and candy on top. She had no difficulty telling the difference between the cookies that Rachel had decorated and the cookies that Declan had decorated. The ones Declan had decorated were adorable—in their messy, dripping-icing sort of way.

She took one of the cookies he had decorated and took a bite, giving an exaggerated sigh and saying, "This is amazing" around the bite of cookie. Then she passed the tin to Eloise, who did the same.

"Do you two want to come inside?" she asked as she swallowed the first bite of cookie. "Eloise and I were just decorating the Christmas tree."

Rachel met Lisa's eyes and then nodded. "Just for a little while."

"I'll put the kettle on," Eloise said. "Want some hot chocolate, Declan?"

"Yeah!" he said, already working to take off his coat and boots while Roxie licked his face.

The four of them settled into the living room, each with a cookie and a mug of hot chocolate topped with two fluffy marshmallows. Lisa looked up at the little infant ornament atop the tree. She felt Mitchell's presence with them.

She wished he could've been with them in person, but for the moment she felt a sense of comfort and peace settle through her.

His loss would always be a chasm in her heart, but she could perhaps still spend time around friends.

She looked at Rachel—at the soft curls that fell around her face, at the way Rachel's cheek dimpled when she smiled, at the way her eyes lit up. She blushed when Rachel turned and caught her admiration.

No, it wasn't an afternoon with friends. They were more than that. She *wanted* them to be more than that. She wasn't sure she was ready, but the afternoon felt so comfortable that for the moment she wanted to ignore the fears that quelled inside her. She wanted to enjoy the soft glow of happiness—the light she saw for the first time after a long stretch of dark.

She took a sip of her hot chocolate, and watched the way Rachel's whole face brightened when she smiled and the way Declan told stories around the cookie in his mouth, colored icing smeared over his upper lip.

She tried to ignore her fears and hesitations and enjoy the moment. The rest could be figured out later.

Chapter Twenty-Two

Rachel finished buttoning Declan's white dress shirt and adjusted his little red and green bow tie. She smoothed his hair, trying to tame the unruly strands. He looked so grown-up in his little suit. She just watched Declan, her heart aching with how handsome her little boy was. She couldn't resist allowing herself to kiss his perfect forehead.

"When's Daddy going to get here?" he asked, fidgeting as Rachel finished getting him ready for the school's Christmas concert.

She didn't want to let him know she'd been wondering the same thing. "He'll meet us at your school. He's got a long drive, but I'm sure he'll be there."

If he didn't show up, Rachel might kill him. She hated the doubt she saw in Declan's eyes. He'd already been let down by Joey too many times.

The doorbell rang and Declan lit up, pulling away from Rachel to answer the door. He nearly tripped over his feet as he raced down the hall. Rachel watched his shoulders slump ever so slightly at the sight of her dad.

"Hey, Grandpa," he said, not unhappily, but still his disappointment was clear to Rachel. It wasn't *his* dad, and it should've been.

"Hey, kiddo. All ready for your big performance?" If Frank Murray noticed Declan's disappointment, he didn't let on. He radiated excitement—Declan's biggest fan.

Declan nodded. "I've practiced lots. I know all the words."

"I'm gonna be cheering for you," Frank said. "You look toward the loudest person in the audience and you'll find your mom and me."

He couldn't help but grin with pride, and Rachel ushered them out the door and into her truck before they were late for the concert. When they got to the school, Rachel left Declan with his teacher and classmates, and she and Frank found seats in the audience. She picked the edge of a row, and saved an empty seat for Joey, although as each second passed she grew more and more concerned she was going to have to explain to Declan why his dad did not attend his Christmas concert. She was already trying to find the words in her mind.

With ten minutes left until the concert was set to begin, Rachel excused herself and stepped outside to give Joey a call.

The phone rang.

He had better answer and tell me that he is parking as we speak.

Another ring.

Rachel's stomach clenched.

Joey answered after the third ring.

"Hello?"

"Where are you?"

There was a long silence, and then he said, "Shit."

Her stomach sank. Joey wasn't coming, and Declan would be devastated. He couldn't look forward to anything, it seemed, without Joey finding a way to ruin it.

"I marked it on my calendar, but work was crazy busy this week, and when I got home I just crashed. I didn't even think about the concert. Ah, fuck, Rachel, how can I make it up to you?"

"It's not me you have to make anything up to," Rachel said tersely.

"I'll find a way to make it up to him." Another false promise.

"You're always saying these things, Joey, and you're always letting him down."

"It was an accident," he said. "I swear. I wanted to be at his concert. I feel terrible."

Rachel could hear the regret in his voice, but that didn't change a thing. It didn't matter how bad he felt because none of that would ease the pain Declan felt. She leaned against the wall outside of the school gymnasium.

"Your kid is about to get expelled from school," she said. "Every time you let him down, it affects him, you know. He acts up, gets in trouble, and now the school wants to kick him out. There's nowhere else for him to go. You don't get how much damage you're doing to his life. You waltz in and out of his life when it suits you, but it *affects* him."

"Come on, Rach. He's a kid. Kids act out. You can't blame me for that."

"I do, though! I do blame you!" Her voice was strained, and she tried to keep from crying. "You're always disappointing him. You've got to decide if you can be in his life or not. And if you decide you *are* going to be in his life, then you need to be there. Not some of the time. Not just when you feel like it or when it's convenient for you. *All* of the time."

"I'm doing the best I can," he argued. The same tired argument. She was the one that was going to have to see Declan's heartbreak when he realized his dad had missed his performance.

The first few notes of music drifted from the auditorium, providing her the escape she needed.

"I hear the concert starting. I have to go."

Joey said her name, but she hung up the phone before he could say anything else. Then she returned to take her seat next to her dad, ready to watch Declan's performance of "Frosty the Snowman."

"Everything okay?" Frank whispered.

Rachel nodded even though nothing was okay. But she would fake it for the evening. When Declan took the stage, she smiled and cheered for her son, and hoped the fallout from this disappointment wouldn't get him kicked out of school.

She smiled and for the hour-long concert pretended everything really could be all right.

Chapter Twenty-Three

Christmas Eve came quickly, and as much as Lisa had hoped to avoid the holiday she found herself getting at least partially into the holiday spirit. She'd gone shopping and picked up small gifts for Kara and Susie, which she'd mailed off to Toronto a few days earlier to ensure they made it to her brother's home in time for the holidays. And she had been guilty of putting on the occasional Christmas record as she worked on her art. Still, she was glad she opted for the quiet of the island as opposed to having to put on a cheery front and spend the holiday doting on the girls. Her heart ached to think of the Christmas that should have been. She wanted to settle into the hurt and create new art, rather than pretend everything was all right and put on a fake smile while opening presents and eating turkey.

The morning of Christmas Eve, she took her sketchbook to the dining-room table where she sipped on eggnog and worked on a new sketch. She drew a fireplace with stockings hanging above it. In the middle was an empty nail where a stocking was meant to be. She sketched a child's room with an empty crib. She sketched a woman in front of a small grave, a small gift with Christmas wrapping paper placed next to the headstone. A series of quick sketches to capture the emptiness she felt—the wrongness of the holiday without Mitchell. Then she sat back and looked at the sketches.

She tore the images from her sketchbook and tucked them in

the bottom of her art folder. She didn't intend to share them. They were for her eyes only. They were her way of surviving the holiday.

Even staying on Cape Breton Island away from family, she realized that she couldn't completely hibernate through the holiday. She'd wrapped a gift for Eloise and placed it beneath their tree, and while she was shopping she found something for both Declan and Rachel. She wasn't entirely sure why she felt so compelled to get them each a small gift, but it had made her happy, and so she didn't stop to analyze that desire. By late afternoon, she decided to swing by the Murrays' place and give Rachel and Declan their gifts. Casually. She'd just drop by, say "Merry Christmas" and be on her way. She didn't have to read anything into it.

Bundled up, gifts in hand, she walked the few blocks to Rachel's home. It was a warm, sunny afternoon, and she watched the sun reflect diamonds in the snow. The town was beautiful, like a scene from a snow globe. She thought about what it would've been like to pull Mitchell down the streets in a sled as they looked at all of the Christmas lights, but as soon as the image popped into her mind she pushed it away. There was no use thinking about the could-have-beens that would never be.

She felt suddenly shy as she knocked on the door. She didn't know how she would explain the gifts and hoped that it didn't seem too forward. It had seemed the natural choice when she'd purchased them. And yet, standing on Rachel's porch with gifts in hand, suddenly it all seemed so intimate.

Rachel opened the door, and a smile spread wide across her face.

"Merry Christmas," Lisa said softly, feeling herself smile in return. She extended the gifts toward Rachel.

"What are those?" Rachel asked as she took the presents from Lisa.

She shrugged. "I wanted to get both you and Declan something small."

Rachel smiled, and warmth spread through Lisa.

"We're just about to head out to the Christmas festival," Rachel said. "Why don't you join us? Then afterward we can open the gifts. Declan and I each have a little something for you as well."

She *should* say no. Stay in, as she'd planned. And yet she didn't want to. She wanted to spend the evening with Rachel and Declan. It didn't make sense when she was avoiding any kind of celebration with everyone else. Somehow, it didn't hurt to think about spending the evening with them. It felt right.

"I'd like that," she said.

Before Rachel could respond, Declan was at the door, grabbing Lisa's legs in a hug.

She bent down and hugged him back.

"Declan, can you go put these under the tree and then get your coat on so we can head over to the festival?"

He took the presents, but made no move to leave, staring at the package with his name on it. "Can I open it?"

"You can open it when we get home," Rachel said.

He frowned, but set them in the living room and returned a moment later with his jacket.

"Are you coming, too?" he asked.

Lisa nodded. "If that's all right with you."

"Yeah!" He grabbed her hand, pulling her toward Rachel's truck. She found his excitement contagious.

She could always leave early if need be. She didn't have to stay out long. But surely the Christmas festival had to be healthier than staying in and thinking about everything she had lost.

Still, the evening felt like a dangerous high-wire act. She was balancing carefully between falling into the despair of not having Mitchell with her and falling into the pull of intimacy with Rachel and Declan.

Pain and love were both more than she could risk, but as long as she could stay balanced and not fall into either, the night out would be fun. So she climbed into the passenger seat of the truck while trying to ignore her mind shouting warnings about the dangers.

Even as an adult, Rachel found something magical about Christmas Eve. She had been alight with holiday spirit all day, excited about the annual festival in town. It was one of her favorite town activities of the year. With Lisa beside her in the truck, and Declan in his booster seat in the back, heading to the festival felt complete. Rachel listened to Declan and Lisa chat back and forth. Well, Declan was doing most of the talking, and Lisa worked in a few words here and there to show she was listening. The sound of their conversation caused a warmth to settle low in her stomach and her chest to tighten. She cast the occasional glance over at Lisa, trying to decipher where Lisa's head was at, but if Lisa was uncomfortable with the Christmas celebration, she hid it well. Still, Rachel was very aware of the fact that a large part of what she loved about Christmas was watching Declan's excitement, and she couldn't imagine the grief that Lisa felt on the holiday. That was why she had not invited Lisa to the festival sooner. Lisa had not shown much interest in the holiday. Rachel had wanted to respect that and not push her beyond her comfort zone. But then when Lisa showed up at her place with Christmas gifts, the invitation had slipped out naturally. It felt so right to have Lisa there with them.

"What's Eloise doing tonight?" Rachel asked.

"She went out to the festival about an hour ago with a neighbor. We might see her there."

"I hope so," Rachel said. "I'd like to get the chance to wish her Merry Christmas." She pulled her truck into the overflow parking near where the festival was being held at the center of town. It was still relatively early in the evening, but already a crowd of people had gathered. She helped Declan out of the backseat.

The town choir was singing carols, and the sound of the music carried through the crisp evening air. The winter wind was not overly biting, and the smell of popcorn wafted over from a cart that was parked at the start of the vendors.

"This is cute," Lisa said, and Rachel turned to see her wide-eyed and taking it all in.

She had attended Craghurst's Christmas festival since she was a child, and while it was still special, she'd come to take the tradition for granted. It was a tradition that she loved, but she didn't look at the festival with the same sense of wonder she saw on Lisa's face. She was glad to be able to share it with her.

A sad expression passed across Lisa's face, but she turned to face Rachel and said, "I'm glad I'm here."

Rachel saw the wistfulness in Lisa's eyes, but also a flicker of something else. Hope perhaps. "I'm glad you're here, too."

Declan, unaware of the shared moment between the two adults, grabbed Lisa's hand and pulled her in the direction of the gingerbread house display. Rachel laughed and watched the two of them look over the gingerbread houses being auctioned off.

"Do people get to eat these?" Declan asked in awe.

"I don't know," Lisa admitted. "They look too nice to eat."

"I'd eat it. Especially this one," Declan declared, pointing to the largest of the gingerbread houses, which was propped in the center.

Lisa laughed. "I think that snow is made of pure sugar."

"Uh huh," Declan agreed, fixated on the house.

"I'd eat this little one on the end." Lisa pointed to the smallest of the gingerbread homes. "I love candy canes, and it's got the most of them. And is that tree made of taffy? Yum."

Declan giggled.

"You'd both get tummy aches," Rachel joked, rolling her eyes at the two of them.

"Oh, come on." Lisa elbowed her lightly in the side. "You wouldn't want to eat one of these?"

Rachel shook her head.

"Oh really?" Lisa asked, her disbelief clear.

"Okay," Rachel admitted. "I'd eat the one with the Oreo pillars."

"Hah," Lisa laughed. "I knew it."

Declan bounced with excitement and asked his mom if they could *pleeeease* get one of the houses to eat.

The lady at the table made her way over to the three of them. "You know," she said, clearly sensing that they were salivating over the edible homes, "all of the money made in the gingerbread auctions goes to charity."

"Really?" Lisa asked.

The lady nodded. "Every year we pick a different charity. This year we're raising money for Sick Kids hospital in Toronto."

Lisa didn't hesitate. She reached for a pen and put down a bid on the little gingerbread house.

Rachel didn't mean to look at the number she wrote, but she saw two zeroes behind the number. Even the largest gingerbread house in the center only had a $40 bid on it so far.

"Thank you," the woman said with delight when Lisa put the pen down. "Merry Christmas."

"You too." Lisa stepped away from the table, the earlier cheer gone from her voice.

Rachel gave Lisa's hand a squeeze. She'd only meant for it to be a quick reassuring touch, but when Lisa's hand closed around her own, she found herself unable to let go. They both had thin gloves on, but still she could feel the warmth of Lisa's hand around her own.

Lisa wasn't letting go either, and that knowledge made Rachel turn away to hide her smile.

"If you win, can I help you eat it?" Declan asked, still looking at the gingerbread houses.

Lisa laughed, the mood lightening once again. "Of course. I can't eat an entire *house* all by myself."

Declan grinned.

"I have to say," Lisa said as they began walking around the square, Declan running up ahead of them, "that's the biggest Christmas tree I've ever seen."

Rachel nodded. "They'll light it up soon. At 7 p.m. on the dot they turn on the Christmas lights, the choir sings a couple of songs, and then Santa comes to visit the kids."

"I wish I could've brought Mitchell to this," Lisa said.

Rachel turned to look at her, surprised at her casual mention of Mitchell. Lisa's eyes were sad, but she didn't seem encompassed with grief.

"I wish that, too," Rachel said genuinely.

"Where's your dad?" Lisa asked, breaking the eye contact to look around.

She recognized Lisa's desire to ease the heaviness, and so she gave a playful grin. "Can you keep a secret?"

Lisa laughed. "Sure."

Keeping her voice low so that nobody would hear, she leaned over and whispered, "My dad is Santa."

"So that's why he's not here," Lisa whispered back with a knowing smile.

"That's why he's not here *yet*," she agreed.

"Very cool," Lisa said.

She nodded. "Declan has been going through this weird thing the past week or so where he's wanted nothing to do with Santa. But I think when he sees him that will change. *Every* kid loves Santa."

"It's true," Lisa agreed.

Up ahead of them a volunteer dressed as an elf handed Declan a blue and white candy cane.

"Do you think those are just for kids, or can I go get one?" Lisa asked.

Rachel laughed. "I'm sure if you ask really nicely and remember to say please, they'll give you a candy cane, too."

She bumped Rachel with her shoulder. "I'm a sucker for candy."

"Good to know," Rachel said and gave a soft laugh.

Declan ran back with his candy cane. "Mom, I need help opening this."

She reluctantly let go of Lisa's hand and peeled off the wrapper, careful not to snap the candy cane. When she looked up, she saw Lisa receiving a candy cane from the elf girl as well.

Declan popped the tip of the candy cane into his mouth and took his mom's hand as they walked.

Lisa winked as she walked back with her own candy cane.

The choir began to gather around the Christmas tree. "They're about to start," Rachel said, and the three of them moved in to watch the performance.

It didn't last long, but by the end the children in the crowd were beginning to grow antsy. The choir sang a couple of short Christmas songs, the multicolored lights on the tree were turned on, and with a big dramatic entrance in came Santa Claus in a sleigh pulled by horses that had been given antlers.

"I want to go home," Declan said, pulling hard on her arm. His eyes were wide, and he looked desperate for an escape.

"Declan. Don't you want to see Santa and tell him what you want for Christmas?"

He shook his head furiously side to side, continuing to pull on Rachel's arm.

She knelt in front of her son, the snow cold on her knees through her jeans. "What's wrong, honey?" she asked. "Why don't you want to see Santa?"

"I hate Santa," he spat.

She frowned, not knowing what to say.

He continued trying to pull away until his hand slipped from his mitten and he took off, running through the crowd.

She tried to scramble to her feet and go after him before he became lost in the crowd of people, but Lisa had already hurried off after him.

With a sigh, she pushed herself off the ground and followed after the two.

"What's up, buddy?" she heard Lisa ask as she approached. Neither Lisa nor Declan seemed to notice she was there.

"I don't like Santa." He was clearly very upset, his eyes watery.

"How come?"

He said nothing, clearly struggling to hold back his emotions.

"Santa really likes you, you know," Lisa said. "I bet he really wants to see you."

"No, he doesn't," he said. "He hates me. He's not going to bring me any presents because I'm on the bad list."

"What?" Rachel asked incredulously, cutting in and kneeling next to Lisa in front of him.

He frowned. "Patrick said so. He said that he went to visit Santa at the mall in Sydney, and he asked Santa if I was going to get any presents, and Santa said no. He said I'm on the bad list because I'm always getting sent to the office."

She stepped forward with a frown. "Was that why you punched Patrick in the stomach a couple of weeks ago?"

He hung his head, ashamed, and nodded.

She burned with anger at the injustice of it. Declan had been sent to the office and threatened with expulsion while that little punk Patrick had gotten away with being so cruel to her child.

"Why didn't you tell me?" she asked, feeling helpless.

He gave a small, sad shrug. "Patrick was right. I *am* a bad kid. Mrs. Harvey is always mad at me. And I'm always in trouble."

She grabbed him and pulled him into a hug. "No, you're not, sweetie. I promise you're not a bad kid. Patrick was lying. Santa never said anything bad about you."

"How do you know?"

"I just know."

He didn't look convinced.

"I went to visit Santa the other day," Lisa interjected. "I told him that if he hadn't finished making his list yet, he should be sure to add Declan to the 'good' side because he's the best kid I know. But he told me not to worry because you were already at the top of that list."

He looked uncertain but hopeful.

"Let's go see him," Lisa suggested, "and you can see for yourself."

Rachel watched him think it over before nodding.

Lisa stood and Declan took her hand.

"Thank you," Rachel whispered, following the two of them to where her dad was dressed in a Santa Claus outfit, complete with the fake white beard. Children were lined up, eager to visit him.

Declan held Lisa's hand, and when Rachel looked down at

him, she could see how nervous he was. He could hardly stand still, and he made sure to stand with Lisa between him and Santa at all times.

She wished Declan had told her. Patrick was a bully, and it wasn't fair for Declan to get in trouble because of it. Unfortunately, it seemed that Patrick knew just how to push Declan's buttons to get him in trouble, and because of the school's zero-tolerance policy for violence, Declan got punished while his reasons for punching Patrick were ignored.

The closer they got to the front of the line, the more visibly scared Declan became, and her heart broke for her little boy.

When it was his turn, he froze in place, eyes wide with fear and his lower lip pulled between his teeth. He looked ready to run or cry or both. She wanted so badly to scoop him up and just hold him. He looked small enough. Still her baby.

"I want to go home." His little voice was shaky.

"How about you wait here with Lisa, and I go ask him if it's okay if you visit with him?" she suggested.

He nodded, hiding behind Lisa, and peeking around her at Santa. Rachel smiled reassuringly and stepped up to where her dad sat in his big Christmas throne.

Rachel whispered a quick explanation of the situation.

Frank looked over at Declan and said in the biggest voice he could, "Why, I can't wait to visit with Declan! I've got his presents all ready to go tonight."

Declan lit up, and she heard him say to Lisa, "Did you hear that?"

Lisa nodded, and he let go of her hand, stepping up toward Santa and crawling into his lap.

"Am I really on your good list?" he asked.

Rachel smiled as her dad nodded vigorously. "Absolutely. Top of the list. I've heard that you like to help your grandpa with all the food shopping for the restaurant and that you're always really friendly to all the customers."

He nodded proudly, then chewed the inside of his cheek as nerves once again took over.

"I got sent to the office a bunch of times this year," he admitted.

"Everybody makes mistakes," Frank answered as Santa Claus, "but you've done a lot of good things this year."

Declan smiled and threw his arms around Santa in a big hug, before listing all of the things that he hoped to get for Christmas. "Santa" was careful to make no promises, saying it was already Christmas Eve and the sleigh was packed. She watched with a smile and turned to see Lisa with a matching expression on her face.

Rachel warmed at the sight. She knew it was hard for Lisa to be around Declan without being forced to confront the realization of everything that she'd lost. If their positions had been reversed, Rachel didn't think she'd be spending Christmas Eve with someone else's child. But despite the pain, it was clear that Lisa cared about Declan.

It was clear Lisa cared about her, too.

Lisa turned and met her gaze. "What?" she asked.

"Nothing." She wasn't ready to admit how deeply she cared for her.

Declan pushed between the two of them, happily grabbing both Rachel's hand and Lisa's.

"Did you see that?" he asked. "Santa doesn't hate me. He said I was good. He's still going to bring me presents."

"I didn't have a doubt in my mind." Rachel gave his shoulder a squeeze.

"Want to go get hot chocolates and wait until they announce the winners of the gingerbread auction?" Lisa suggested.

"Yeah!" he exclaimed, and Rachel nodded.

There was no way Lisa wasn't about to win that gingerbread house, though, and if Lisa was indeed planning to share, Declan was not going to need more sugar. But it was Christmas Eve, and one of the most perfect evenings that she could remember. She followed along to the hot chocolate booth, and Lisa ordered all three of them drinks.

Declan eagerly took his hot chocolate, blowing on it to cool it off, and using his teeth to pick out the marshmallows and eat those first.

"This is the best Christmas ever," he said.

Rachel agreed with him.

Lisa tore a piece of cookie from the roof of the gingerbread house. The cookie was covered in white icing snow and cloyingly sweet, but she took her time savoring as though it was a small bite of an expensive chocolate or some rare treasured dessert. Declan didn't take the same slow approach. He was chewing on a piece of licorice and had blue icing smeared over the top of his upper lip. She tried not to laugh, but watching him enjoy the candy was one of the highlights of the night.

The three of them sat on the floor of Rachel's living room, fire roaring in the fireplace, each with a glass of milk in hand as they picked at the gingerbread house on the coffee table in front of them. A Christmas cartoon played in the background, and Declan laughed while helping to devour the gingerbread house.

Lisa looked around the living room that had been decorated for the Christmas season. Rachel's place was even more cozy than usual, and she took in the various decorations adorning the room: a stuffed snowman, colored tinsel, a thread of red and green lights strung over the fireplace.

She felt the grief and the panic in the pit of her stomach. The warmth, the coziness was damn near suffocating. A framed photo of Rachel and Declan hung above the fireplace, the two of them smiling together for the camera. Mom and son. Just as it would've been for Lisa and Mitchell. Her chest was a cavern, unfilled space, where hurt echoed endlessly. And yet something else resonated within her as she looked at the photo of Rachel and Declan, something that separated them from mere reminders of the life she should've had. They were more than just shadows of what should've been, even if Lisa couldn't put into words yet what Rachel and Declan were to her. She sat back and settled into watching the movie and eating gingerbread, feeling not whole but maybe not so broken.

When the movie ended, Declan crawled over to the tree and went to the two boxes Lisa had brought with her earlier. He found the one with his name on top and brought it over to her and Rachel.

"Can I open this now?" he asked, looking at his mom with wide, pleading eyes.

"You can open the present Lisa brought for you," Rachel said, "and then you'd better get to bed so Santa can come visit."

He smiled and nodded, the bedtime request not met with any kind of argument.

"It's not much," Lisa said as Declan tore open the wrapping paper. "I just wanted to get you both a little something."

"You didn't have to do that," Rachel said.

She met Rachel's eyes. "I know. I wanted to."

Rachel's face flushed a soft pink, barely visible in the firelight.

"Wow!" Declan exclaimed, interrupting the moment as he pulled out the sketchbook and set of colored markers. "Mom, look! I have my very own art book, just like Lisa's!"

She laughed at his excitement.

"That was really nice of you," Rachel said, casting a tender glance her way. "What do you have to say to her?"

"Thank you!" Declan said, opening the set of markers.

Lisa went to the tree and picked up the second gift she'd brought, for Rachel. "Your turn."

Rachel gently removed the wrapping paper and pulled the framed sketch from the gift bag.

Lisa's heartbeat quickened as she watched Rachel's gaze travel over the sketch, taking in all of the details. Lisa worried that the gift was perhaps too intimate. She had framed the sketch she'd created of the two of them sitting on the cliffs in the highlands, looking out at the ocean. There was nothing particularly romantic about the picture. It was two friends sitting side by side with beer and sandwiches. But as she watched the emotion pass over Rachel's face, she wondered if perhaps the gift might have been too much.

"It's us," Rachel said.

Lisa nodded.

"I love it."

"It's okay if you don't. I just thought, I don't know . . . it was a fun afternoon. It meant a lot to me and I wanted to capture that on the page." She was rambling, and yet she couldn't seem to stop.

Rachel rested her hand on Lisa's knee and repeated, "I *love* it."

"There's more."

Rachel eyed her suspiciously as she reached back into the bag and pulled out the small cookbook.

"What is this?" Rachel asked with a laugh.

"I think it's pretty self-explanatory," she said with a grin.

Rachel glared, but her attempt to appear angry failed and only served to send Lisa into a fit of laughter.

"You work in a restaurant and can't even manage mac and cheese," Lisa said. "It's not right. This book will help you."

When Lisa had seen *I Can't Cook*, she hadn't been able to resist.

"Thank you," Rachel said, sarcasm lacing the words.

She grinned. "You're very welcome."

"Declan," Rachel said, changing the subject, "why don't you bring Lisa the present you have for her?"

Declan looked up from the sketchbook he was already breaking in and nodded. He raced off and returned a minute later with a piece of paper in his hands.

"I drew this for you." He held the picture out in front of him, and she took it carefully. In the picture were three stick people, all with big smiles on their faces, and what appeared to be a dog standing down near the bottom of the page.

"Is this us?" Lisa asked.

Declan nodded. "Yeah. And Roxie."

"I love it," she said, and it was true. In the picture, all of them were happy. They were all together and smiling. Even the sun in the drawing had a smiley face. "I'm going to put it on my fridge."

He beamed.

"Should we put out milk and cookies for Santa?" Rachel asked.

He nodded and followed his mom to the kitchen.

Lisa waited in the living room, looking at the picture Declan had drawn for her. She couldn't help but notice they looked like a family. She knew that wasn't how Declan intended the picture, but it struck a note of panic in her. And yet, simultaneously, she was incredibly touched. Grief for Mitchell and caring for Declan, the constant tug-of-war inside of her.

He walked back into the living room carrying a small plate with two sugar cookies and a handful of carrots. Rachel followed with a tall glass of milk. They each set the goodies down on the edge of the fireplace where Santa would easily find them.

"What are the carrots for?" she asked.

"The reindeer," Declan explained, matter-of-factly, as though it was obvious and she shouldn't have asked such a silly question.

"I see," she said. "Can't forget about them. They must get hungry pulling that sleigh all night."

"Uh huh," he agreed.

"All right, it's time to be getting to bed. Santa can't come and bring you your presents until you're fast asleep," Rachel announced.

Lisa smiled as she watched Declan race out of the room.

Rachel returned a few moments later, taking a seat on the floor next to Lisa. "One night a year I get to put him to bed without a fight."

Rachel laughed, settling back against the couch.

"I had a really great night," she said.

"So did I," Rachel agreed.

"Really," she stressed. "I was going to stay in and pretend that Christmas wasn't a thing, but I'm glad I came out. I enjoyed the company and the festival, all of it."

Rachel's gaze was warm and tender, and Lisa shifted under the intimacy of it.

"I should probably get going," she said, about to stand. "I'd imagine Declan's going to have you up at the crack of dawn tomorrow."

"Wait." Rachel reached for her hand and pulled her back down. "You can't leave yet. I haven't given you the present that I got you."

She sank back into the couch, and this time Rachel stood. "You couldn't have thought all you were getting was a picture from Declan."

"I love that picture," Lisa said. "I don't need anything else."

Rachel smiled but disappeared into the other room. A minute later, she returned with a small box, covered in snowman wrapping paper.

Lisa held the box in her hands, trying without luck to figure out what it could be.

"Open it," Rachel urged.

Lisa did, slowly pulling away the snowman paper. Once the wrapping was off, there was a plain cardboard box that she opened to reveal a necklace with a small wooden angel charm.

"A lady in town makes them," Rachel said. "They're all made out of driftwood from the beaches here."

"It's beautiful," Lisa said.

"She says that all of her carvings have the life of the ocean in them. This one made me think of Mitchell. I know you don't like to talk about him, but I wanted you know that I'm here when you do want to talk, and he can be here with us."

Lisa turned the angel over in her hands, tracing her fingers over the smooth wood and the tiny, intricate details in the feathered wings and gentle facial features.

"I love it," she said, not able to take her eyes off of the angel charm.

"I hope it's not too much." Rachel had her lower lip between her teeth, and she peered at Lisa with concern evident in her soft gaze.

"Help me put it on?" Lisa asked.

This time she looked up, and Rachel nodded, sliding closer while Lisa turned so she could fasten the clasp at the back of her neck. Rachel's fingers were gentle as they brushed Lisa's hair out of the way, grazing over the back of her neck and sending a shiver down her spine.

"There," Rachel said against her ear, and let the necklace settle against Lisa's chest.

She clutched it to her. She clutched *Mitchell* to her.

"I should lay out Declan's stocking and presents," Rachel said. "But you should stay. It will just take me a few minutes, and then we can watch a movie or something."

"Are you sure?" Lisa asked.

"I don't want you to leave," Rachel said, her voice so soft it was nearly a whisper.

Her breath caught in her chest. She *should* leave. A part of her felt like she *needed* to leave. But, all at once, she didn't *want* to leave.

Rachel stood and left the room, returning a moment later with a little stocking that had Declan's name across the top. Little toys and candies poked out of the stocking. Rachel placed it against the fireplace and set a few larger presents in front of the stocking: a DVD, a teddy bear, and a box of crayons.

Rachel turned on the stereo, and soft jazz versions of Christmas classics filled the room. She picked up the plate of cookies and carrots and the glass of milk and settled in beside Lisa. "Here, you get to help me eat these."

She laughed. "So, this is why you wanted me to stay."

Rachel grinned. "You caught me. I don't even know if I can stand to eat one more sugar cookie, let alone two."

She laughed and reached for a carrot instead of the other cookie.

"Cheater!" Rachel exclaimed, nudging Lisa with her leg.

She just grinned at Rachel and took a bite of the carrot.

Rachel frowned at the sugar cookies but picked one up and took a bite. "This wouldn't be so bad, if we hadn't already eaten most of that gingerbread house."

"Does Santa really *need* two cookies?" Lisa asked. "I mean, I'm sure he's as tired of sweets as you are after going to millions of houses to drop off toys, with all of those other kids leaving him cookies as well. I'm sure he's starting to get a bit of a stomach ache."

"This is true," Rachel said. "I wonder if Declan would buy that next year. Probably not. Everyone knows Santa *loves* his cookies. Can't make Santa mad and miss out on a good toy."

Lisa shook her head. "We definitely don't want to upset Santa."

"The things we tell our kids," Rachel said with a dramatic sigh, and then she looked up with concern visible in her eyes as she realized what she had said.

The statement caused the familiar stab of grief, but she wanted to reassure Rachel. "It's okay." Any little thing, it seemed, could bring that hurt rushing back. It was hardly Rachel's fault. "You don't have to apologize for being a parent. You can talk about Declan. I care about both of you."

"Thank you," Rachel said.

Lisa met her gaze. The look Rachel gave her was tender, and she felt herself drawn in. She should have said that she had to get going for the night. She should have said it was getting late. She should have said something, anything. Instead, she took in the way the soft golden glow of the firelight caressed Rachel's skin. She memorized the way her hair hung in haphazard curls that framed her face. She wanted to brush her fingers through those curls, and trace them over the line of Rachel's jaw . . .

Rachel bit the corner of her lower lip.

As if of its own accord, Lisa's body turned ever so slightly closer toward Rachel.

Her breathing grew heavy. Her mind screamed at her to move, to get up, to stop what was surely about to happen. But those thoughts were drowned out by the pounding of her heart.

She didn't get up. She rested a hand on Rachel's knee, as if to steady herself.

"Rachel." The thought ended there. She didn't know if the single word had been uttered as a warning or a sign of encouragement.

Rachel leaned toward her, and rested her hands on Lisa's hips. Warmth spread through her at the touch.

She needed to feel more.

She closed the distance and captured Rachel's lips with her own. The heat that had been building between the two of them sparked into a flame.

Rachel deepened the kiss, her lips parting and her tongue brushing over Lisa's lips, causing Lisa's stomach to clench in anticipation. An unfamiliar moan slipped out of her mouth before she met Rachel's tongue with her own.

Desire clouded her thoughts, and her body took over. She leaned into Rachel and pushed her down onto the couch.

Rachel pulled Lisa down over top of her, and she tumbled into a dizzying whirlwind of sensation.

Rachel's body soft and warm beneath her.

Breath hot against her lips.

Fingers digging into her back.

She slipped her hands beneath the hem of Rachel's sweater, feeling the impossibly soft skin that awaited her underneath. God, she wanted more. She needed more.

"Lisa."

The sound of her name didn't even register through the desire, at first.

Another light kiss and then she heard her name again.

She opened her eyes to Rachel gazing at her with sea-green eyes heavy with desire.

"Bedroom?" Rachel asked, her eyes widening hopefully.

She knew what was being offered and panic constricted around her chest, but God, she didn't want to say no. She didn't want to leave. She swallowed hard and nodded.

Rachel stood first, and Lisa felt the loss instantly. But then Rachel was pulling her up and leading her to the bedroom. She shut the door behind them, and pressed Lisa against the wall, kissing her neck, and jaw, and ears. Rachel was pressed flush against her, so warm and right, and Lisa couldn't think of a single reason why this could have been wrong.

No, she wasn't going to stop this time.

Rachel closed the bedroom door behind them and turned to Lisa, gasping as Lisa pulled their bodies flush against each other and began brushing her lips over Rachel's jaw. She tangled her hands in Rachel's hair, and Rachel closed her eyes and tilted her head back, breathing in Lisa's soft scent, her mind closed to everything but the feel of Lisa's lips on her skin, Lisa's body flush against her, Lisa . . .

She could feel Lisa's desire in the way she reached for her, pulling her closer, tasting her and touching her.

Desire emboldened her in response, and she pressed Lisa against the wall, anchoring Lisa with her thigh, as she met her kisses with more urgency than earlier, restraint gone as she let the desire take over.

"Please." Lisa breathed into her mouth.

The word was almost all that she could take, but she didn't push things further. She continued to enjoy the deep, languid kiss. She wouldn't be the one to set the pace. She had been clear about her desire from the start. She'd wanted Lisa for months, while Lisa had been clear about all of the reasons "they" could never happen. If anything *were* to happen, it needed to be Lisa who took the lead. She needed to know Lisa was ready.

But, God, the restraint was hard when Lisa moved against her, her hips pressing into Rachel, her hands settling on Rachel's hips.

Then, Lisa's hands were pushing beneath her shirt, leaving a trail of fire across Rachel's skin as her fingers brushed up Rachel's sides and across her back. She arched against Lisa with a small gasp that she almost didn't recognize as coming from her.

In the morning this will all be over. She squeezed her eyes shut against the warning that echoed in her mind, but closing her eyes did nothing to relieve the fear that bloomed in her chest.

Lisa's hands slid higher, brushing across Rachel's bra and causing her nipples to harden against the fabric, and all thoughts were gone. There was only desire.

Lisa tugged Rachel's shirt up, and she raised her arms to help shrug it off, needing the clothes gone. For a moment, the air was cool against her burning skin, but then Lisa was there, kissing her chest and touching her stomach without the fabric barrier between them.

She half expected nervousness to set in, but with Lisa she didn't feel awkward or shy or inexperienced. She felt safe and *wanted*.

She reached out and pulled Lisa's shirt off as well, needing to feel Lisa's skin against her own.

Lisa guided her toward the bed, all the while kissing her neck and throat and shoulder, pushing away her bra strap to kiss the skin there. Lisa's tongue trailed over Rachel's skin, and her stomach tightened in anticipation.

When the back of her legs hit the bed, she sat down, taking a moment to look up and meet Lisa's tender gaze before trailing her own gaze over Lisa's gentle curves, taking in her smooth skin and full breasts, clad only in a soft lilac bra. She slid her arms around Lisa's waist, hooking her hands into the back pockets of her jeans to pull Lisa closer.

She kissed Lisa's stomach, her lips and tongue flirting with the possibility of moving lower. But Lisa's hands were unfastening Rachel's bra, and her hands went to Rachel's breasts, and all she could do was inhale sharply, arching her back into Lisa's hands. She closed her eyes and bit her lip as Lisa's fingers found her nipples.

She wanted more. So much more. She slid back on the bed and Lisa followed.

Lisa settled over her. *God.* It was the only coherent word her mind could form. All other thoughts were gone. Nothing else mattered except how right they felt together.

Lisa's weight settled over her, and Rachel felt her heart expand at the feeling of complete comfort in that moment. There was no place she'd rather be. Lisa kissed her slowly at first, but the kiss built. She began to slowly rock her hips against Lisa, pressing closer, reaching for contact where she needed it most. Lisa responded, pressing against her.

Their damn jeans . . . She needed them gone.

She reached for the buttons, but Lisa took her hands and pinned them over her head, while continuing to kiss her, slow and deep. Rachel let her take charge, giving herself over to Lisa.

Then Lisa pulled back, reaching behind her to remove her bra.

"My God." She swallowed hard as she watched Lisa reach down to unbutton her jeans, agonizingly slowly, before pushing them down her legs, stepping out, and standing naked before her.

She ached to have Lisa's smooth, soft body against her own. She groaned and bit her lip when Lisa's fingers brushed across her stomach to unbutton her jeans and finally pull the denim barrier away.

"You're so beautiful," Lisa whispered, and she looked down with a gaze that sent heat through Rachel's entire body.

In that moment Rachel believed her. She lay there naked and vulnerable and felt no shyness at Lisa's gaze.

Lisa lowered herself back over her. Skin against skin. Warm and perfect. Everything Rachel had imagined and so much more.

Lisa kissed her ear, her tongue teasing Rachel's ear lobe, sending a shiver of pleasure through her body.

"Please," Rachel sighed.

Lisa trailed her fingernails up her thigh, and Rachel gave a soft moan in response.

"I need you," she whispered, guiding Lisa's hand to her.

Lisa stroked her and gave a small moan. "You're so wet," she said, before finally sliding into her.

She pressed herself harder against Lisa's hand, needing more.

Lisa's body covered hers, and they found a rhythm, rocking against one another. Their hips moved together, while Lisa's fingers found exactly where she needed her. Lisa's breath was hot against her neck, her breathing heavy, matching Rachel's.

She gripped Lisa's back tightly, gasping for air as Lisa pumped inside of her. When her thumb found Rachel's clit, she cried out, pulling Lisa against her, sweaty and desperate for release.

"Harder," she said with a gasp, and Lisa obliged, bringing her closer and closer to the edge.

Rachel felt the orgasm build, and for a futile moment tried to fight it. She was both desperate for relief and wanting to prolong the pleasure. But Lisa felt so right with her body pressed against hers, their breasts flush against each other, their hips rocking in tandem, and she couldn't stop herself from tumbling over the edge.

The orgasm hit her hard, her entire body contracting with the force of it. Lisa held her, continuing to thrust inside of her until Rachel's body fell still. They lay there together, breathing heavily for a long moment before Lisa slipped her fingers from Rachel slowly.

Lisa propped herself up on her elbows, and Rachel gazed up into her warm, hazel eyes.

"Lisa," was all she could manage to say. She couldn't form words. There were no words to describe the rightness of the moment. All she could do was bury herself in Lisa while her breathing returned to normal.

As she came down from the orgasm, however, doubt began to creep back in, replacing pleasure.

This doesn't mean anything to her. It can't. So, it's just sex.

But to her it was more than sex. Everything with Lisa had always been more.

She couldn't keep denying that.

Chapter Twenty-Four

The little boy ran toward the ocean, just out of reach, as Lisa sprinted after him.

"Mitchell," she called. "Wait for me."

The boy kept running, gangly legs pumping hard, his blond hair blowing back in the breeze.

She needed to stop him. To keep him from reaching the water. She grabbed for him, but he was a couple inches beyond her fingertips.

His laughter carried musically on the breeze, rich and carefree. Such beautiful laughter.

Ahead of them, breakers crested and rolled toward the sand. The soft sound of rushing surf. The caw of seagulls. The splash as a pelican hit the water in search of a fish.

But the laughter . . . the beautiful laughter sang above it all.

She stopped to listen to that laughter. To take it in, while she watched her son, so full of joy. So happy.

He ran to the water's edge.

And then the wave appeared. The wall of water rose from nowhere. Time slowed to a crawl.

She froze as the wave grew and towered over her little boy, who could do nothing more than stare at it.

"Mommy!" he called.

But they were both frozen.

"Mommy!"

"Mommy!"

The voice again.

She opened her eyes, but the room was dark. She didn't know where she was.

Where's Mitchell?

She felt for him, but felt nothing. Her son wasn't there.

And then the dream was gone, and she was awake, and she knew where she was.

Her eyes adjusted to the dark, and she saw Rachel pulling on a shirt.

"Rachel?" she asked, the only concrete word her mind could form.

"I'm sorry he woke you," Rachel said. "Go back to sleep. I'll be right back."

"Mommy, my tummy hurts."

This time she recognized Declan's voice drifting in from the room down the hall.

Rachel sighed. "I'll be right back. I knew I shouldn't have let him have so much candy last night. He probably just needs me to rub his back until he falls back to sleep."

Lisa nodded numbly as she sat up in bed, wrapping the blankets around herself as Rachel left to check on Declan.

Mitchell's not here.

She could feel the emptiness, the hollow in her chest, the deep ache in her bones.

Her hands went to her belly, as they had when she was pregnant.

Not here.

Not anywhere.

Gone.

She closed her eyes. The wave was still there. Towering above her child.

Just a dream, she told herself. But she didn't know if that brought relief or more grief. The wave, the threat, was never real. But neither was the child. She'd never get to see him as a boy. He was never there.

A different wave—panic—swelled within her. She could feel it build, but was powerless to move out of its path, to stop herself from getting swept away.

He's gone.

The wave grew.

I need air.

Bigger.

This is not my home. Not my son. Never my son.

She would never hear Mitchell cry out for her.

The wave of desperation crested and bore down on her. She gasped for air but there was none. She was drowning, gasping, reaching for anything solid she could find.

As Rachel had expected, Declan was fine. He was merely uncomfortable from a combination of the sugar he'd consumed the night before and his anticipation of Santa Claus. In fact, the second thing he'd said after "my tummy hurts" was "did Santa come yet?"

She had assured him that Santa had not visited their house yet and rubbed his back until he was asleep no more than five minutes later. She was glad he'd fallen asleep quickly because she wanted to get back to bed herself and snuggle in next to Lisa.

She had tried to get up quietly so as not to wake her, but Declan's continued cries woke her anyway. As she walked back to the bedroom, she noticed a light shining from beneath her door, telling her Lisa was awake.

"I'm sorry about that," she said as she stepped back in the bedroom.

She stopped when she saw Lisa pulling on her pants.

"Lisa?"

Lisa didn't look at her. She didn't even seem to *hear* her. She looked distant and scared as she fought with the zipper of her jeans.

She rested a hand on Lisa's to stop her. "Hey. Talk to me."

Lisa's eyes contained everything Rachel needed to know. They were wide and full of pain—pain so deep that Rachel thought she too might drown in it.

"Talk to me," she urged again.

Things between them had changed over the past month. Lisa had opened up to her. She'd been happier. Rachel ached to see *that* Lisa, but she feared the grief had consumed her again. She didn't want the wall between them, but more than that, she didn't want the grief to pull Lisa back into that dark place, so full of despair.

Lisa shook her head, but Rachel couldn't tell if it was directed at her request to talk or if she was trying to shake away her demons.

"I thought it was Mitchell," Lisa said, her voice small and thick with unshed tears. "I heard him, but it wasn't him; it was Declan."

Realization dawned on her, and her heart grew heavy in her chest. Lisa had woken to cries for Mommy that weren't from her child.

There was nothing she could say, but she couldn't watch Lisa go so she tried desperately anyway.

"Come back to bed," she begged. "Let me hold you."

The words felt wrong even to her ears, but she didn't know what else to say. She put her hands on Lisa's. She tried to ground her in the present, but Lisa's eyes were distant.

"Please," Rachel begged.

But the request fell flat. It was not enough. There were no right words.

Rachel had Declan. Lisa would forever be without Mitchell.

Lisa buckled her belt and reached for a pair of socks. She looked like she was on the brink of tears. Crying would be better. She could comfort crying. But Lisa didn't cry. She didn't let Rachel in. She just left.

Rachel watched her go, helpless to stop her, and then fell to the bed, overcome with her own tears.

Chapter Twenty-Five

What the hell was I thinking? Lisa walked through the empty streets aimlessly. *I should never have slept with her. I should never have let myself get so close to her. I should have kept my damn distance from the start.*

The self-defeating thoughts played over and over in her mind like a mantra, fueled by the image of the hurt on Rachel's face, an image she feared might be forever etched into her mind's eye.

She and Rachel were a dangerous combination. The connection between the two of them had been too intense from the start, the attraction a spark they never could have contained. She'd felt it, and she'd known Rachel felt it, and yet somehow she'd thought that they could control it. *Stupid.* She should've stayed away. Now she had hurt Rachel. And she had hurt Declan. And she had never wanted to hurt either.

I didn't mean to, she thought, futilely trying to defend herself against her own self-admonitions. *They're the last two I would ever want to hurt. I love them both.*

The words echoed through her chest, and she stopped, doubling over as if she'd been punched. She shook her head.

"I can't. I can't. I can't," she repeated, as she continued to walk through town, not knowing where she was going, just knowing she had to chase the ache out of her chest.

The wind outside was a heavy cold, the moisture from the ocean thickening the air. Cold in her skin, her lungs, her bones. The icy numbness that settled into her was a relief.

She made her way back to the center of town where the festival had been the night before, but the area was now abandoned. The Christmas tree still stood, but the lights were off. The tables with crafts and baked goods for sale had all been taken down. There were no families, no children, no couples. The place felt as empty as she did.

She didn't stop. She was scared if she stopped, that same echoed thought would creep back in: *I love them both.*

Declan wasn't Mitchell. Her son was gone, and she didn't want to fill that void with another child. She didn't want to love any other boy. And at the same time, she did love him. Not as a replacement child. As his own person.

I love them both.

She loved *Declan*, the little boy who was sweet and sensitive, with huge feelings that got hurt so easily, but who loved so easily and so freely anyway.

And she couldn't stand to be another person in his life, one like his dad, who couldn't be there for him in the way that he deserved.

She kept walking, her feet propelling her forward. She didn't have a destination in mind; she only knew she couldn't face going home yet.

The roads took her closer to the ocean, and the sound of the violent surf drew Lisa in. She found herself climbing down the rocky embankment to the small beach below. The moon was full and bright enough for her to see where she was going, and she carefully stepped over the snow-crusted rocks.

When she reached the bottom, she brushed the snow off the top of a large piece of driftwood, sitting down and staring out at the water. She didn't move, she didn't think, she just stared at the rolling waves in the gray light of the moon.

Tears slipped from her eyes, completely effortlessly, before she even realized she was crying. The tears were hot as they trailed down her cheeks, immediately being chilled by the cold December air.

She lifted her hand to wipe her face, but acknowledging the tears only made them worse. A hard sob ripped its way from her chest and she began to cry. Her body heaved violently with the force, and she gasped for air.

The more she cried, the more she wanted to cry. Her emotions were a dam that had broken, and she knew it would be hard to push them back into check. Impossible even. She'd kept too much bottled up for too long.

She got up from the piece of driftwood and picked up a large icy rock. With all her might she heaved it into the ocean, letting a shout tear its way from her chest as she did so. Then she lifted another rock. And another. Each rock was thrown with a guttural cry.

When her arms shook like her body had nothing left to give, she sunk down on the piece of driftwood once more and her sobs began to still. Tears leaked from her eyes but the violence of the crying had gone out of her.

The ocean continued to surge. The wind continued to blow. The surf continued its steady ebb and flow. A simple melody. A steady beat.

"Mitchell?" Lisa breathed deeply and wiped her eyes. "Are you out there?"

She waited for a response, as though one were possible. As though an answer would carry in on the wind. She heard only the staccato crashing of the waves, the predictable pattern of crescendos and diminuendos.

Her body felt limp, her muscles cold and tired. The fight in her had died. It was time to accept what was.

She couldn't be with Rachel and Declan anymore.

They were gone.

Mitchell was gone.

She was alone.

Without thought she reached into her pocket and fished out her cell phone, dialing the familiar number.

"Lisa?" her brother answered.

"Andrew," she said, trying to keep her voice together. "Merry Christmas."

"Merry Christmas," he said. A long pause. "Lisa, do you know what time it is?"

She looked at the still-dark sky, and dropped her head and shoulders, the realization hitting her that it was still the middle of the night.

"Oh shit. I'm sorry. I'm so sorry." She hung up the phone and fell to her knees on the beach. Guilt and grief and loss all swirled inside of her, a violent storm, and she rocked in on herself as though she could protect herself from the onslaught of emotions.

Her phone rang.

She hit "answer" and wordlessly lifted the phone to her ear.

"Is everything okay? Lisa, talk to me."

She fought the urge to respond with her usual "everything's fine" lie. Everything *wasn't* fine, and they both knew it. She was kneeling on frozen sand, calling her brother in the middle of the night on Christmas.

She'd walked out on Rachel.

Tears returned, and through them Lisa choked out, "I'm a mess."

"Talk to me, Lisa," Andrew said again, his voice thick and comforting with sympathy.

"I miss Mitchell," Lisa said. And then the wall broke, and all of the words came pouring out. "I miss him so damn much. I should be celebrating Christmas with him, and instead I'm sitting on the beach all alone. I'm all alone. I should be with her, and I can't. I met someone, and I can't be with her because she has a kid, and all I can think about is Mitchell. *My* child. My child who died. He died."

Sobs hit her harder at the word, as though saying that he died made it real all over again. She was back in the hospital, rocking her lifeless infant, rocking back and forth on the sand, time and space overlapping, the same scene stacked atop itself.

"He did," Andrew said. Then softly added, "And it's really fucking unfair."

She rocked back so she was sitting on the sand, and she wrapped herself inward, hugging her knees with one arm and holding her phone to her ear with the other. She held and rocked herself as if she could comfort her own broken soul.

"Come home," Andrew said.

She nodded against her knees. She wanted her brother. Her parents. Her family. She had wanted an escape, but the loss had followed her. It wasn't something that could be left in Toronto.

"Yeah," Lisa said quietly, nodding against her knees. "Okay."

Home.

She had to stop running.

Chapter Twenty-Six

Declan eagerly tore open his gift from Santa, pure unadulterated joy etched across his face. Rachel wanted to be happy with him, to be present in the morning. It was *Christmas Day*. She was opening gifts with her dad and her son. It should've been the happiest day of the year. And all she could think about was Lisa.

She kept replaying over and over in her mind that moment when she'd walked back into the room and seen Lisa getting dressed to leave. The hurt had been palpable. *Lisa's. Her own.* The air had been thick with pain. She vacillated between her own hurt at Lisa leaving, and hurt for Lisa, of watching the grief regain its grip on her. The walls had been coming down, Lisa had been slowly opening up, and Rachel had watched as the walls all fell right back into place. And there'd been nothing she could have done to stop or prevent that from happening.

"Whoa!" Declan said as he pulled the wrapping paper off of the remote-controlled car that Rachel had given him "From Santa." "This is awesome. Grandpa, help me get it out of the box."

When she had purchased the car, she'd been so excited to watch Declan open that gift, and now his reaction barely registered past the haze of hurt and loss. She wished life came with a pause button. She wished for time to stop so she could process everything and come back and be with her family in this moment.

Frank Murray laughed. "Slow down, bud. I think I see a present with your mom's name on it. Why don't you pass it to her? After breakfast I'll help you get the car working. We're going to have to find some batteries for it."

Declan frowned down at the car, but then crawled across the floor and found the gift addressed to Rachel. The tag told her this gift was also from Santa, but she knew it was really from her dad.

She held the small present in her hands, trying to muster the energy to fake enthusiasm. She didn't want to open gifts, to have her dad and son watching her. Declan wouldn't see the hurt, but her dad would. She had no doubt the pain was etched very visibly across her face.

She took a breath and unwrapped the paper, exclaiming her gratitude for the gift. Her voice sounded distant to herself. She didn't know if she had managed to fake happiness or not. Declan, thankfully, acted as a buffer and reached for another gift, taking the spotlight off her.

Frank opened his gifts from Rachel and Declan. Declan opened the other small gifts that he'd received. Once the gifts had been opened, Frank went to make the French toast for breakfast. It was their Christmas morning tradition. He would show up bright and early. They'd open gifts, eat breakfast, and then spend the day doing something as a family—staying in with a Christmas movie, going out skating, taking snowmobiles out on the trails . . . a tradition carried over from Rachel's own childhood. It was one of her favorite days of the year. She got to spend the day with the two people she loved more than anything without the pressures of work and school. This year it was incomplete. Someone she loved was missing.

Rachel froze at the realization. *Love.* She shook her head, and realized she had stopped breathing. *No.* She couldn't. She *shouldn't.*

Lisa had never wanted to be included. Lisa had never wanted Rachel to fall in love with her. She'd made the impossibility of the two of them clear from the start.

She struggled not to curl up and cry. She wanted to spend the day in bed. She didn't want to put on a happy face and pretend it was the best day of the year. She was fairly certain she was not that good an actress.

She'd gone and fallen for Lisa, despite every attempt not to. And now Lisa was gone.

She was never here. But images of the night before pressed their way back into her mind, and she knew not to believe those thoughts. It had never been one-sided. Lisa had felt it too. Not that it mattered.

She squeezed her eyes shut, trying to block out the thoughts. When she opened them again, she fixed her gaze on her Dad and Declan making the French toast. Her dad had helped Declan up onto a chair in front of the stove and was showing him how to flip the toast in the pan. Declan looked so proud, helping with the breakfast. The smell of cinnamon drifted from the kitchen into the living room. Tears burned at her eyes, and she wiped them away with the back of her hand.

Not now, she told herself.

It had been a hard year. For all of them.

The last thing she needed was heartbreak. She didn't have time. She told herself she couldn't be heartbroken at the moment, as though she could somehow will the feelings away.

She tried to swallow the pain, but she could feel it extending from her heart and out into her body. A general ache she felt in every muscle. She felt drained. Tired. Empty.

She didn't *want* to feel those things. It was Christmas morning. She had a family who also wanted to be happy and have a good day. Declan deserved a happy Christmas. He *needed* a happy Christmas. He'd been sad so often. Rachel owed him this day.

She put Christmas music on the stereo.

Later she could fall apart.

Chapter Twenty-Seven

The highway stretched in front of Lisa—a long, lonely ache of a road. The hills began to flatten as she moved farther away from the Cape Breton highlands. Hoar frost embossed the trees with an almost eerie, empty white. Everything was still and silent, buried beneath the freshly fallen snow. All that moved was her car. The tires kept spinning, kept her moving forward. Forward toward the airport in Sydney. Forward toward home. The tires kept spinning, hurtling her backward. Backward into the pain she'd tried to escape from. Backward into the past. She didn't know which way she was going, but she kept her foot on the gas pedal and hoped she was moving in the right direction. The fear that tightened like a vise around her tempted her to turn around, while also encouraging her to press forward. It was time to face her grief. As she drove, the white canvas of the highway faded away, and instead she saw a different road in front of her. A different drive.

It was sunny and warm on the green, vibrant streets, the sun so bright it burned her red-rimmed, tear-stung eyes. Andrew drove. She wouldn't have been able to get behind the wheel. She could only stare out at the cruel daylight, numb. She kept her arms wrapped around her stomach, as though she'd be able to feel the tiny flutter of kicks once more. But she was empty. Mitchell was gone.

She kept her gaze fixed on the blur of trees outside the car, forcing herself not to turn and look at the empty car seat in the back. She had bought the car seat earlier in her pregnancy. Before the doctor had come in with the somber look on his face and told her in no uncertain terms that she would never bring her baby home. He had been clear, but still she held onto misplaced hope and refused to remove the car seat, just in case.

Just in case.

Just in case her baby destined to die had somehow lived.

Beat the odds.

There were never any odds to beat. Just a tragic certainty.

The emptiness screamed at her from the backseat. It was deafening. She wanted to turn her head, but she'd be blinded by that emptiness, as well, if she were to turn to it.

She blinked and tried to focus on the white winter trees. The here and now. She'd learned to do that in the counseling she'd gone to in the month after. Breathe. Focus on tangible senses in the present. The winter road. The cushion of the car seat. The rush of the hot air blasting from the air vents in a desperate battle to keep the car warm against the chill of winter outside the thin metal frame. It was a way of staying grounded when the thoughts and emotions took over, but the technique was currently failing her.

When she had finally had to leave her house, when she'd finally had to get back in that car, the car seat had been gone. Andrew must have removed it.

For a sharp instant, she had hated him. But the car seat wouldn't have given her Mitchell back. It wasn't the car seat she wanted. It was her son. And he was gone.

She had slumped against the steering wheel and sobbed until her chest ached. Then she'd started the ignition.

Fresher hurts flooded her, joining the other memories that haunted her. She thought back on the pain etched into Rachel's features when she'd left. She'd run away. Running was about the only thing she was good at. She had run to Cape Breton Island because she couldn't face her life in Toronto without Mitchell. She ran from Rachel because she couldn't face the thought of a future with a little boy who wasn't Mitchell. She was good at running.

She was a coward.

"You're here. You got up in the morning. That took courage."

She remembered her therapist's words. But it didn't feel like courage. It never had felt like courage. She was just a shadow, going through the motions. A ghost.

She followed road signs toward Sydney. Forward. Backward. She wasn't sure which direction she was moving in. But at least she was moving somewhere with purpose. She *wanted* to live. There was a future waiting for her. She just didn't know how to get there. But she was trying.

Lisa's apartment didn't smell like home anymore. It didn't feel like it either. After she left, she always thought she'd return, but now she looked out her window onto downtown Toronto, no ocean in sight, and she knew she didn't want to live in this space again. The friend subletting the place while she stayed on Cape Breton had let her in and offered her coffee or tea.

Lisa shook her head and left her waiting in the living room as she headed toward Mitchell's closed nursery door. As much as she didn't want to open the door, she needed to. She couldn't keep all of the hurt and grief locked in that nursery. It permeated her life regardless of whether the door was open or closed. She had her hand on the doorknob, which she hesitated to turn, in case opening the door triggered a backdraft of emotions that would incinerate her with their intensity.

With a deep breath to steady herself, she slowly pulled open the door and stepped into the nursery.

It was dark and musty in the room with closed curtains and air that hadn't circulated properly in over a year. She blinked at the gray against the backdrop of her son's belongings and felt the darkness hit her as a punch to the stomach. Mitchell's teddy bear sat cloaked in shadows inside his crib, a sad little prison. She almost couldn't stand the sight, and she rushed to open the curtains and allow daylight to fill the small room.

She picked up that teddy bear, lifting the stuffed animal from its cage. It was a small brown bear, with puffy fur and blue eyes. It was the first thing she had purchased when she'd discovered she was pregnant. She'd found the little bear in a shop on the way home from the doctor's office, and she had known immediately that the bear was meant for her child. She pictured a baby mouthing the bear's small nose, coating the fur with drool. She pictured her toddler, dragging the bear around the house. Her child, holding the bear at night when scared after a bad dream.

The bear had never been held by a child.

Lisa pulled it close, and imagined the bear grieved that fact as much as she did. A mother without a son. A bear without a boy.

She took the teddy and sat in the rocking chair next to the crib—the chair that had been meant for nursing her baby in the night. She sat and rocked and held the bear, and eventually she cried.

As she cried, she thought of Rachel. She wished Rachel were there to hold her. She felt safe and comforted and loved in Rachel's arms. *Loved.* Lisa hadn't wanted to fall for Rachel and Declan, but she had, and she knew the feeling was mutual. She had heard it in the desperation as Rachel had asked her to stay—begged her to come back to bed. She had wanted nothing more than to curl up beneath the covers again and allow Rachel to just hold her. Leaving hadn't been a choice. It had been a *need.* She hadn't been able to breathe.

Mommy. The word had kept echoing. Mitchell. Declan. She didn't know who was speaking.

And so she'd run. Rachel had Declan. Lisa had Mitchell. And in that moment, the distinction had seemed like an ocean that could never be bridged. It felt like being with Rachel would mean choosing between the two boys.

Except Lisa knew that it was a false alternative. She would never be choosing Rachel and Declan over Mitchell. Mitchell was gone. And if he had lived, there would never have been a question about being with Rachel. Still, her heart ached with the loss, with what would never be, and she didn't know how to be whole enough to have anything to offer Rachel and Declan.

She held the teddy bear close to her chest as though it was Mitchell, and she could hold him close and block out the rest of the world.

"Mitchell's gone," she said out loud to the empty nursery. Her voice broke with the words, but she needed to say them. She needed to *hear* them. "He's gone. I love him, but he's gone."

She could keep holding a ghost forever, or she could allow herself to move forward and love the living boy in her life.

She clutched the teddy bear tighter, and she rocked while she cried. She took a long moment, but eventually she had to set the bear down. She had to leave Mitchell's nursery.

She had to say good-bye.

After leaving her old apartment, she drove to her childhood home, where her parents still lived. Obligation brought her to the two-story brick home in the suburbs, and she sat out front, idling the car for a while before she got up the nerve to turn off the ignition. The sun had already set, and she watched her breath puff in front of her, as she knocked on the door and waited for it to open.

It's not too late to run, she said to herself. She was expected at her family's New Year's Eve party, and after missing Christmas it had been more or less demanded. The thought of facing all of her extended family was beyond overwhelming, and her feet ached to carry her in the other direction. But even as the fear hammered in her chest, she held her ground until Andrew opened the door and pulled her into a big bear hug.

"I didn't think you'd actually come," Andrew said, grinning at her. *Neither did I.*

Before she knew what was happening, a pair of arms and legs wrapped around each of her legs, nearly throwing her off balance. Both of her nieces had grown about half a foot since she'd last seen them.

"Girls, let go of Auntie Lisa so she can get inside and take her boots off," Andrew's wife, Sarah, said as she stepped into the foyer, laughing and taking her daughters' hands.

Lisa shrugged off her coat and boots, lining the boots up neatly by the door and hanging the coat in the closet. Music and voices carried from the living room, and she braced herself for the crowd of people at the Whelan family's annual New Year's Eve party. She hadn't seen most of her family in months, and she'd been bad about returning calls. She expected nothing short of an interrogation from her family members. Almost all of her extended family was at the event, perhaps with only the exception of Auntie Eloise who hadn't made the trip from the coast. Her cousins, aunts, uncles . . . all of them wanted some sort of update on her life.

"We've missed you, Lise," was all Andrew said.

She met his eyes and nodded. "I've missed you, too."

Sarah stood with her hands around her visibly pregnant belly, the move triggering a flash of muscle memory as Lisa's hands went to her own stomach. She remembered standing that same way, treasuring the life growing inside of her. It was such a habitual move, a subconscious shift. Sarah still had a couple of months to go, but she was far enough into her pregnancy that she would be able to feel the flutter of feet as her baby kicked inside of her. Her arms were already preparing to hold her baby.

She saw Andrew watching her gaze and looked away, feeling naked in her grief. She tried to keep it inside, lest it all spill out. "Have you thought of a name?" Lisa asked. She wanted the focus shifted away from her. She felt her pain leaking into the foyer. Only Kara and Susie were oblivious to it, running off to find toys to play with or trouble to get into.

"We're thinking Daniel for a boy," Sarah answered. "Or Lauren for a girl."

"Those are nice names."

"Thank you," Sarah said.

Something tugged in Lisa, and without thought she reached out a hand and asked, "May I?"

"Of course." Sarah stepped forward to let her place a hand on her belly.

Lisa's breath caught in the back of her throat at the feel of the tight skin. She placed her other hand beside her first, and then she felt the tiny kick against her palm.

She pulled back as though she herself had been kicked in the chest, but then she returned her hands to Sarah's belly, feeling the tiny flutter of feet against her palm—her little niece or nephew. When the kicking subsided, she stepped back, tears brimming in her eyes.

"Thank you," was all she could manage, as she tried to swallow the tidal wave of emotion that surged through her chest. Too many emotions to untangle.

She knew that Andrew was looking at her with concern and sympathy and sorrow, and she avoided looking up to see the expression she knew all too well.

"I'm going to go say hi to everyone else," she said, making her way to the living room to face the rest of the family.

As expected, she was met with a barrage of hugs, and the questions began flying her way. She answered them as concisely as possible. Yes, she was staying with Auntie Eloise. No, she didn't know when she'd move back to Toronto. Yes, she'd gone out there to work. No, she wasn't ready to talk about her new project, but she would let them know when she was.

Keep it surface level, she coached herself. That was all anyone really wanted in response anyway. They didn't want to hear the truth. They didn't want to hear she was broken. That she was stuck. That she didn't know how to move on. Not when they'd all done so, effortlessly. They had been sad about losing Mitchell, of course. But life hadn't stopped for them. It kept going.

Mundane conversation.

Cheese plates.

Setting resolutions that would be forgotten in a month.

It all felt so forced now. So empty.

She impatiently waited out the hours until midnight, just as she waited out the rest of the hours of her life. She wanted to go home. Go to sleep. Wake up and start again.

Finally, the clock ticked down the remaining minutes of the year, and Andrew opened the champagne, pouring everyone a glass, except Sarah who got apple juice.

Every year the Whelans went around and toasted to one thing they were thankful for from the previous year and one thing they hoped for the upcoming year.

She held the champagne in front of her, staring at the bubbles, only half listening to the others. She tried to think of what she was going to say. One thing she was thankful for. One thing she hoped for. She wondered if she'd be able to get away with saying nothing. The past was pain, and she didn't allow herself to hope anymore. Everything was a day at a time.

She didn't hear what the others were saying. She just stared at her drink, trying to think of *something*, as the toast moved around the room, getting closer to her turn to speak.

Beside her, Andrew was thankful for his wife and daughters and looking forward to meeting his new child. The room cheered and sipped their drinks.

Silence then as the family waited for Lisa to speak.

Lisa felt the eyes on her. They all wanted some simple answer. She could have said she was thankful for time on the coast. She was hopeful about her new project. She had the words ready. But other words came spilling out instead.

"I hate this toast," she said. "I don't want to do this."

Andrew moved forward, about to stop her, but Lisa shook her head and kept talking.

"Last year, I didn't come to our New Year's Eve party, because of this exact toast," she said. "I couldn't do this. I couldn't reflect on the year I lost Mitchell. I'm supposed to say what I'm thankful for? What I'm hopeful for? I've got nothing . . ." She trailed off.

All eyes on the room were on her, but nobody said anything, all stunned into silence, she was sure.

The emotions rose in her chest and she took a drink of her champagne before continuing. "But last year, I guess, I did have something to be thankful for. It was a year that I had Mitchell with me. I carried him inside of me. I held him in my arms. It was the year he died. But it was also the year he lived. This year I had to spend three hundred and sixty-five days without him. Next year, another three hundred and sixty-five days." If she didn't do something, if she didn't move forward, it would be on and on like that forever.

She thought of Rachel and Declan. She was going to spend the next year without Mitchell, that was a given. But the realization slowly settled in that she didn't want to spend it without them as well. Furthermore, she didn't *have* to spend it without them. She stared at her champagne and took a long moment before continuing.

"I'm thankful for all of the people in my life who have been patient and given me space to grieve, and I'm hopeful that they're still there waiting," she finished.

She met Andrew's gaze, and his eyes were misty. She gave him a slight nod to let him know that she included him in that.

She set her champagne down.

"I have to go," she said.

She wanted to move forward. It wouldn't be easy, but she couldn't keep living in the past. Not forever. Not even for another year.

Chapter Twenty-Eight

Rachel wished she could wake up without the now-familiar empty ache in her stomach. She kept telling herself it was stupid how much she missed Lisa, but that didn't take away from the constant hurt. Stupid or not, she'd fallen for Lisa. Every day she woke up, and the first thing she noticed was that Lisa wasn't there beside her. The emptiness was jarring. She began each day in pain.

She could only imagine how Lisa felt, living every day without her *child*. That was the worst part. She *understood* why Lisa couldn't be with her. She wished she could have felt anger, but she couldn't even imagine the depth of grief she would feel if she lost Declan, and so she couldn't be mad at Lisa for being unable to move forward into a life with the two of them. Had the tables been reversed, she'd have run, too. The chasm between them could never be bridged. But, God . . . anger would've been preferable to the sad acceptance of what was never going to be. This was just . . . emptiness . . .

The unfairness of the situation weighed heavily upon her. She'd never fallen for anyone the way she'd fallen for Lisa. She hadn't even believed that kind of connection was possible. Then there was Lisa, attractive, kind, and empathetic. She was great with Declan, and the two of them connected so easily and naturally. Lisa fit into her life as if she had been meant to be there from the start, which made the situation all the more cruel.

The worst part was knowing that Declan missed Lisa as well. At first, he'd asked about her, asking Rachel if Lisa could go tobogganing with them again, or if she could come over and watch a movie, or if he could go visit Lisa and show her his art. Every time she had to let him down the hurt intensified. Eventually he stopped asking. He had been irritable in the weeks since, and she knew his foul mood was in direct connection with losing someone he cared about. That part made her burn with anger. Anger at Lisa partly, but mostly anger at the injustice of it all.

She prayed Declan's first day back to school after Christmas break would go smoothly, and his irritability wouldn't get him kicked out of school, but when she tried to get him ready for his first day of classes, she found her hopes dwindling by the second.

"I'm not going!" he screamed from the floor of his bedroom, surrounded by the clothes he was supposed to be getting changed into.

She tried to will some patience into herself, but she felt the pressure to get him out the door so that she could get to work.

"Declan," she began, as calmly as possible, "you don't have a choice. You need to go to school today."

He folded his arms across his chest and shook his head. The last thread of her patience snapped.

"You either change right now or I'll carry you to the truck and you can go to school in your pajamas."

He began to cry but as he did so he changed into his clothes. Once he was dressed, she sat down beside him, exhausted, hurt, helpless.

"I know you don't want to go to school. If it were up to me, we could both stay home all day, watch movies, and eat junk food. But you need to go to school and I need to go to work, and then afterward we can cuddle up on the couch and watch a movie together. I'll make popcorn, and you can even have a cream soda. How's that sound?"

"I hate school," he said through his tears. "Everyone's so *mean*."

Rachel wanted to ask what Declan meant, but he continued before she got the chance to form a question.

"You're mean, too."

She felt like he'd punched her. "What?"

"I said you're mean, too." His voice broke and hiccupy sobs echoed through the room.

Tears burned in her own eyes, but she blinked them back, determined not to cry in front of him.

"You made Lisa go away." And there it was. The elephant in the room. The conversation she should have had weeks earlier.

She looked over at him. He looked small and sad and scared.

"I didn't make Lisa go away," she said, her voice soft. "I miss her, too."

"I heard you talking to Grandpa. You said you wanted to call her, but that you shouldn't. You said it's best if you don't call her."

"It's complicated," Rachel said.

"No it's not. You won't call her, and now I don't get to see her."

If Rachel thought calling Lisa would in any way fix things, she would've been on the phone weeks ago. Lisa needed her space. Lisa couldn't be in a relationship. Lisa had made that choice . . . if it was even a choice. It felt more like some cruel fate.

"You're mean," he said through his tears. "You're mean and I hate you."

This time, she couldn't stop the tears. She turned away so he couldn't see them.

"Declan, honey," she said when she finally found her voice. "I didn't make Lisa go away. I want Lisa here with us more than anything."

"Is it because she doesn't like *me?*" he asked, his voice heavy with pain.

"No, baby. I promise you it's not that."

It wasn't that Lisa didn't love Declan, Rachel knew. It was that Lisa couldn't.

But that was a small distinction he would never be able to

understand. He cried, and she put her arm around him and pulled him close. That was all she could do. There were no magical words that could fix things.

She dropped Declan off at school and prayed she wouldn't get the call from his principal. *"Come pick him up. He's been expelled. Find him a new school."*

Just don't hit anyone. It's that fucking simple. Except it wasn't. He was trying. She knew his emotions burst from him, too big to be contained. And they were both raw with emotion. All it would take was being called a name, or having his seat taken at circle time, or even an unpleasant look from a classmate.

She had lost her patience with him that morning, and he was not going to be met with the same understanding and empathy at school. When she dropped him off, she pulled his teacher aside and let her know it had been a hard Christmas break, and he was having a rough time. Mrs. Harvey was slightly more open to hearing what was going on than his principal was. Rachel left the elementary school and drove to work, all the while hoping that it would not be her last time dropping him off.

When she pulled up at the restaurant, a familiar black truck waited out front. She frowned as she watched Joey get out of the driver's side and wave at her.

"He started back at school today," she said.

"I know," Joey answered. "I'm here to talk to you. Can we go inside?"

There was a seriousness in his tone, and she wanted to shake her head. She wanted to get back in her truck and drive away. She nodded, though, and led the way into the restaurant. Frank and Eloise were in the kitchen. The dining room was empty except for the two of them, and Rachel showed them to a table.

He sat across from her and rubbed his hands together, cracking the knuckles on both of his thumbs, something he'd always done when he was stressed or nervous.

"Why are you here?" she asked. She hoped her tone didn't

sound too brisk, but she didn't have the patience for more bad news, which was clearly what was about to follow. Tension knotted between her brows, and she rubbed the bridge of her nose as if that could take away the burden of whatever Joey was going to say.

"I met someone, Rach. And, um, it's going really well. I've asked her to marry me."

She sat back, some of the tension falling away. She had been waiting for some terrible announcement, the way he sat there looking so somber. This was not something Joey should have been scared to tell her. She had never expected or wanted him to stay single forever. "I'm happy for you."

"Yeah, um, the thing is," he continued, "all of her family lives out in British Columbia. I've already put in for a transfer and it's been approved. We're moving out there."

"To the other side of the country," she said, the understanding dawning on her.

He nodded.

"And Declan?" Rachel asked, already knowing Joey had made his decision and his son clearly didn't factor in.

"He can come visit me sometime. I could show him around. There's lots of cool stuff to do out there. He'll love it." His voice lifted with excitement, which only sparked her anger. He didn't get it. He *never* did.

"So, you're just going to disappear from his life." It wasn't a question. It had never been a question. Joey had been walking out on Declan since the day he found out Rachel was pregnant. At least this time he'd stay gone and stop getting Declan's hopes up every other weekend only to leave him crushed.

"I'll still call. We can Skype. I'll fly him out to visit when I can afford it. Maybe I'll come out here from time to time."

She shook her head. She couldn't believe what she was hearing. "He's going to be devastated."

"I'm really sorry. I am. But this is what's right for me and my life, my future. I have to do this."

"You're telling him."

He nodded, casting his eyes down at the table, looking somewhat regretful for the first time since getting his big announcement out. "I know."

She hated the relief she felt. She was angry and disappointed and hurt for Declan, of course, but beneath it all she couldn't deny the relief. She was so tired of doing *this*, of explaining to Joey why he sucked at being a dad, and then watching him hurt her son. Over and over again.

"You can come by the house when I'm done work. Come by at seven."

Joey nodded. He looked sad and tired, and finally said, "He's going to hate me, isn't he?"

Declan couldn't hate his dad. Rachel didn't feel compassion enough to tell him that, so she merely shrugged. Declan would be angry, but at himself more than at Joey. He'd be left wondering why he wasn't enough to keep his dad around. Just as he'd asked why he hadn't been enough for Lisa.

But they'd move forward—Rachel and Declan. They had each other. And that was all they'd need.

Declan kicked off his snowsuit and raced to the living room. "I want to watch 'Cars,'" he said, already grabbing for the DVD.

Rachel had forgotten about her promise to watch a movie when they were done with work and school, but Declan clearly had not.

She sat down on the couch and rested her elbows on her knees. "Your dad is coming over."

He looked up, confusion etched in his features. "Today?"

"Yeah. He's got to talk to you about something."

A smile broke across his face. No matter how often Joey hurt him, he still lit up whenever he'd get to see his dad. Rage simmered inside of her, knowing how crushed Declan was going to be later. She half wanted to tell him herself. To prepare him. To keep him from getting his hopes up. But this was Joey's job. Declan needed to hear this from his dad.

As if on cue, the doorbell rang, and he scrambled to the door to open it.

"Dad!" He threw his arms around Joey.

She stood back, at the end of the hallway, watching the exchange.

Joey looked at Rachel, then turned to Declan, kneeling to pull him into a hug. "Hey buddy! How's it going?"

"Good! Can I show you the new car that Santa brought me?" He radiated excitement.

"Sure, buddy," Joey said. "Why don't you go get it and bring it to the living room? You can show me the car and then I've got something that I want to talk to you about."

Declan nodded and raced off.

"I should go," she said. "You two can talk alone. I'll be in another room."

"Please, Rach. Stay?"

She didn't want to help him out. She didn't want to make this conversation easier or more comfortable, but she nodded and sat back on the couch. He sat next to her, and she scooted an inch away, not wanting to appear a united front. This was all Joey.

Declan returned with his toy car. He showed Joey how the remote worked and then set the car on the floor so that he could demonstrate how to drive the car.

"It goes really fast, and sometimes I crash it into things," he said, as he drove the car into the leg of the coffee table. "I can't wait until the snow is gone and I can drive it outside!"

"That's a really great car," Joey said.

Declan beamed and picked the car up, holding it to his chest. "Do you want to try?"

Joey looked at him and slowly shook his head. "I need to talk to you about something first. Come sit with me?"

First. As though he'd be driving cars with him after.

Declan set the car down and climbed into Joey's lap.

Joey just held him for a long moment. He ran a hand through Declan's hair and kissed his forehead.

Declan looked confused, but sat quietly, seeming to understand that this conversation was going to be important.

"I'm getting married," Joey said. Not the pertinent part of the story.

She watched Declan look up at his dad. He didn't appear to know how to react.

"You've met Amy. I asked her to marry me, and she said yes. But the thing is, her family all lives really far away, and we're going to move out to BC so she can be close to them."

"You're moving?" Declan asked. His eyes were wide, and he sat back, staring up at his dad with what she could only describe as a look of betrayal.

Joey nodded. "I'm really sorry, buddy. We'll still see each other. But it'll be less often because I'll be pretty far away."

Tears welled in Declan's eyes as the full understanding settled in. "You're already far away. Now you're going to be farther?"

"Yeah. I am. But when you come see me, you'll get to fly on an airplane. Won't that be cool?"

She wished he would stop talking. What, did he expect that she was just going to send Declan on a plane every other week? It wasn't going to happen. Joey knew that. He knew the choice he was making.

Declan, however, did not appear placated by the lure of an airplane. He shook his head, visibly fighting tears. "I don't want you to go."

"I know, buddy. You're my number one little man. I would live closer to you if I could."

"No you wouldn't!" Declan said, his voice rising in anger this time.

"Declan—" Joey began, but she held up a hand to stop him. Declan deserved to have his anger.

"You're a liar," he said, getting up off Joey's lap and standing in front of him. His hands were balled into fists, and his brows were furrowed together. "You never come visit me when you say you're going to. You're going to move away and I'm never going to see you."

"That's not true. I'll visit when I can."

Rachel believed Joey believed that to be true. She knew a part of him *did* really love Declan and wanted to be able to see him. But she also knew Joey was better at making plans than at keeping them. He had big plans and no follow-through. Ever. She could see Declan knew that, too. He had fallen to the floor, and folded in on himself, crying quietly.

Joey slipped from the couch and sat next to him, resting a hand on Declan's back. Declan pushed him away.

"Go away," he shouted through his tears.

"Please believe me. I love you *so* much."

"Liar! Go away!"

Joey looked at her for help, tears misting his eyes as well.

There was nothing she could say that would make things better.

Joey stood, wiped his eyes with the back of his hand, and walked toward the door. She followed.

"I don't want to say good-bye like this," he said.

"He gets to be sad and angry right now."

Joey nodded.

"I didn't want this. I never wanted to hurt him."

"I know." But that didn't change anything.

He pulled on his jacket and stepped outside to go. "I'm sorry."

She shut the door behind him and leaned against it for a moment before she went to check on her son. She knew that at the moment he wasn't okay.

And she felt helpless to make it better.

Chapter Twenty-Nine

Lisa stood in the loft bedroom of Auntie Eloise's home. The warmth of the room embraced her. The small house on the coast had become her safe haven. It was more her home than her apartment in Toronto. The coast was more her home than the city. She'd only arrived on Cape Breton Island four months earlier, but it felt like a lifetime. Surely she was a different person now than she'd been when she arrived.

Four months earlier, she'd been running from her grief. She had wanted the sea to free her—she had thought the sea *could* free her—simply by her being there. Now she understood she couldn't run away from her grief. It had waited for her in her apartment in Toronto, and it also waited for her in the safe-haven loft bedroom. This time she was ready. She wasn't going to run. It was time to accept the grief.

Lisa pulled out her cell phone and dialled her agent. Natalie answered on the third ring.

"Lisa, hi. How are you?"

"I'm good," she said, and for once she wasn't saying those words as an expected response. "I went home for a bit. I'm ready to give you the more personal art."

"Lisa—" Natalie began, but Lisa cut her off.

"I thought about what you said, and you were right. The work I sent you *is* flat on its own. But you were also right about the direction I could take the work. Those sketches, they matter to me, and I think they could maybe matter to others. But I only sent you a part of the picture. They don't make sense on their own."

Natalie was quiet on the other end of the line, waiting for her to continue. Lisa took a deep breath and told her about the project she had outlined on the flight home. Even just telling Natalie about the details made her want to lock her work in a safe somewhere, where nobody could see it.

But it was time to be vulnerable. It was the only way to heal.

She needed to share her story. It didn't mean letting go of Mitchell. He would always be with her. But keeping him locked up inside of her was only keeping herself locked up as well. They were both trapped.

When she finished explaining her idea there was a long pause, and then Natalie said, "Are you sure? I think you've got a great idea, but are you really ready?"

She took a breath before answering. "I am." Truthfully, she hadn't been more sure about anything in a long while.

"Okay," Natalie said. "Let's make it happen."

They talked over a few more details, and then ended the call, Lisa promising to send some frames by the end of the afternoon. She felt lighter already by the time she hung up the phone.

She stepped over to the closet where she kept the most personal reminders of Mitchell and gently pulled the items one at a time from the top shelf and set them on the bed. She would look at them all later. There was one item in particular, set at the very back of the closet, that she reached for.

She reverently pulled down the marble urn. It was small and light, with most of the weight, she knew, coming from the marble. She held it in her hands, turning it over, taking in every whorl in the stone. A lump formed in her throat.

"Mitchell." She traced her fingers over the urn as if caressing her baby.

For days after the funeral home had given her the ashes she sat just holding them and crying. The urge to do the same now was overwhelming. She wanted to clutch the urn to her chest—

clutch Mitchell to her. But it was time to set him free. She pulled the urn close to her, and carried it downstairs. She dressed in a heavy jacket, boots, and a toque, then stepped out into the cold.

The sun shone brightly in the mid-morning sky, and the snow glistened over the rocks, crunching under her feet as she made her way toward the same spot where she had sat with her grandfather decades earlier.

"Mitchell's not in there," she said quietly to herself. "He's out here."

She carefully opened the urn and poured some of her son's ashes into the palm of her hand. She felt the soft ash, closed her fingers momentarily, and then tilted them into the wind.

Unbidden tears filled her eyes as she watched the ash carry off into the ocean breeze and disappear. And yet, somehow, she did not feel the great overwhelming sadness she'd always thought she'd feel when the day came that she could finally bring herself to scatter Mitchell's ashes. Instead, a deep sense of peace filled her. Mitchell was with the sea. It was where he belonged.

She took her time, releasing the ashes little by little. The cold settled into her bones, but she was in no hurry to go back indoors. She couldn't be rushed.

When the last of the ashes had been scattered into the wind, she closed the urn, and set it at her feet. She stood facing the ocean with her eyes closed and listened.

The winter seascape was far more silent than in summer. There were no ships or gulls, no distant voices and laughter. There was the soft gusting of the wind, and the sound of rolling waves breaking against frozen shores. A gentle, rocking lullaby.

She did not know how much time had passed before she finally moved to go inside. When she did, some of the heaviness had left her limbs. Her heart was lighter. Mitchell would always be with her, but the grief didn't need to be a prison anymore. They were *both* free.

She set the empty urn back in the top of the closet, pulled out her sketchbook, and began to draw.

Chapter Thirty

Rachel sat in one of the restaurant booths watching the snow fall outside. Eloise and Frank were in the kitchen watching television while Eloise prepared a pot of chowder. Declan was at school. There had been a few customers over the lunch hour, and Rachel was enjoying the quiet lull before dinner when a few more would trickle in. She needed the quiet, the time to process everything that had happened over the past month. Lisa leaving. Joey leaving. Both she and Declan were heartbroken, and the pain was palpable in the air at home. The restaurant offered somewhat of a reprieve.

The restaurant had first been her mom's dream. Then, it had been a way for her and her dad to remember her mom. Gradually, over the years, it had become more than merely a connection to her mom. It had become her own love and passion. The restaurant was hers. Her home. Her heart.

She ran her fingers over the knots in the wood of the table. She'd wiped down the tables countless times. She'd cleaned tables after breakups, she'd wiped down the remains of engagement celebrations and marriage proposals, she'd cleaned up after so many big events in people's lives that had taken place in this restaurant. Her own life events had unfolded there as well. She'd told her dad she was pregnant at the booth farthest from the door, terrified of what her traditional father was going to think about having a daughter pregnant at nineteen years old. She'd told him she was gay in the same conversation when he had tried insisting that she and Joey get married. She'd watched Declan grow up, taking his first shaky steps in the kitchen, then toddling around the dining room, and finally chatting up a storm with the customers.

Just as he'd talked Lisa's ear off when they first met her—also in the restaurant.

She tried to push away the memory. It hurt too much to think back on that moment. She had felt the pull to Lisa from that first day in the diner and had been falling in love ever since. From the very start.

Declan had been falling in love with her from the start, too, and between Lisa leaving and his dad leaving, her son had way too much loss to carry in his heart. He'd been listless and quiet, going through the motions. No energy left to even get in trouble at school. She'd continued taking him to his counselor, but there was nothing she could do to truly erase his loss.

She watched the snowflakes illuminated by the hazy circle of sunlight peeking out from the clouds and focused on their gentle descent. A hypnotic distraction from the hurt. She wasn't sure how long she sat numbly staring at the snow.

Eventually, she was pulled back into the present by the sound of the front door chiming as it opened. She looked up and her breath left her.

Lisa stood at the door, holding a binder in her arms. Her hair was windswept, her cheeks rosy, and damn if she wasn't prettier than Rachel remembered.

"Eloise is in the back," she said, not sure how she managed to form words.

Lisa's gaze was steady, apologetic, and completely disarming. "I'm not here to see Eloise." She stepped closer to the booth and motioned to the seat opposite Rachel. "May I?"

She shook her head. "I don't think that's a good idea." Her voice was small and on the verge of breaking.

"Please?" Lisa asked.

The hope and the hurt in the single word undid her, and she nodded despite the fear that boomed inside of her.

Lisa slid into the booth across from her and set the binder on the table. "I have some frames outlined for my new project. I need you to be the first to see it."

Rachel looked at the small blue binder. She shook her head.

"It's important," Lisa said. "If you look this over and never want to see me again, I'll go. But please . . . I need you to see what's inside."

Rachel hesitated. Fear and curiosity warred within her. Fear was winning, but she saw the longing look on Lisa's face, and she reached out and pulled the binder toward her.

Carefully she lifted the cover. The first image she saw was a black and white professional-quality photo. A tiny infant resting in Lisa's arms. She knew what the photograph was before she ever read the caption beneath it.

"Mitchell Adam Whelan–June 12th, 2016–6lbs 11oz"

She traced her fingers over the photograph, emotion thickening in her throat. She flipped through a couple pages to confirm the book was, in fact, Mitchell's story. The binder was full of sketches Lisa had drawn with the occasional photograph mixed in as well. The captions were brief, the artwork doing most of the speaking, though there were some captions containing details of Mitchell's short life.

Her eyes misted at a close-up of the tiny infant.

"Mitchell was born with a tumor encasing his heart. His doctor discovered the tumor during an ultrasound six weeks prior to his birth. Mitchell was given a terminal diagnosis. He lived for only a few hours post-utero. The hours felt like minutes, and yet they are my entire lifetime. There is no before. There is no after. There is only this frozen moment."

She looked up, reached across the table, and took one of Lisa's hands in hers before she continued reading. Another photograph of the tiny, perfect infant, eyes closed, head resting across two forearms, cradled in his tiny wrinkled hands.

"After his diagnosis, it was my doctor who suggested hiring a photographer. During that time, I was too broken to think, let alone prepare, but I took her advice. The first photo was prior to his passing.

This photo was taken just after. Until now I've kept it tucked away in my closet, only taking it out for my own eyes on the really hard days. This is my beautiful boy. I'll forever remember his soft features and tiny hands. Only once did he ever grasp my finger in his little fist."

A lump formed in her throat. It was one thing to know Lisa had lost a child. It was another to see the photos and to truly be invited in to see the depth of her loss. Mitchell was small and puffy, but even so, she could make out the resemblance to Lisa. The faint wisps of hair were light enough to hint at the same wheat blond hair. His nose was tiny, but the same curve was vaguely visible. Somehow she knew he would have had the same golden hazel eyes.

She quickly wiped the tears from her eyes, and looked up at Lisa as she tried to find some words.

"I couldn't keep hiding," Lisa said. "I was trying to run from my grief. I thought that was how to be happy. I realized that was only making me hurt worse. I think now that maybe sad stories need to be shared. Maybe grief doesn't need to be fought, but rather embraced, in order to ever heal."

"Lisa—" she began, but Lisa held up a hand to stop her.

"There's a lot to say, but take it all in first. Then we'll talk."

She nodded, and looked back down at the binder on the table in front of her. She looked at the beautifully intricate sketches Lisa had drawn. The images were raw and vulnerable and captured Lisa's grief, her love for Mitchell, and the dreams she'd had for him. The images reflecting the hurt made the pain almost palpable. The metaphorical drawings were brutal in their symbolism. She took in the sea monster trying to pull the ship into its black depths with the caption, *The struggle to stay afloat.* Then there were tender images based more in realism, sketched memories of a tiny baby, of the boy he might have grown to become, of the man Lisa had hoped he'd be.

Near the end was a sketch of a woman standing near the sea and tilting ashes into the wind. The ash scattered from her hand and carried off into the sky, forming the figure of a little boy.

She moved to the last image, which caused her heartbeat to quicken in her chest.

There were three people in the picture: two women and a little boy. Rachel knew immediately the sketch was Lisa, Declan, and herself. They were sitting in front of a Christmas tree with the little boy opening a present. The woman Rachel knew to be herself was watching the boy with a smile while the other woman looked at her with a tender gaze. The caption for the sketch was a single word:

Hope.

Rachel read it again and again, as though the repetition would give meaning to the word. She felt as though she was reading another language. The word didn't make sense to her.

Lisa squeezed her hand, but Rachel couldn't stop looking at the picture.

"I'm sorry that I ran."

The words brought her back from the sketch into the room, and she turned to meet Lisa's eyes.

"I shouldn't have stayed the night until I was ready to stay the morning. I'm ready now."

Rachel tried to process what Lisa was saying, but she shook her head, terror clutching her chest. "It's not just about me and you. I've got Declan, and I let him get hurt again. I know why you can't commit to him. I *get* it, really. He can never replace Mitchell, and the grief is a canyon between us that can't be bridged. But Declan? He doesn't get that. It's okay. We just weren't meant to be."

Lisa turned so she was fully facing her and shook her head. "I thought that, too. That the grief would always be between us. But these past few weeks . . . my grief isn't lessened when I'm away from you and Declan. After I left, I was grieving the loss of *three* people instead of one. I *have* to spend my life without Mitchell. That's not a choice that I get. But I don't want to choose to spend it without you and Declan as well."

Rachel searched Lisa's eyes for any sign of doubt. She saw none, but she was still scared to let down her walls and hope. "We

227

fell in love with you, both Declan and I. When you left . . . it didn't just hurt me. He's had a lot of disappointment in his short life, but losing *you*, that hurt the worst."

"I know," Lisa said. "And I don't have any excuses. I feel horrible for hurting both of you. I never wanted to. But I had to leave and face my grief."

"And?" Rachel asked.

Lisa motioned to the book with her head. "I hope you can see I *have* dealt with my grief this time. I wish more than anything that I had Mitchell here with me. I love him, and it hurts every day that he died. It will hurt me for the rest of my life. But I don't want that to stop me from loving you. Because I do. I love you. And I love Declan. My life is still going, and I want the two of you to be in it with me."

She so badly wanted to believe what Lisa was saying. She'd dreamed of this conversation since Lisa had left. But she and Declan had been so hurt, and not just by Lisa. She needed to be certain.

As if sensing her fear Lisa moved to her side of the booth. Rachel slid over to accommodate her, her breath catching as Lisa's hand gently cradled her jaw.

She searched Lisa's eyes for any sign of doubt. She saw none.

Lisa leaned in and softly captured Rachel's lips with her own. The kiss wasn't hurried, and it wasn't driven by lust or passion. It was slow, a promise, and with it she understood that this time Lisa wasn't about to run.

"I love you," Lisa said again when she pulled back, her eyes pleading when they met Rachel's.

This time, she nodded. Tears welled in her eyes. "I love you, too."

She looked back at the picture and once again read the caption: *Hope.*

She let it sink in.

Epilogue

"Okay, now run," Lisa said. Wind whipped her hair in her face as she held the kite in the air. Declan took off running down the beach with the spool of string in his hands. When the string became taut, the kite caught the air and accelerated upward, bringing giggles of delight to Declan whose legs pumped as he ran faster. Lisa smiled and breathed in the briny ocean air, digging her toes into the cold sand while watching the kite lift higher.

"It's flying!" he exclaimed with glee, and she laughed with delight as well.

"You're doing it," she called. "You don't have to run now that it's in the air."

He stopped and turned to look up at the kite, his eyes wide as it floated high above them, red and blue streamers trailing behind.

She looked over to where Rachel sat on the checkered picnic blanket they'd spread out. She caught Rachel staring at her with a tender gaze and gave a small smile and wave. Then, once Declan had the kite safely in the air, she took a seat next to Rachel. She kissed her on the cheek and took Rachel's hand, turning back to watch Declan fly the kite.

It was his first day of summer vacation, and both she and Rachel had scheduled the day off to celebrate with him. The rest of the school year had been by no means easy, but his behavior had improved enough that he had been able to stay at the elementary in Craghurst, and he'd even scheduled a few play dates with some classmates toward the end of the year. The three of them had decided to get up early to secure their little corner of the beach and enjoy the day together.

It was a rare day for them to just relax and have fun. The summer tourist season had brought a rush of people to the island, and the sleepy little town was once again bustling with life, keeping Catherine's Restaurant packed from open to close daily. Lisa's book had been approved by her publisher, and she was busy finishing getting it ready for a winter release. She still felt nerves at the thought of people reading her story, but she also had a sense of lightness, having let it go out into the world.

She watched as Roxie followed Declan along the beach, tail wagging. Occasionally, the dog bounded off, barking at the seagulls that landed on the shore, and he giggled, calling her back to him.

It was the perfect morning, her favorite people in her favorite place.

Lisa felt the warm sun on her face, and she tilted her face up into the warmth and closed her eyes. She no longer had to work to hear the melody laced over the rocking rhythm of the waves. She closed her eyes and heard that song her grandfather had told her about. She heard Mitchell in the crescendo and diminuendo of the water and in the staccato bursts of laughter. It was his song in the languid whisper of the breeze and the soft percussive sound of footsteps along the rocky shore.

He was with them.

She reached up and traced her fingers over the little driftwood angel she wore around her neck.

She *heard* him.

"Do you have a song stuck in your head?" Rachel asked.

She turned to her and smiled. "Something like that."

She kissed Rachel and leaned her head on her shoulder. She listened to Declan's laughter and the sound of his feet splashing as he ran along the water with his kite in tow. She listened to Rachel's steady breathing and sighed.

Music.

It wasn't the song she had once envisioned, but she was happy with the melody.

About the Author

Jenn Alexander was born and raised in Edmonton, Canada. She holds an M.S. in Counseling from the University of North Texas, and she is currently living back in Edmonton where she works as a play therapist. Jenn is a 2018 graduate of Golden Crown Literary Society's Writing Academy, where she was the recipient of the Sandra Moran Scholarship. She lives with her dog, Delia, and her cat, Molly, both of whom try their best to distract her while she tries to write. When she's not writing, she spends her time playing the drums, skiing, or looking for adventure. You can find her online at www.jennalexander.ca

Acknowledgements

I would like to start by thanking my publisher, Salem West, and the wonderful team at Bywater Books who believed in this book and helped me see it through to publication. Rachel Spangler, my amazing content editor, provided invaluable feedback to strengthen this book and really bring the characters to life—I am so appreciative of her support in helping to bring my vision to life. Additional thanks go to Lynda Sandoval for providing an initial read-through, and suggestions for the content edits. I would like to thank Elizabeth Andersen for her copy edits, Nancy Squires for her proofing skills, Kelly Smith for typesetting, and Toni Whitaker for the e-book conversion. I am also incredibly grateful for the beautiful cover that Ann McMan created—she captured the setting and the feel of the story perfectly.

I would probably still be spiraling in rewrites if not for Beth Burnett, Joy Val Stralen, and the GCLS Writing Academy. Beth was the first person in the lesbian fiction community to read part of my novel and see something in it. I held onto her early comments often when the self-doubts crept in and told me to restart or quit the whole thing. It was an honor to have received the Sandra Moran Scholarship which provided tuition for the Writing Academy, and allowed me to work one-on-one with a wonderful mentor throughout the year. This book is miles better than it would have been otherwise thanks to this generous scholarship.

Susan X. Meagher was a pleasure to have as a mentor, and her thoughtful feedback on early drafts of this book helped bring it to life in ways I had not imagined. I am so thankful to have been able to work with her, as her insight into character motivation and emotions was incredible.

I am forever grateful for all of my wonderful artistic and creative friends who inspire and motivate me daily. Writing can be a very solitary and isolating pursuit, and this book exists because of the friends who have spent time with me writing in coffee shops, acting as a sounding board for all of my plot problems, and helping to workshop scenes to get them as tight as possible.

And last, but certainly not least, a big thank you goes to my family, for always showing encouragement and enthusiasm for my writing. Thanks for skipping over the steamy bits.

FULL ENGLISH

"Ms. Spangler's characters are deep and multidimensional."—CURVE

"Spangler's novels are filled with endearing characters, interesting plot turns, and vivid descriptions. Her readers feel immersed in the worlds of her novels from start to finish." —THE OBSERVER

Full English by **Rachel Spangler**
Print 978-1-61294-155-4
Ebook 978-1-61294-156-1

www.bywaterbooks.com

Bywater
BOOKS

At Bywater Books we love good books about lesbians just like you do, and we're committed to bringing the best of contemporary lesbian writing to our avid readers. Our editorial team is dedicated to finding and developing outstanding writers who create books you won't want to put down.

We sponsor the Bywater Prize for Fiction to help with this quest. Each prizewinner receives $1,000 and publication of their novel. We have already discovered amazing writers like Jill Malone, Sally Bellerose, and Hilary Sloin through the Bywater Prize. Which exciting new writer will we find next?

For more information about Bywater Books and the annual Bywater Prize for Fiction, please visit our website.

www.bywaterbooks.com

CPSIA information can be obtained
at www.ICGtesting.com
Printed in the USA
LVHW012028020719
623042LV00003B/4

9 781612 941516